A SPECTRE IN THE STONES

T0351622

A Spectre in the Stones

THAMES RIVER PRESS
An imprint of Wimbledon Publishing Company Limited (WPC)
Another imprint of WPC is Anthem Press (www.anthempress.com)
First published in the United Kingdom in 2013 by
THAMES RIVER PRESS
75–76 Blackfriars Road
London SE1 8HA

www.thamesriverpress.com

A CIP record for this book is available from the British Library.

ISBN 978-0-85728-004-6

Cover design by Sylwia Palka

This title is also available as an eBook

A SPECTRE IN THE STONES

John Kitchen

THAMES RIVER PRESS

CHAPTER 1

No one would ever accuse Lloyd McKenzie Lewis of being superstitious, but he felt uneasy now.

He'd heard a lot about the children's home they were heading for, and there was no smoke without fire.

"This place," he said.

"Yes, what about this place?" said Robin.

Robin was his social worker; lean faced with thinning wispy brown hair. He was taking him there.

He and Robin weren't exactly best mates, but with so much going on in his head, Lloyd needed to ask somebody.

"Kids have said stuff. It isn't that good there, is it?"

"In what way?"

"People getting sick? Lee Peddar said some of them go mental."

"That's garbage," said Robin. "I never had you down as a guy who'd be taken in by that sort of junk."

"Yeah, but it wasn't just Lee Peddar. Other kids said stuff… about curses and that."

Robin glanced at him as he manoeuvred down the narrowing road. "Your mates are winding you up," he said. "And I thought you were tougher than that. I mean, not even the most intimidating of Housefathers can ruffle you, can they? So, what's all this nonsense about curses?"

"Haven't you heard stuff then?" said Lloyd. He looked at Robin. "I bet you have. You'd be scared blind if you was going to stay there."

"It would take more than a few stories dreamed up by your so-called mates. Sarson Hall's just like any other kid's home. If it wasn't, the inspectors would have closed it down." Robin glanced across at him again, and this time he attempted to show more understanding. "It's nerves, that's all. It's always a bit of a thing going somewhere new. And don't worry about it – being nervous. It shows you're human. It's a relief to know there's a chink of weakness in you. You play the tough guy so much, it's quite refreshing to see you've got a softer side."

Lloyd didn't say anything. He didn't fall for all that rubbish. There was something bad about this place. His mates knew it, and he knew it, and, as they got nearer, he could feel it in the air. It had felt like spring when they set off, bits of green shooting on trees, and flowers in the hedges – daffodils, primroses, that sort of stuff. But the nearer they got to Sarson village, the darker the sky became, and now the trees were just leafless skeletons – a bare mesh of branches. Where there'd been clusters of flowers, there were only mud patches, and the grass looked sparse and frost-burnt. When they got to the village, the houses seemed to cower in gloomy copses and there was an eerie stillness everywhere.

They were driving past a high stone wall now, with an algae-stained pavement running beside it. There was a break just ahead, with a couple of posts topped with rounded stones, supporting a heavy iron gate.

"This is it," Robin said, stopping the car.

Beyond the gate, trees lined the driveway, black and bare, and the driveway plunged into a tunnel of darkness. There were brackish pools of standing water, and the tree trunks were mosaicked with sun-starved moss.

"Okay. I need the gate opened," said Robin.

Lloyd got out. It had the feeling of the Victorian workhouse about it and the gate scuffed on the drive, fighting his efforts.

His mates were right about this place. The birds weren't even singing, and there was no wind, no flowers and no leaves.

As Robin eased the car into the driveway, splattering the puddles in the process, hints of uncertainty nagged at Lloyd. Robin had said that it was nerves because this was a new place; but he'd been to half a dozen new places in the last thirteen years.

He couldn't remember when he came to be in homes, but the social workers told him his mum had quarrelled with her parents back in Jamaica and they'd kicked her out. That was before he'd been born. She'd come over to England and she'd lived in a commune; one of the guys there was his father. But she'd been on drugs and that had killed her. They'd put his dad in prison because it was him that had given her the drugs.

Social services had contacted his grandparents, but they didn't want to know. They had this religious idea about the sins of the parents being visited on the children, so he'd been put in a home and from then on he'd been shunted from one kids' home to another.

He'd never felt like this though, not about any of the other homes. He pushed the gate shut and clambered back into the car.

"It's real cold out there," he said, buffing his hands. "It wasn't like that when we left."

He noticed that Robin had put the headlights on. "It's only March, kid," he said. "The seasons can change from summer to winter in five minutes this time of year."

They rounded the bend and, for the first time, he saw the house. It glowered menacingly across the grounds. The windows were dark and the stonework blackened by age. And everything was cast in the lurid purple of the sky. The door was in shadows, shielded by a pillared porch. There were no shrubs on the gravel forecourt and there seemed to be an utter desolation hanging over the place.

"There you go. Nothing wrong with that," Robin said. "Sarson Hall. It's got history. Parts of it go back to Tudor times, you know?"

"Yeah, whatever," said Lloyd. He shrugged and got out of the car. All he wanted to do now was get in there, face what had to be faced, know the worst and deal with it. That's the way he always handled things – front on, no messing.

Robin went to the boot and emptied out his possessions. There wasn't much, just a battered suitcase he had picked up at some charity do, and an emerald-green cabin case, bought by the sweat of his own brow. He'd saved for that by delivering papers. It was for when he went travelling around the world, because that's what he was going to do one day. The cabin case, with its trolley wheels and retractable handle, was the first step.

"You stay here. Look after this stuff while I go and find someone," Robin said. "And when I say stay, Lloyd, I mean stay. No wandering off."

He went through to the inner porch and Lloyd was left alone, staring at the scowling façade. It dwarfed him.

"You the new boy?"

He started. He hadn't noticed someone coming around the corner and he took a pace closer to his luggage.

"What if I am?" he said. "You going to make something of it?"

It was a boy about his own age, and he grinned at Lloyd. He was Asian, olive skinned, with a shock of jet-black hair.

"No," he said. "I never take on people that might be stronger than me."

Lloyd pulled himself up to his full height. He was taller than the Asian kid. Neither of them displayed many signs of adolescence as yet, but Lloyd was more sinewy and muscular. He was proud of his wiry strength. He relied on it. It was one of his trusted means of survival, one of the weapons he depended on to deflect whatever life might throw at him. He stared at the boy. The boy seemed okay, but Lloyd didn't smile. He wasn't in the mood for smiling.

"As long as we've got that sorted," he said.

The boy offered his hand and Lloyd took it tenuously. At the homes he wasn't used to this type of formality, not with the other kids.

"I'm Rudi," the kid said.

"Why aren't you at school?" said Lloyd.

Rudi shook his head. "Off sick." And that made Lloyd's antennae twitch. It was what Lee Peddar had said.

"Yeah? What way, sick?" he said.

Rudi shrugged. "No appetite, not sleeping, it's…"

He tailed off and there wasn't time for any more, because the door opened and a sour faced woman appeared at the top of the steps.

"You Lloyd Lewis?" she snapped.

Lloyd glanced around with a gesture of mock enquiry. "You Lloyd Lewis?" he said, looking at Rudi.

Rudi grinned. "No."

"Seems like I am then." He turned, looking back at the woman. "This guy here said it isn't him, so it must be me. Yeah."

Her face tightened. "Don't get lippy with me, son." She glanced at a card she was holding. "Lloyd McKenzie Lewis?"

"That's what I said, didn't I?" said Lloyd.

"Then you've got to come with me. Bring your cases. Rudi, you'd best give him a hand."

She opened the door and the boys scrambled up the steps. Lloyd took the cabin case. No one else was getting their hands on that.

They went through to a dark hall and there was a smell that hit the back of his throat, and stillness drenched with portents of hidden menace.

He looked around him. The hall was clean enough; the hallstand and the oak settle, and the dresser standing against the wall, all polished, and the wood block floor was shiny. The carpet on the stairs had been brushed to near extinction, but... the smell, it was sickly sweet, mingling with the odour of disintegrating stone, and that was what got to him more than anything.

It made him want to gag.

"Down here," snapped the woman. "You don't want to keep Dave Trafford waiting – and don't try getting smart with him. You'll find you've taken on more than you can handle if you try it on with Dave."

She pushed open an oak-stained door and shoved him through. Rudi sat outside with the cases.

"Don't go touching that cabin case," Lloyd said. "That's special and I don't want no one messing with it."

"A cabin case? A man of property," said Dave. He was sitting by the window behind a heavy, paper-strewn desk. He was balding, but the hair that fringed his head was blond. There was no hint of grey. His face was puffy, but unlined. He couldn't have been that old, but his eyes, behind rimless glasses, were steel blue and there was more sneering sarcasm than friendship in his tone.

"I don't like my stuff being messed with," Lloyd said.

There were forms to fill in, but it was all so familiar he hardly took any notice. He looked around the room with its high ceiling. There was an embossed plaster rose around the light fitting. There was no light shade, just a bare double-tubed low-energy bulb. There were a couple of worn leather armchairs in the corners of the room, and a glass-fronted bookshelf with hundreds of books, all boring stuff on education and psychology. And, even in here, there was the smell.

Robin did most of the form filling with Dave. Dave was the Housefather and his wife, Marion, was Housemother. Any domestic problems, Lloyd was to go to her. Any other stuff and he must come to Dave.

It all just flowed over him.

"Any questions?" Dave asked.

"Yeah. What's the pong?"

Dave sniffed. "Can't smell anything."

"You've got to be joking. It's everywhere, man. What do you reckon, Robin?"

Robin shook his head. "I can't smell anything." He looked at Dave with an expression that made Lloyd want to smack him one. "He seems to have developed a fantasy about the place. Ghouls and ghosts. In fact he's beginning to show a fertility of imagination that I've never seen in him before – smells and curses and the place being possessed."

Dave laughed. He had a neat row of tiny teeth and Lloyd wanted to smack them too. "Okay. You can go now," he said. "And don't go tripping over any ghoulish phantoms, and for goodness' sake don't tell Cook about the smell. It's probably her dinner."

Lloyd headed for the door where Rudi was waiting. "Christine said I've got to show you round," Rudi said. "But we'll take the cases up first. You're in with me."

"Who's Christine?" Lloyd said, looking at him quizzically.

"The woman that brought us down here."

"The one what's got the face like sour milk, you mean?"

"They're all like that," Rudi said. He picked up the suitcase and they headed down the corridor towards the hall.

At the top of the stairs, they turned left down another corridor. There was a room about halfway down. It wasn't big, but it had four beds. There were windows on the left – sash windows, set deep in the wall. There were no windows on the other walls – just blank plasterwork, painted with cream emulsion. At the far end was a sink between two dark stained wardrobes, and it all looked as barren as midwinter.

On the furthest bed a boy was splayed. He had loose, dark curls and his eyes were closed. His head made convulsive movements in time with an iPhone. He looked up when Rudi and Lloyd came in, but there was no smile, and his eyes were dull and distant. Lloyd had noticed the same about Rudi's eyes when they'd first met.

"This is Martin," Rudi said.

The boy slid off the bed and removed his earpieces. He was bigger than Rudi and Lloyd. His face was strong, carved with encroaching adolescence.

"Is he coming in here?" he said.

Lloyd kicked off his trainers and threw himself onto a bed. "Seems like it, don't it? You not in school neither?"

Martin shook his head.

"Don't nobody go to school round here?"

"He's got the same as me," Rudi said.

"Only three of us in here, then?" said Lloyd.

Martin nodded. "Yeah, kids don't stay that long."

"How long you been here?"

"A year. That's longer than most."

It was all pointing in the same direction. Sick kids, no one staying for more than a year...

"Shall we unpack, or do you want to look around first?" said Rudi.

Martin lunged back onto his bed making it clear he wasn't planning to help with any unpacking.

"Let's have a look around first," Lloyd said.

Rudi looked at Martin. "We got to. Christine said." And Martin rolled over, grabbing his trainers.

They headed down the stairs, taking in the bathroom and showers. Then they went into the dining room where there was just one long table, laid for dinner.

"Everybody sits together," said Rudi. "One big family." And Martin gave an ironic laugh.

The television lounge was next, and that seemed okay.

Then they went out into the garden where the sky was as bleak as when Lloyd had arrived. It looked as if the garden was frozen into permafrost.

Robin's car had gone and suddenly he glanced across at the other two and said: "My mate at the old place, Lee Peddar, he said this place was cursed."

He saw the look Rudi gave Martin, tense and uneasy, but neither of them spoke. Martin had his hands in his jeans' pocket and his foot scuffed at the gravel, while Rudi looked up towards Dave Trafford's office. "Yes, we know what people say," Rudi said. "But Dave said it's nonsense – kids getting hysterical. He said you get noises and stuff in all old houses – but…" He tailed off, and Lloyd's curiosity stirred.

"But what?" he said.

"Dave reckons it's a kid that's doing it," said Rudi.

"A kid that's doing what?" Lloyd persisted.

"Just stuff," Martin said.

They were hiding something, Lloyd was certain, but just then they rounded a corner and there was another building. It was attached to the main hall – only this one was different.

"What's that place?" Lloyd said.

"The North Wing," said Martin. "It's got bedrooms in there for kids that need to be kept on their own."

It wasn't like the rest of the house. It seemed a lot older and there was something about it that was even more menacing than the main house. It was grey and dank – low slung –not neat and squared off like the other building. The stones seemed randomly placed, they were raw and they looked roughly cut. The windows were smaller too, with diamond shapes set in lead, and it was as if the roof was sagging

under the weight of slate. Even the walls sagged. Lloyd shuddered –
but he was curious.

"Can we go in there?" he said.

Rudi seemed uneasy. He glanced towards Martin. "We shouldn't,"
he said. "It's only bedrooms and locker rooms and Dave said we've
got to be supervised if we go in there."

"So?" Lloyd said, and he could see Martin had no qualms about
Dave's rulings. He didn't look easy about it though.

"Okay," he said at last. "There isn't no one around, not till the rest
get back from school."

There was nothing on the door to keep them out – no security
locks or anything, and that seemed odd seeing as no one was
supposed to go in there. Lloyd followed the others and pushed
into a dark, low ceilinged passage. There were doors leading off
on either side and the smell was worse than in the main building.
It seemed to bear down on him – damp with degenerating stones,
and a stench of decay and must. It nearly made him choke, and
he couldn't help himself. He coughed convulsively and the others
stared.

"What was all that for?" Martin said.

"The smell. It made me gag. It's gross in here."

"It's nothing," said Martin. "It's a bit musty – that's all."

In the room to their left was a stairway leading to the first floor.

"You want to see some of the bedrooms?" Rudi said.

They climbed to a low ceilinged landing. There was only one
small window at the far end. There was a silence up there, so thick
you could almost touch it.

They pushed through into one of the bedrooms and straight away
the cold bit into him. It clawed through his clothes and it wasn't like
anything he'd ever felt before.

The others were very quiet, but they didn't seem fazed and he
knew if they played it this way, that's how he must play it too. That
was the way he dealt with stuff anyway. The place felt old and sick,
but it was okay. It was natural for something this ancient to feel like
this. He had to live here for the next year or so after all so no way was

he going to be taken in by all Lee Peddar's talk about curses. "Yeah, it's okay, this is," he said.

Martin looked at him and there was a hint of a sneer in his voice. "Thought you was gagging at the smells a minute ago."

"I could get used to that, couldn't I?"

"We going down the cellar then?" Martin said.

He saw an expression of uncertainty in Rudi's face, but – bedrooms, cellars – it was all the same to him. One was above ground, the other below ground. It wasn't any kind of a big deal. "Yeah, why not?" he said.

At the end of the passage downstairs, there was a door – an old, wooden thing, held closed with a metal latch. Martin pushed at it and flicked a switch on the wall, and somewhere, from the bowels of the building, Lloyd saw the disembodied glow of light glimmering on the stairwell. He couldn't see the light itself and it felt eerie.

When they reached the bottom, there were no windows, and the cement, or whatever it was that bound the stones, had crumbled, forming dust piles on the floor. There were massive holes between the stones – rat runs most probably. And what lit the place was a forty-watt bulb, with clear glass. The filament was burning yellow inside like a glowing spider's web. The light was hanging from a worn flex, and the shadows it cast seemed to dissolve into the general gloom.

The stillness hummed in his ears, and he looked at the others.

There was still a strain on Rudi's face, and nothing moved, not even the air.

Then, in the far corner, where the light barely reached, he saw something that made him start – just the faintest disturbance of the dust to begin with, but slowly the movement strengthened, as if a wind was whipping the dust into a spiral.

There was no sound, but the dust carried on swirling, growing into a vortex, like a small tornado and he gasped, "Did you see that?"

Martin looked blank. "See what?" he said.

"Over there."

He watched as Martin shrugged. "What we meant to be looking at?" he said.

The tornado had already died back though and now there was nothing.

"It was the dust," said Lloyd.

"Everywhere's dust," Rudi said.

"But this… it come up like a whirlwind, didn't it?"

The others shook their heads and Martin stared at him.

It was all getting too much. Suddenly he turned towards the stairs and said: "Let's get out."

It hurt him to say it. He never showed weakness – but spirals of dust rising out of the ground for no reason? That wasn't natural. He needed to be out in the air to get his head around something like that.

CHAPTER 2

When they were outside, he was aware of the other two watching him – and it wasn't them that had chickened out.

Admittedly they hadn't seen the vortex but they still didn't seem bothered by the cellar or the North Wing.

He could see that neither of them were mental like Lee Peddar had suggested, and whatever was going on here, they appeared to have developed some kind of strategy to cope with it.

Martin's, he suspected, was easy. He let it flow over him, and whatever didn't flow over him, he denied. He couldn't work out Rudi's strategy though. Apart from the dull eyes, Rudi was totally sane and Lloyd knew that's just how he had to be.

It would be no problem to cope with the atmosphere and the smell. That was the breathings of an old house disintegrating. He could let that flow over him like Martin did. Spirals of dust in the cellar though, that took some explaining – but he'd battled with mountains and chasms for the last thirteen years… and he'd done that by getting his head around stuff. He grasped what was going on and then he controlled it.

That's what he would do now.

"Would there be some sort of air vent down there?" he said suddenly.

Martin's stare intensified. "What are you talking about – air vent? What's an air vent got to do with anything?"

"I mean, making that whirlwind, with the dust."

He saw Martin kick at a divot. He was looking irritable. "You're always on about weird things," he said. "It's creepy down there, okay, but there wasn't no whirlwind, was there, Rudi?"

Rudi shrugged. "I didn't see anything," he said.

"Well I did," said Lloyd. "I just figured, if there was some sort of air vent, it would explain it, that's all."

"The only thing that would explain it is your sick head," Martin said. "Because I was down there, and there wasn't no whirlwind."

"You saying I'm mental?" Lloyd said. He gave Martin the full benefit of his face. "There isn't nothing mental about me, and I don't go winding people up – not like that. If you didn't see it, that's your business. I seen it. And you want to make something of that, it's okay by me."

Martin looked at him and there was a weariness in his face. He pulled his coat around him and grunted, "It's freezing out here. I'm going in."

"You've seen just about everything now, anyway," Rudi said. "You'll have to put your cases in the North Wing when you've unpacked."

"Not my travel case, no way," Lloyd said. "That's staying with me."

"Whatever," said Martin. "The guy's only telling you how it is. It's no big deal. You do what you like with your travel case." Then he slouched off across the lawn towards the main building.

Lloyd thought he knew what to expect when the other kids came back. There would be shouting and laughing, kids shoving each other, glad to see the back of school, coats and bags being dropped in untidy heaps. The carers would be doing their heads in, shouting at kids to pick up stuff and tidy it away. In every home he'd been in since before he could remember there'd been laughing and joking, and a cheerful chaos.

But when the kids came back this time it was different.

There was noise, although it was more like insurrection. No one was laughing. There were quarrels and arguments. Dropping coats and bags was a preliminary to kicking coats and bags, and it was other people's coats and bags the kids were kicking.

Nothing was good-natured and that applied to the carers too. You could feel the tension. When the carers shouted for them to pick up their stuff, the kids just kicked it out of the way and walked off. Some retaliated with jibes like, "You pick it up if you want it picked up."

No one spoke to him. One or two looked, as if to register that someone was there who they hadn't seen before, but the looks ranged from indifferent to hostile.

Dave came out of his office and yelled, "Will you kids shut up? I'm trying to work in here!" Then he slammed his door, while a girl on the stairs took another girl's bag, ripping it away and hurling it at a boy in the hall. The boy kicked up – mainly to make trouble for the girl, and one of the carers bawled, "Caitlin Jamieson. Come down here and pick that up."

But the girl just swore and headed off towards the bedrooms. Eventually it took two carers to hold her down.

They dragged her off to Dave's office, and Rudi looked at Lloyd. He grinned.

"That's Caitlin," he said. "She's in the North Wing. She's got one of the single rooms. None of the girls will have her in their bedroom."

Lloyd stared. "I thought I was bad," he said. "But this lot, they're off the wall, man."

"It's what happens. You're expected to be like that," Rudi said.

"Yeah? You telling me you do this stuff?"

"They'll have you if you don't."

"Who'll have you?" Lloyd said. He glanced at the seething mob and Rudi nodded towards a tall kid. His hair was shaved right down to his skull and he was standing away from the rest, watching the chaos with a sideways smirk.

"Craig Donovan. You really want to watch him."

A few kids wandered off to their bedrooms, while the rest pushed into the television lounge, shoving past Rudi and Lloyd. The carers started clearing up, hanging up coats and stashing bags, and slowly the tension eased, but it didn't go away. And dinner was seismic.

When the gong rang, it was one big scrum. Lloyd had to get stuck in or he'd have been flattened, but he did manage to get a place by Rudi.

It wasn't in his nature to cling to one guy. He could mix it with the best in other homes. But this was a whole different ball game.

He needed an anchor. The place was like a bear pit, and everything seemed barbed with spite. Kids kicked each other under the table and, when the staff weren't looking, they chucked food. A couple even got into stabbing with their knives.

Most of them headed for the television lounge after dinner, and the dining room looked as if it had been subjected to an exploding bomb. Normally he would have gone to the television lounge too. He liked watching TV but, even before dinner, there were rows about what to watch, and the kids who lost kept winding up the ones who won. Then, when Craig Donovan came in, he took over completely, grabbing the remote, and it was clear that no one was going to argue with him. The carers didn't do anything, other than join in the shouting, and Lloyd reckoned, with a whole lot more in there now, he'd rather be somewhere else.

He decided to go into the garden, but as he made for the front door, there was a voice. "Lloyd Lewis."

Christine was standing behind him.

"Where do you think you're off to?" she demanded.

He gave her a look to match any he'd seen here and he said, "I'm going in the garden. No law against it, is there?"

"You stay in the grounds, then. You go wandering off and you're in big trouble," she said.

"I said I'm going in the garden, didn't I? And if I did want to go anyplace else, there isn't nothing you could do about it."

He pushed through and slammed the door, putting four centimetres of solid oak between him and the chaos.

He knew Christine wouldn't follow, but he wished he'd grabbed a coat. It was freezing and he clasped his arms around himself to ward off the cold.

He'd got a lot to get his head round – the resentments, the sickly smell, the tensions and hate, that whirlwind of dust in the cellar. If he was going to survive in this he needed to be on top of it – and, to be on top of it, he had to understand it.

The wild behaviour might be down to Dave. He'd been in places before where they had weak house parents – where kids didn't have any bounds. But, even in these places, it wasn't as bad as this. In these places the kids didn't seem to hate each other, and it didn't go on all the time. Then there was the smell and the icy chill of the North Wing. That could be Lee Peddar and the rest back at the other home planting stuff in his head.

The vortex though, that wasn't Lee Peddar. The only thing that would explain that was something physical. He knew he'd have to go down the cellar again to check it out.

He was deep into his own thoughts, and when he heard a voice it startled him. "You okay?" the voice said. "I haven't seen you before. You new?"

The sky was darkening, and it was hard to see, but he could just make out a figure stepping from behind some shrubs.

It was somebody on the staff by the look of it – some young guy with long, loose hair. As he came nearer he could see the hair was fair and it might have been natural, because the guy's eyes were an amazing blue. There was a small mole above his top lip, on the right, and he had a fantastic smile.

But he was holding a shears, so he had to be staff. Lloyd didn't trust any adults, especially those connected with social services and children's homes, and he found the best way of keeping them at bay was to be as offensive as he knew how.

"Any of your business, is it?" he said.

He waited for the face to cloud and the barriers to come up. But this guy was still smiling and his teeth gleamed white and even – totally right for that massive smile. "It's just – I haven't seen you around, that's all."

"Well you've seen me now. Make you happy, do it?"

The boy put his shears down, and he was still unperturbed. "What's your name?" the boy said.

"That isn't none of your business neither. You one of them carers?"

He laughed and his long hair shook. He didn't have the sour look that the others had, and he didn't have that irritating "we're trying to relate, here" attitude, the trademark of all the social workers. "Do I look like a carer?" he said.

"Dunno. What do carers look like?"

"Not like me, I hope."

Lloyd didn't speak straight away, but then he said, "If you aren't a carer, what you doing here?"

"I work in the garden mainly," the boy said. "Trying to give it a bit of life."

"Well, if you just work in the garden, why you asking for my name? You weird or what?" He flinched, because he'd gone as far as he dared – and he waited for the retaliation. But all the boy did was shrug.

"Wouldn't get a job here if I was," he said. "Police checks and all that stuff."

"You *do* work here then," Lloyd said.

"I told you, I do the garden. Aren't you cold?"

"Yeah, a bit. But I wanted to get out. You married?"

The boy laughed. "Give us a break. I'm only twenty."

"Got a girl then?"

"Not so as you'd notice. Why?"

"Just wondered," Lloyd said. He paused. He was beginning to be wary. This was getting too much like friendly conversation. He needed to watch his mouth. "Thought you might have kids, that's all."

The boy laughed again. "I told you, I'm twenty. I've got things to do before I get stuck with kids."

"What's your name then?" Lloyd said. There was a rough garden seat by the wall. They wandered towards it.

"Justin," he said. "You going to risk telling me your name now?"

"Lloyd McKenzie Lewis," Lloyd said. "That enough information?"

"Lloyd would have done. I didn't need a full CV," said Justin. "So, what do you make of this place?"

"The biggest dump I've ever been in, if you want to know."

"You been in many places?"

Lloyd gave him another intense stare. "You planning to write my biography or what?" he said. "Five or six, if you must know. I've been in homes all my life. What about you?"

"Lucky I guess," Justin said. "I had parents. They were okay. Still are, really."

"You still living with them?"

He shook his head.

"Living in, then?"

"No way." And immediately Lloyd knew. This guy understood. "I've got a flat in the village. I could have lived with my parents if I'd wanted to. They don't live far away, but… I like my independence I guess."

"So why don't you live in?" Lloyd said.

Justin laughed. "What independence would I get if I lived in?"

But that wasn't what he meant and Lloyd knew it – and he didn't have to say anything either. He just looked and straight away Justin said, "Okay. Like you said. It's a dump. No way would I live here."

There was a cold wind scudding across the bench and Lloyd gave an involuntary shiver.

"I tell you what, man, there's something really bad going on in there. My mate at the other place, Lee Peddar, he told me there was some kind of curse on the place, like it makes kids go mental. And there's that gross smell. Have you smelt that smell? Then, down the cellar…"

"You've been down the cellar?" said Justin.

It wasn't an accusation. It was more curiosity, and Lloyd didn't feel threatened.

"Yeah. Me, Martin and Rudi."

Justin smiled again. "Rudi? He's all right. He's a nice kid."

"He's the only one that's not sick in the head around here, if you ask me," said Lloyd. Then he added, "You always want to be a gardener?" And Justin shook his head.

"I dropped out of university."

"What you do that for?" Lloyd was staring at Justin for another reason now. For Lloyd education had always been the perceived escape route. Dropping out of university was beyond reason. "Education – that's important," he said.

"Yes, but I didn't think university was right for me," said Justin.

"So you left, just like that?"

"I suppose so."

Lloyd frowned. "What did your dad say?"

"He wasn't too pleased, neither was Mum."

"Is that why you don't live at home?"

Justin leaned forward and gave a guilty laugh, as though he'd been caught out. "Partly, I suppose. I wanted to be free to do what I liked, but – I guess there was a bit of tension with me dropping out and everything – and I hate that kind of thing."

"Me too," Lloyd said.

"That's tough then, isn't it?" said Justin. "I mean, this place is nothing but tension."

"I'll get my head around it," said Lloyd. "That's the way I deal with stuff, getting my head round it."

But then he got up. He'd said enough. He looked at the fair-haired boy and said, "I got to go. It's getting cold and I haven't got no coat."

Justin nodded and he got up too. "Yes, and it's getting dark," he said. "I've got stuff to sort before I'm finished."

He headed back to the shrubs, and Lloyd watched him pick up his shears and disappear into the gloom.

For the rest of the evening Lloyd braved the television lounge.

Craig was in charge. He had football on, and that was okay.

But there was an evil tension. Caitlin Jamieson kept flinging magazines around and rows erupted until she was taken off by one of the carers.

Martin went to bed early and by the time Rudi and Lloyd got back he was asleep.

Lloyd couldn't understand how he managed that, because the noise in the corridor and the other bedrooms was horrendous. Kids were shouting, running from room to room. A couple of bedrooms seemed to be on a permanent war footing, with boys from one raiding the other, hijacking pillows and bedclothes. There were windows being banged and, judging by the shouts, a gang from one bedroom had chucked their adversaries' bedclothes out of the window. Carers were yelling and kids were screaming back.

He shifted his still-packed cases off the bed, found his toilet bag and then braved it to the bathroom. But he wished he'd brought his wellies, because there'd been some kind of water fight down there. A couple of kids still in their underclothes, were wrestling in the shower, pushing each other – and all this would have been okay, but there was no goodwill in any of it.

He and Rudi talked when he finally got to bed. It was inconsequential talk – about school and football – and about Justin. Neither of them probed each other's lives and Lloyd thought it prudent not to mention curses and smells.

Eventually the stampedes died down. The carers screamed their final threats, Dave's voice shrieked abuse from the foot of the stairs for the last time, and Sarson Hall sank into some sort of restless repose.

For some time Lloyd grasped at sleep, but his senses were wide-awake. Now he and Rudi had stopped talking, the smell seemed to intensify in his nostrils. It hung over him like a repulsive gas, clogging his lungs and making his stomach lurch.

Neither Rudi nor Martin had fallen into a deep sleep. They were constantly sighing and groaning – especially Martin. Occasionally he shouted out and there seemed to be a repressed fear in his voice.

Lloyd tried pulling his pillow over his head, but, as the night got deeper, nothing could shield him from what was going on outside his bed.

Sometimes, when Martin turned over, his cries sounded more like sobbing.

It wasn't just Martin's cries that disturbed him either.

He knew all old houses made noises… but it was hard to believe they made noises like this. Floorboards groaned. The door creaked so that he shot up in bed for fear that someone was coming in. There was running water, like a spring, gurgling under the floorboards.

He distinctly heard a chair scraping across the room, but when he peered into the blackness there was nothing. Outside, a window banged, and then the window in their room began to rattle.

He told himself it could be the wind, or his imagination. Everything could be his imagination – the smell – the natural groanings of an old house, magnified in his head.

He turned over and pulled the pillow tighter around him. That was it. An old house groaning under the burden of the night. He squeezed his eyes shut. Then, with his pillow over him, he curled tightly into the foetal position and, because his brain couldn't take any more, he drifted into a shallow sleep. But, like Rudi and Martin, his sleep was restless, deprived of any real peace.

When he woke up, it was full daylight.

The other two were still sleeping and he decided now would be a good time to unpack his cases.

Rubbing the tiredness out of his eyes, he sat up… then he breathed in sharply, because both his cases were gone.

There were clothes strewn around the floor, and his eyes widened. For a while he couldn't take anything in. Objects were there, registering on his retina, but not getting through to his brain.

During the night someone had nicked his travel case.

Then his eyes took in the wider compass of the room and he saw his cases dumped on top of the wardrobes, his old suitcase in the far corner, the travel case just above his head, and they were both open, with clothes spilling out, draping over the edges.

He was confused, because he couldn't think how it had happened

Rudi wouldn't have done it. It wasn't in Rudi's nature… and then red fury welled in his head, swirling simultaneously with a launch from his bed – and he was shaking at Martin's shoulders like a dog with a rat.

"You're dead meat, man," he hissed.

It took a few seconds for Martin to emerge from the grip of sleep and he muttered, "Get off, you loon. What you playing at?"

"You've been messing with my cases. You've been through my stuff and I'm going to punch your lights out."

He pulled back a clenched fist, but Martin grabbed it and sat up. He was still disorientated. "You some kind of a nut case or something?" he mumbled.

"It's not me that's a nut case," Lloyd said. "You look at that." He pointed to the wardrobes. "Them cases didn't get up there on their own, and no way did Rudi do it."

Martin looked, but his face didn't register surprise. It was more a resigned glazing of the eyes, and he shook his head. "That hasn't got nothing to do with me. It's what we told you yesterday. Dave said about it. There's some sick guy in here that winds kids up. It's always happening."

Rudi was awake too now, and he was looking at the spilling suitcases. "Yes, we told you," he said. "Someone must have snuck in when we were asleep."

Lloyd extricated his fist from Martin's grasp and stared.

"Well, I'm telling Dave," he said, but that just brought an ironic sniff from Martin.

"You're wasting your time. Dave won't do nothing. He'll just say what we said."

"'Don't dignify this joker's pranks by making a fuss.' That's what he'll say," Rudi said. "'The less reaction you give, the less likely he is to try it again.' He always says that."

Martin nodded and flopped back on his bed. "Yeah, so, quit the threats and let me get back to sleep." Then, as if nothing had happened, he rolled over, pulling his duvet around his shoulders, closing his eyes in an attempt to grab a few last moments of repose.

CHAPTER 3

Rudi clambered out of bed. "Seeing as someone's started the job, we may as well finish it," he said. "I'll help you unpack."

But Lloyd shook his head. All this talk about some kid doing stuff to everyone was nothing but a cover-up. He knew no one had come into the room last night. The only explanation for the suitcases was lying in bed just across the room.

"It's okay," he said. "I'm leaving it like it is, and I'm going to see Dave."

"We told you what Dave will say," Rudi said.

"Yeah, well, Dave don't know me, do he? He may give you all that rubbish – but I don't believe none of it. Martin done this and that's what I'm telling him."

"You reckon?" A voice came from under the duvet. "You tell him what you like. He'll only say what we told you."

"Yeah, right. And don't touch my stuff neither, because I want him to see just what kind of mess you made of it," Lloyd said.

There was a resigned sigh from beneath the duvet and Martin's voice said. "It wasn't me, and it won't make no difference."

He was only wearing his underpants when he headed for Dave's office, and there were a couple of girls in the corridor who gave a few whoops and shouted "Streaker" – to which he made an appropriate gesture.

He only held back at Dave's door long enough to knock – certainly not long enough for any summons from within.

Dave was sitting at his desk labouring over some paperwork and he looked up. Then he sat back, making an arch out of his fingers, pressing the tips together, and said: "Three things, Lloyd Lewis. One, no one ever barges in here – not until I've invited them. Two, do you think it's appropriate to parade around the house in that state? There are young girls and ladies out there, you know, and I'm sure they don't want to see you running around half-naked. And three, you never come into my office unless you're fully clothed, is that understood?"

"Yeah, right," said Lloyd. "I only just got out of bed, didn't I? And someone's been messing with my stuff."

Dave leaned further back, maintaining the pose with pursed lips and fingertips. "What do you mean, messing with your stuff?"

"When I went to bed last night, I was tired, right? I didn't unpack. I left my case and my travel bag at the bottom of the bed. When I woke up this morning they'd been shoved up on the wardrobes and someone had been through my stuff. It was hanging out all over the place."

"And that's such a big issue, is it?" Dave said. "So big you've got to come storming in here semi-naked. Have they taken anything?"

"I don't know. I mean, I came straight down here, didn't I? And it don't matter if they took stuff or not. It's mucking around with my property. That's the thing. No one's got the right to mess with my stuff and I reckon it's Martin. You've got to sort him out."

Dave's eyes were closed now. "It is not Martin, Lloyd," he said. "It's some joker. It's always happening." And that made Lloyd start. He hadn't believed Rudi – but Dave had said exactly the same as Rudi.

"What do you mean, some joker? If someone's always doing it, then you should sort him. He might have nicked stuff for all you know."

Dave radiated a tired boredom. "Do you really want to make a fuss about it?" he said. "Do you honestly want to dignify his pranks by making it an issue?"

Rudi had said that too, and Lloyd was beginning to wonder about what had gone on last night.

He wasn't going to be driven off course though. "Yeah. Why shouldn't I?" he said.

"It'll just give him the satisfaction of knowing his stupid japes have had some effect. Whoever it is, he's just doing it for attention, believe me."

"So?" Lloyd said.

Dave opened his eyes and wove the fingers of his two hands into a gesture of prayer. "If we acknowledge he's made some sort of an impact, it'll give him the positive feedback he's looking for. He'll do it again."

"Well he *is* doing it again. You said so yourself. He's always doing it," Lloyd said. He was getting really mad with this guy. Dave was supposed to be in charge of the place. "Ignoring him isn't working is it? So this time, you sort him, okay? I don't have people messing with my stuff and it's your job to stop them."

Dave sat up at that, and his face was red.

"I'll deal with it my way, if you don't mind, Lloyd Lewis," he snapped. "When you're old enough and mature enough to sit where I'm sitting, then you can dictate the strategies, but no thirteen year old is coming in here telling me how to do my job – is that understood?"

"But you don't do your job. That's the trouble."

Immediately Dave leapt to his feet. "Right. You've said enough," he barked. "Now go and get showered. Then put some clothes on and, after breakfast you come back here ready for school. And I'll have some respect from you in future. Do you understand?"

"You get respect when you done something to deserve it," Lloyd said, and he scurried for the door. He didn't care what he said to this guy, but he was in no hurry to be around for his response.

He heard a bellow of, "Get out," but he was out already, and now he had the bit between his teeth.

If no one else was going to sort all this – then he would.

Nobody messed with his stuff and the quicker they realised that, the better.

Normally he would have gone to school with the others in the minibuses, but today he had to go with Dave in the car because he had to be registered, and the journey was grim. After droning on about how he expected him to behave, and uphold the reputation of Sarson Hall, Dave completed the journey to Brookley in stifling silence and Lloyd thought he must be a couple of studs short of the full football boot to think the kids in Sarson Hall had any kind of a reputation to uphold. The guy was totally spaced out.

There was a bog-standard feel about Brookley school; random redbrick buildings, metal-framed windows and flat-roofed prefabricated slabs, sprawling across the playground, making irregular incursions into the school field and nudging towards the requisite pair of football pitches.

They went through to the entrance hall where the walls were lined with notice boards and some arty display tables. There were teachers standing around, like members of the politburo, watching the movements of the kids, and their faces were grim.

Dave steered him to the secretary's office and she ushered them into the head – a florid woman with short, dark hair that curled out at the ends. She had a brown mole protruding from under her left eye, and she was a lady who clearly had no taste for exercise or calorie counting.

Judging by the colour of her face Lloyd assessed that she was suffering from hypertension and a bad reaction to heat, and when Dave introduced her as Mrs Cherry, he nearly laughed out loud.

Even at the best of times he wouldn't have warmed to her – and these weren't the best of times. He had no difficulty being surly and answering with insubordinate monosyllables.

He could see Dave trying to catch his eye – but that egged him on. He was careful not to say anything that could be pinned down as rude, but he did just enough to unveil his contempt.

Mrs Cherry assigned him to a tutor group and instructed one of the secretaries to take him to his class.

There were two other kids from Sarson Hall in his tutor group, Rudi – he was glad of that, and Caitlin – which didn't please him quite so much. And it didn't take long to see that Caitlin had as much attitude in school as she had at the home. She scowled when she saw him and, while he was being shown to his desk, she managed to tear a page out of her book and make a paper dart, which she scudded across the room. Her brown hair was dishevelled and she had an unwashed look about her. Her eyes were filmed with lethargy and they looked heavy.

As he passed she muttered: "Baa baa black sheep," and he reckoned that was being racist. But the teacher ignored it.

"I'll put you next to Rudi," the teacher said. "He's from Sarson Hall. It'll be someone familiar to help you settle."

He grunted and sat down.

"What we doing then?" he asked, deliberately bypassing her and addressing his question to Rudi.

"Maths," Rudi muttered and Lloyd thrust his hand in the air and shouted:

"Can I have a book to do my calculations in, please, teacher?"

The teacher was delving in a cupboard and she said, "I'm getting one, Lloyd. Just be patient. And it's Miss Webb – not 'teacher.'"

He splayed himself wearily over the desk in a gesture of premeditated insolence and said, "Whatever."

Miss Webb swung around and gave him a warning glance. But she didn't say anything. She just fetched a maths notebook.

"Do you have writing implements and a geometry kit?" she said.

"Yeah, in here somewhere." He poured the contents of his bag across the table.

He was beginning to suspect that Miss Webb ran her class by avoiding confrontation and that took some of the velocity out of his strategy. When she didn't retaliate and went back to her interactive white board, he just gathered his stuff and settled.

He felt tired and his equilibrium had been disrupted. Someone back at the home was messing with his stuff, and Dave wasn't doing anything about it. What with that and the weird noises and the bangs and crashes through the night; he was irritable and he was spoiling for a fight.

Miss Webb was directing them to a page in the workbook now so he shouted, "I can't turn to that page, teacher, because I haven't got no workbook."

He saw her flash him another look, but he didn't flinch.

"It's Miss Webb, Lloyd, and you can share with Rudi for the time being. I'll get you a workbook at the end of the lesson."

He pulled Rudi's workbook across so he could see it, and said, as loudly as he dared, "Sorry mate. I know this book's your property and all that, but teacher said you was to share. Is that okay with you?"

Rudi winced and looked at him with a sideways glance. It was clear he wasn't into baiting teachers and Lloyd didn't want to embarrass him, so he settled and scanned the page.

He worked quickly, and when he'd finished he looked over at the scrawled calculations on Rudi's page. Then he shoved him with his elbow. "Done it, look," he said, pushing his own book across the desk.

Rudi whispered, "Shshsh," and Lloyd began to figure Miss Webb might deserve a bit more respect. It was really quiet – apart from some heavy breathing from across the aisle. Caitlin, he noticed, was splayed over her books. She was completely out of it.

He elbowed Rudi again. "Look at Rip Van Winkle over there," he whispered. Then, from the back of his notebook he removed a page, rolling it into a tight ball.

It caught Caitlin across the cheek and, immediately, she leapt up. "What's that?" she shouted. She really looked a mess, and her face was contorted with spite. She grabbed the ball of paper and held it up. "Miss, someone chucked this." Then she looked around, and Lloyd could see she was hell-bent on creating mayhem. "It's paper out of a maths book, Miss. Someone's tore it out"

Miss Webb looked at Lloyd, and immediately he was on his feet, throwing his hands in the air. "Why you looking at me, Miss? Just 'cause I'm new. It could have been anyone."

"It could have been anyone, but it wasn't, was it, Lloyd? It was Lloyd McKenzie Lewis."

"Yeah, it was him, Miss," Caitlin said. "He's always picking on me."

Lloyd looked at her. "How could I always be picking on you? I only come yesterday. That's rubbish."

"Lloyd," Miss Webb said. She was coming over now but she still didn't look fazed. "You do not conduct arguments across my classroom. If you've got something to say, you talk to me. Did you throw the paper?"

Lloyd shrugged. "She was sleeping, wasn't she?" he said. "I just wanted to wake her so she could get on with her sums. I was being nice."

Caitlin flashed him a look. "Yeah, that's a joke, and I wasn't sleeping."

"Snore when you're awake, do you?" Lloyd said, and Miss Webb held her hand up.

"That's enough," she said. She was still calm and Lloyd respected her for that. "I've been patient with you, Lloyd, but I can't have this anarchy in my classroom. Now settle down and get on with your work and I'll see you after class."

She did see him after class too, but she didn't make a big thing of it. She just repeated what she'd said before, but what was filling Lloyd's head was Caitlin. She'd stirred it for all she was worth and she needed sorting for that. He could see she was more tired than the other Sarson Hall kids. That made him curious because he knew she'd been in the North Wing all night. All the same, he still didn't reckon that was any reason for her to be so ratty. If anyone had the right to be ratty it was him. It was him that was stuck in a bedroom all night with some guy who was messing with his stuff. She needed speaking to about stirring it and at break he made a special point of seeking her out.

"What you playing at?" he demanded. "You *was* asleep. You know very well you was asleep. I only chucked the paper so you wouldn't get in no trouble."

She scowled. "Yeah. You think I'm stupid or something? You was set on winding teacher up – as soon as you got in class, and you can mess with her as much as you like – but you try messing with me and I'll have you."

He shrugged. "Whatever," he said. "Next time you're splayed out on your desk, snoring like a pig, I'll just leave you. What you sleeping in class for anyway? You not getting enough sleep or what?"

She glared at him and then turned her back. "That's none of your business," she snapped, and she began to walk away.

But he wouldn't let her go. "You're in North Wing, that's right, yeah?" he said, grabbing her arm.

"Don't touch me." She flinched, and her face was snared with venom.

"I'm just asking," Lloyd said. "There's stuff going on back at the home, and I want to get my head around it. Someone mucked around with my cases last night."

"So? You accusing me?"

"No, but the only reason you got for being so foul-mouthed is if stuff was happening to you down the North Wing too. Is there something messing with you down there, keeping you awake?"

A look of fear crossed her face. "You trying to wind me up or something?"

"No, I just want to know, that's all."

But she pulled away. "Get lost."

"I want evidence. I want to find out who's doing this stuff."

By now though she had her hands to her ears, and she was shouting some wild chant to drown him out and that took him by surprise. She was almost crouching too, as if someone had hit her in the stomach. Suddenly she swung round, and landed him a thump on the arm. "You're nothing but a sicko," she yelled. "Get your head sorted." Then she stormed off into the crowd, leaving him staring after her.

It didn't make sense. He only wanted to find out what was going on. It was no big deal. The kid was off the wall. But her reaction made him even more curious. Something had kept her awake. Something had made her stop her ears and scream.

Christine was waiting for them when they got back. She was standing on the steps, her hands on her hips, and her face sour.

Even before Lloyd scrambled off the minibus she was shouting his name.

He was in no mood for Christine though. "What?" he said. "You been waiting there all day?"

"Don't give me lip, boy," she said. "I went in to check your bedroom this morning. Do you call those cases unpacked?"

The other kids were rampaging up the steps, barging past her and she grabbed at the doorpost to steady herself. Then she turned to Lloyd again. "You stay where you are, Lloyd Lewis. I haven't finished with you yet."

"I told Dave about that this morning," he said. "Someone's been messing with my stuff so I left it like it was. Don't you lot ever talk to each other?"

She snorted. "There's only one person that's messed with your stuff, Lloyd Lewis, and that's you. Looking for your school clothes more than like. And you don't leave your bedroom in that state – not when you're here, you don't."

"You'd better not have touched nothing," he said. "That stuff is my property, and I'll flatten anybody what touches it."

"It's just as you left it," she snapped. "And before you do another thing, you get up there and pack it away. I'll be up to see it's done in half an hour, and you'd better believe me, if it's not sorted by then it won't be your stuff I'll be laying my hands on."

He stared right through her. "You lay a finger on me, Missus and I'll have welfare on you faster than your tongue can bitch. And I'll sort my stuff when I'm ready, and that's when I've had my snack."

He pushed past her, barging into the dining room for his Twix and orange squash.

It was only after he'd finished that he went to his bedroom, and one glance told him the case and the travel bag were just as he'd left them. Even the clothes that had dropped to the floor were lying untouched.

He found a couple of empty drawers and reached for the big case, sorting his socks and stacking his underwear and T-shirts. He was methodical. Apart from his travel case, his clothes were the main sum of his worldly property and, if he didn't look after them, no one else would. Shirts, jeans and trousers went into the wardrobe. Then he put the case to one side to be stacked in the North Wing.

There were more T-shirts and underwear in the travel case, and there was other stuff too – special stuff – but, as he removed the clothes, his hands froze.

His main possessions, other than his clothes and travel case were a couple of photos, one of his mum, taken just before she died, and a picture of a family. It was some place where he'd been fostered when he was six. It was the only time he'd ever lived in a proper home, and that time had been special. He'd thought it was for real – that he'd live there forever.

But social services weren't in on his plans, and they dragged him off to another institution. He still kept in touch with his foster parents, Bill and Jean, and the other special possession was a small bundle of letters he'd had from them. Those photos and the letters, along with the travel case were his most treasured possessions. And the photos and letters weren't there anymore.

He rummaged through the T-shirts and underwear. Then he grabbed a chair to look on the tops of the wardrobes. And a red mist flooded him. Suddenly it was as if there was a hole where his gut should be, and only one name shouldered through the turmoil.

With one bound he leapt off the chair and out into the corridor.

He was down stairs before two thoughts had passed through his head. Then he was in the television lounge where Martin was curled into an armchair, and he was on him, ripping him from the chair and grabbing his arms. The whites of his eyes shone. "You got my photos and my letters," he shouted. "What you done with them?"

The assault caught Martin off guard and his body had barely adjusted from prone before Lloyd had him back in the chair again, pinning him with his knees, and he was baring his teeth in fury. "You've been messing with my stuff. You've got my letters and my photos."

Martin stared, confused. He tried to wrestle his arms free, but, even though he was bigger, Lloyd's strength was fuelled by a rage that was beyond Martin's capacity.

"I'm going to punch you senseless if you don't tell me where my stuff is," Lloyd hissed.

Martin tried to kick out and shake him off. "What you on about? What photos and letters? Your girlfriend or what?"

With a blinding swipe Lloyd brought a fist down on his face and that was enough.

In a second Martin was out of his chair and Lloyd was pinned to the floor.

There was a trickle of blood dripping from Martin's nose and the strength in his arms and knees was like a vice.

"You do that once more and you're dead," he hissed.

It stunned Lloyd. Martin had always seemed more laid-back than a sloth, but the guy had fight in him, and the sudden display of muscle power brought some kind of respect into Lloyd's head. He looked up from the floor.

"I got two photos in my travel bag, and a bundle of letters, and they've been nicked. I've been unpacking my stuff and they're gone."

Martin released his grip slightly, wiping the blood from his nose, and he sniffed, "That isn't my problem. I told you. I never touched your stuff."

Lloyd looked into his eyes, and he had this sense that he wasn't lying.

"Well, Rudi wouldn't have touched them," he said. "And someone's had them."

"It wasn't me," Martin said. "I told you that this morning."

Pinned to the ground, the anger was seeping away and in its place there was desolation. They were his most precious things, and they'd been nicked. They might never be found, and he could feel tears stinging his eyes.

"They're the most special things I got," he said. "I don't tell people about them. They're personal."

"Like I said, it isn't my problem," said Martin. "And I'm telling you, you come in on me like that again and you're finished."

He stood up and returned to his chair while the others settled back to watch TV.

There hadn't been any carers to intervene but Lloyd had lost face. He saw Caitlin smirking and, as he dusted himself down, he said, "Okay, but when I find out who it is what's nicked my stuff, the thumping I'll give them will make what me and Martin done look like a love-in."

Craig Donovan had been watching from a corner of the room with half a grin on his face, and he sniffed, "It was a love-in, mate. 'Cause anyone but Martin would have left you for dead. You're nothing around here, and you try throwing your fists about like that again and I'll sort you."

"Yeah?" Lloyd said. "You reckon?" But he knew not to push it with Craig, and he shoved his way out of the room.

This stifling dump had done it to him again.

Noises, smells, stuff being moved, vortexes in cellars, his most precious possessions nicked. He was finding it hard to get on top of it.

He wandered into the grounds and if anybody had asked him why he'd gone outside he couldn't have told them. It wasn't for uplift. Out there it was all trees charred with winter cold, void branches, sweeping expanses of flat skies, flower beds that had nothing but the detritus of last summer's vegetation, bland acres of grass smudged by wind and rain – the desolation of the damned.

He wandered across the forecourt, barely lifting his feet. His shoulders were hunched and his hands were deep in his pockets.

He was heading for the North Wing and, without knowing why, he shoved through the door. But, the minute he was inside, something gripped him. It wasn't something reassuring, but it was something – an overpowering feeling, and today it wasn't because he was curious, or because he wanted to prove himself, but he moved inexorably towards the cellar door. He had to. He had to push the door open. He had to turn the switch and, in the disembodied light, he had to clamber down the stairs.

The air was cold and thick, and nothing moved. It was as if all the dysfunctions of history had been compressed into this room and he just stood there.

Then, from the same corner as he'd seen it yesterday, there was a movement, a swirling of the air, silent but palpable. He watched mesmerised as it began to suck up the dust.

This time though the vortex didn't stay hovering in one place. It began to move, slowly trundling towards where he stood.

He tried to step back, but his limbs were rooted. All he could do was stare, and as the vortex wandered, picking up leaves and debris, he gasped in disbelief, because there, swirling in the currents, tumbling and twisting in front of him, were the pages of his letters, and the two photographs. His eyes widened, barely able to take in what they were seeing.

CHAPTER 4

When the vortex had spent itself, there was nothing but an ear-splitting silence. The forty-watt bulb flickered, but it didn't go out and Lloyd was stunned.

There was anger simmering beneath the shock too, because it had suddenly become personal. Whereas before the wheeling vortex and the strange happenings had been a kind of abstract manifestation, now it was aimed directly at him. They were his cases that had been interfered with. They were his belongings that had been spilled. These were his photos that had been taken.

Then he heard floorboards creak and the door upstairs groaned. There were footsteps... and every hair on his body tingled.

Suddenly it was real fear, the fear of a rabbit caught in the headlights. He could barely crack a muscle to move his neck. Prickling with terror, he allowed his eyes to swivel and, in the corner of his vision he could make out a figure standing there... Then he breathed again, because what caught in his eyes was slim, with long hair to its shoulders.

"What are you doing down here?"

He didn't answer. He just pointed at the random pile of sweepings lying at his feet.

Justin crossed the cellar floor. "What's up?" he said, but still Lloyd just pointed.

"It's a pile of rubbish."

"But that stuff is mine," he croaked. "Them letters. Them photos."

Justin bent down to pick up the scattering of papers, shaking off the dust and examining them. Lloyd's first instinct was to grab them out of his hand, but he didn't.

"How come they're down here?" Justin said.

"You tell me. Last I saw them they was packed in my travel case. Then this morning, when I woke up, all my stuff was messed with. My cases had been chucked up on top of the wardrobes, and when I checked this evening, them letters and all that stuff was gone."

Justin looked at the photos and letters again and, for an instant, Lloyd saw him shudder. "Come on, kid. Let's get out of here," he said. "Get some fresh air. We'll talk when we're outside, okay?"

He didn't argue and, outside, even the overcast skies came as a relief.

Justin was still staring at the bundle of paper in his hand.

"Girlfriend?" he said.

"No," Lloyd said, sharply. "And it's none of your business."

He saw him grin. "Sorry. I wasn't prying or anything."

"That's okay," Lloyd said and he wasn't sure what he meant by that. He didn't know if he meant: "That's okay – you're forgiven," or "That's okay – I'm not that bothered if you do pry a bit."

They sat on the bench and, although Justin didn't probe any further, Lloyd knew he was dying to ask.

"I was in a foster home, wasn't I? When I was a little kid," he said. "My foster parents keep in touch."

"You've never been with a family other than that?"

Lloyd shook his head.

"Is this them?" Justin picked out one of the photos, but, straight away, Lloyd snatched the bundle of papers away from him, and then wished he hadn't.

"It's okay," he said. "It's just a bit private, that's all."

"It's just, I was thinking, it's a bit rough," Justin said. "And it makes me feel guilty, to be honest. I mean, a few months with a family, and you carry round letters and photos, and here's me – with parents on call any time – and I'd rather keep out of their way. That isn't right, is it?"

"It wasn't no big deal…" Lloyd said. But then it slipped out. "It's just – when I was there, like… I mean, I was only a kid, and I thought it was going to be forever, that's all."

Any other person would have seen the chink, and they'd have gone in with a crowbar. But all Justin said was, "Well, you would, wouldn't you?" And then he changed the subject. "What made you go down the cellar to look for the letters and photos?"

Lloyd sat up. "That is so weird, man," he said. "I was mad when I couldn't find them, so I come outside. And as soon as I was out here I sort of drifted over to the North Wing. I told you yesterday, me and Rudi went down that cellar, with Martin, and I just had this feeling I wanted to go down there again – on my own"

"And you found your stuff in the pile of dirt?" Justin said.

Lloyd fiddled with the flap on one of the envelopes, opening and shutting it, revealing a triangle of Jean's neatly compacted writing. "This place," he said. "It's bad, man."

Justin sighed. "Yes, there is a bit of an atmosphere about it."

"The thing is, I'm almost starting to think it's worse than that," Lloyd said. "Stuff happens here, and it's hard to get my head around it. Weird stuff – like... unreal."

"The cases, and your clothes, you mean. That could have been one of the kids..."

"That's what I thought," Lloyd said. "I figured it was Martin. We had a punch-up about it before I come out – but... he swore it wasn't him, and then... when I got down in that cellar..." He'd never talked to someone older like this. "You won't believe this – and – I don't mess with people. I mean, I tell it how it is, and, down that cellar I saw like – a whirlwind – and the dust was swirling everywhere. I seen it yesterday too – only, today it was bigger and yesterday it didn't move. Today, though, it was all over the place, moving like a twister, and my photos and letters was in with the dust, flying round in the vortex."

Justin breathed sharply. "Are you kidding me?" he said.

"I told you, I don't mess with people. That's what I saw. I said so to Rudi and Martin yesterday. But they didn't see nothing."

Justin was looking away across the grounds. "You said your cases were messed with," he said "And then there was this vortex thing down the cellar."

"Yeah. You don't believe me, do you?" Lloyd said.

"I didn't say that," said Justin. "It's just, it sounds really weird. What do you reckon it is?"

Lloyd clasped his hands and leaned forward. "It's got to be kids, mucking around. But them whirlwinds – that takes some explaining. I figured some sort of air vent down the cellar, but…"

Justin didn't say anything for a minute and, when he did speak, he sounded reluctant. "You're probably right," he said. "And I'm not saying this to scare you or anything, but it could be something else. Some people think that houses can get sick, especially older ones. It's like, when something bad happens, the – sort of – ambience of the place changes, and sometimes it's so bad it hangs around forever. People say whatever's there can be powerful, so it can create physical disruption, even moving stuff around. I've read about it."

"I'd rather you hadn't said that," Lloyd said. "I mean, I'm here trying to find some rational explanation that I can get my head around and you reckon this place is cursed, just like Lee Peddar said. You reckon what he said is for real."

"Sorry," Justin said. "I didn't want to say anything, but there's something out of sync here. I never figured it was as bad as you said. It's like you can sense something though. It's everywhere."

"Yeah, but what is it?" said Lloyd.

Justin picked up one of the photos again. In the recounting of what had happened Lloyd had absently put the bundle to one side of the bench.

He didn't attempt to wrest it back this time.

"I don't know. It's often something big that's happened in the past – and, let's face it – this place goes back to Tudor times. There's been plenty of space for bad stuff. Sometimes though, it's just an accumulation of bad things that are happening now. I mean, you've got somewhere that's full of kids from broken homes – orphaned kids, disturbed kids – with no families and that and… well – nothing personal, but – they're not the happiest guys in the world, are they? And years of these kids coming and going – that could cause this kind of thing – or it could be one really unhappy person. It could be any of these things, or it might be something different – some natural phenomenon."

Lloyd shook his head. "I don't want to believe that, man," he said. "It's got to be kids, and something down the cellar that's causing the spirals. Anyway, how come you're so well in to this stuff?"

Justin gave another broad grin. "My tutor at university," he said. "He writes books about it, and in a way some of it is tied up with what I was doing – history and archaeology."

They stared out across the grounds. "You should have stuck with that," Lloyd said. "That's a great subject, studying the past."

"I still keep in touch with my tutor," said Justin. " – A bit like you and your foster parents, I guess. He keeps trying to make me come back."

"You won't though, will you? Not yet. Not till I've left here?" Lloyd said suddenly, and Justin laughed.

"Why not?" he said.

It had been an unguarded moment. He'd loosened his grip, like a limpet on the rock taken unawares, and, immediately his defences tightened. "Nothing," he said. "It isn't no big deal. It's just I'm glad to have a guy like you to talk to. The kids here don't talk about nothing."

The front door had opened and Christine was there, sour faced and scouring the grounds. Justin chuckled. "Looks like trouble," he said.

But Lloyd wasn't bothered with Christine.

"Can I talk to you again?" he said.

There was a warmth of kindness in Justin's eyes as he looked down. "Any time, mate," he said and then Christine's raucous voice bawled across the forecourt.

"Lloyd Lewis."

Suddenly Lloyd grabbed Justin's hand, shaking it as if he was sealing a friendship. "Thanks, man. That'll be good."

"Lloyd Lewis?" Christine said again. She was heading towards them and her stout feet were grating harshly on the gravel.

Justin got up, handing the photo back. "See you then," he said. "And show me those pictures again. Tell me about the family. They sound okay."

"Dave wants you inside," Christine snapped, but Lloyd's eyes were fixed on Justin. Only when he was out of sight did he go with Christine into the house.

He was surprised that Dave wanted him. He couldn't think why and he tried quizzing her, but she just looked at him with a knowing expression, vengeful and triumphant.

"You'll find out," she said.

She marched him down the corridor towards Dave's study. He was beginning to feel an aggression every time he saw Dave. The guy was a total waste of space. He sat there now, a smirk on his face, his fingers touching, resting on his lips – a pose guaranteed to get right up Lloyd's nose.

"What do you want?" Lloyd said.

"A bit of respect for a start," said Dave.

"I told you about that already. I only give respect to people what deserve it."

Dave scowled. "I hear you've been in a fight with Martin."

So that was it. "Who told you?" he said.

"Never mind who told me. The fact is, I know, and I won't have it – aggressive behaviour. We don't tolerate it here."

Whatever else he thought of Martin he knew it wouldn't have been him that had squealed to Dave. It must have been Caitlin. That was the kind of thing she'd do. "There isn't nothing you don't tolerate," he said. "My cases and my stuff. All my photos and letters was nicked. You'd tolerate that, no problem."

"What are you talking about, boy," Dave said. "You've got the photos and letters in your hand."

"Yeah, but they was nicked. I just found them, didn't I? And they wasn't nowhere near my cases. You planning not to tolerate that?"

"Was that why you had a fight with Martin? You thought he'd taken them?" Dave leaned back in his chair. "The trouble with you, Lloyd Lewis, is you jump to too many conclusions and you don't seem to have any self control."

"I didn't have to jump to no conclusions about my letters and my case," Lloyd said. "Any fool could see someone had mucked around with them."

"That's not the point," said Dave. "And I've already told you, you're not here to bandy words. You got into a fight with Martin, with no provocation, and I won't have it."

"It's okay. We sorted it, which is more than you did with my cases." He glared at him sitting there complacently behind his desk. "It's me and Martin what gets things done. You don't do nothing. Me and Martin understand each other."

Dave unclasped his hands and then mitred his fingers. "Getting things done with your fists isn't exactly the best course, is it? And quite frankly, Lloyd, I don't think it's a good idea to let you two sleep in the same bedroom. I think – until you've settled – it's best for you to go into a room on your own."

"That's fine by me," he said. "I'll go and shift my stuff now. That suits me, that does, being in a bedroom on my own."

"You can get Rudi to give you a hand if you like – unless you've got designs on a punch-up with him too."

"Me and Rudi, we're okay," said Lloyd, and Dave stood up.

"I'm delighted to hear it." His voice was heavy with sarcasm. "It's gratifying to know that someone's okay in this establishment."

Rudi was in the television lounge with Martin, and Lloyd saw Martin look straight at the photos and letters.

"I got them back," he said. "But Dave's going nuts, because of me and you having a punch-up. He said I've got to move out. He said Rudi's got to help me shift my stuff."

"Where're you going?" said Rudi.

"I got to go into a room on my own, haven't I?"

He saw Rudi breathe in sharply.

"What's up?" he said and Martin eased laconically in his chair.

"We told you about that yesterday. You go into a room on your own and you're in the North Wing – with Caitlin Jamieson. You're going to love that."

Lloyd had forgotten and, for a moment, his stomach lurched, but all he said was: "That isn't no sweat."

The North Wing though, it was certainly worse than the main building and the room he'd been given down there was pokey, with a low ceiling and it only had one small window. The window was letting in the very last dregs of daylight when they went in – and the smell of must and the silence was stultifying.

Rudi helped him stash his stuff and the room generated so much tension that conversation only came in brief snatches.

He was on the ground floor because there was a policy not to allow boys and girls on the same landing.

"Will you be okay?" Rudi said, folding clothes into a drawer.

"Have to be, won't I?"

Rudi looked around, and breathed in, screwing his face into a grimace. "Let me know how you get on anyway – bad or okay. I want to know."

"It won't be bad," Lloyd said. "I survived thirteen years and nothing's beat me yet."

"You will tell me though," Rudi persisted. "Because I'm going to talk to Dave. Get him to put you back with us."

Lloyd shoved socks in beside the T-shirts. "Don't lose no sleep over it, man," he said. But, after they'd finished unpacking they didn't stay in the room any longer than they could help, and – whatever Lloyd said to Rudi, that smell, the must and decay, the degenerating stone – it made him feel very uneasy about the coming night.

There had to be a rational explanation for everything though. He was convinced of that even after the talk with Justin… but he knew as he settled for bed, here in the North Wing, finding a rational explanation would take some doing.

He could explain the cases and the disappearance of the letters – some smart kid trying to frighten him – and the vortexes in the cellar – that could still be a hole in the floor somewhere... it was a long shot – but that's how he'd have to get through it all.

He couldn't lock his door – none of the bedroom doors locked – there was too much risk of kids shutting themselves in, and, when he crept under his duvet there was a coldness penetrating right through to his bones and it wouldn't go away.

He decided to leave the light on. Darkness was a big threat to rational explanations. When you couldn't see what was going on, that was when your imagination played tricks.

He pulled the duvet over his ears and buried his head in the pillow.

But the smell permeated everything, and it seemed to get stronger as the night wore on. Nothing he could do would blot it out. Stuffing his head in the pillow merely suffocated him, so he had to come out for air, and the suffocation on its own was making him feel sick. But, so far, with the light on, nothing seemed too bad. There was an occasional crash from the store room over the way, but, with all the tools Justin had stashed in there, you'd expect that... and thinking of Justin made him feel easier.

He closed his eyes, lying on his back, breathing slowly – deep, gentle breaths, and he tried remembering the two of them sitting out on the bench chatting. He'd been on the brink of telling that guy everything... but, somehow, that didn't freak him out, not like it would have done with others. He felt safe with him. He was only seven years older than Lloyd so it wouldn't be like it was with Bill and Jean.

Through his eyelids he could see the red glow of the light bulb. If he lay very still, he thought, perhaps, sleep would steal over him.

Stillness... and a steady red glow behind his eyelids... and then there was a repetitive crackle, and the red glow began stuttering. He could hear sparks spitting in the light bulb. He sat up and tried to pull his mind together. A short circuit – old houses often had bad wiring. It could happen anywhere.

But he couldn't leave the light on, not spluttering like that. Fireworks in the electric system were bound to keep him awake.

He dragged himself out of bed and, in the darkness, in spite of his bravest efforts, there was a lurch of anxiety.

He knew what he had to do though. He would ride the storm into sleep.

And a storm it was – far worse than the night before in the main wing. First, creaks and groans... but that would be the floorboards contracting in the cold night. Then there were crashes echoing around the corridors – some of Justin's tools being knocked over – probably by rats. He pulled the duvet more tightly over him. That was okay as long as the rats didn't come into his room.

Something touched his face and he jumped – it could have been a moth, something fluttering around the room. The window rattled and the door creaked. He heard it swing open and then slam shut again. That would be the wind. It seemed to have come up quite strongly. Immediately the banging was followed by a rattling against the windowpane. It was almost as if pebbles were being chucked at the glass. A squall of hailstones he thought. What could be more natural in early spring – but... He sat up and opened his eyes. Through the window there was a clear-cut moon, shining, full and gleaming. Then the bed shook. Earth tremors? You did get them in Britain sometimes, but the hailstones were still rattling against the windowpane, even though the moon was out... and the wind was shaking the place with an ice-cold blast, colder than he'd ever felt in his life.

He stared and his brain searched in desperation.

There were shouts now too, cries of anger echoing through the empty rooms, and, immediately, he leapt out of bed.

There was an easy explanation for that. Caitlin Jamieson. The kid was having some sort of nightmare – and that, he could stop.

He pushed through the door and staggered into the passage. There was a wind out there, howling down the corridors like absolute zero, and he felt his way up the stairs to Caitlin's room. Even before he got there though, he knew. The noise wasn't coming from her room. It was coming from somewhere downstairs.

The duvet on her bed was pushed back. The sheets and pillows were disturbed, but she wasn't there.

He felt his way back to the ground floor with the wind ripping through the house and the rattling hailstones on the window panes and he realised the howl of anger was coming from the other side of the cellar door.

Something bad was going on down there and he couldn't let that go unchecked. It would mean going into the cellar again, and that cellar was the worst place in the whole building, with the tornadoes, and now some weird thing that was doing Caitlin's head in.

He thought about fetching Dave, but – no way was Dave going to drag himself out of bed for the likes of Caitlin.

If he knew where Justin lived, he'd go and fetch him… He didn't, though. and really this was just prevarication.

At last he took a deep breath and pushed at the door.

But it didn't give and he gasped with exasperation.

That idiot girl had gone down into the cellar and locked herself in. He tried rattling the door and shouting her name. But still nothing happened.

Then he noticed something that startled him. There was no lock on the door. There was a handle and a door catch, but no lock… and no keyhole.

It must have got jammed somehow.

He pushed at it again but there still wasn't any give. It almost seemed as if some power on the other side was resisting him. Then, with all his strength, he barged, shoving with his shoulder. He ran at the door, but there was still no movement.

If he listened he could catch what Caitlin was shouting. She was practically tearing her throat out down there – and there were words. "Go away," he heard. "Leave me alone" and "I hate you, old man."

He couldn't begin to imagine what was going on and he pushed at the door again, but with no more success than before. All he could do was just stand there, stunned out of his head, and the screaming seemed to go on and on. It was like, when you're in the dentist's chair, and the dentist is drilling… and your brain keeps yelling, "When will this stop? When will it end?"

At last, though, it did end. The hailstones, the wind, the creaks, the shaking of the house, the yells from the cellar, they all stopped at once and a stillness came down on him that was as eerie as the noises had been.

The only sound now was a steady footfall, someone climbing the cellar stairs – slow – regular, like hammer blows.

Then the latch lifted and the door swung back.

He darted against the wall, and Caitlin stood there, her hair a mess, her face pale, her clothes ruffled and, instinctively, he moved towards her.

But she just walked past him as if he wasn't there.

She was treading with even steps. Her eyes were staring and slowly she climbed back to her bedroom.

For a moment he didn't move.

What had happened down there?

Part of him wanted to leg it back to his own room, shut the door and blot it all out. But another part of him wanted to know just what had scared Caitlin.

He put a foot on the first cellar step and switched on the light.

But when he got to the foot of the stairs, there was nothing.

The strong musty smell was there. That always hung around the place though.

There were dust-strewn floors, junk and various furnishings, and the detritus that he'd seen dumped there earlier.

It was certainly colder, but there was nothing else.

He stood, gazing at the crumbling walls, baffled and confused, because something had scared her. He was certain of that. No one could have screamed the way Caitlin did for no good reason.

CHAPTER 5

When he got back to his room there were still noises – banging doors, groaning floorboards, an odd flutter in the ceiling and, upstairs, interminable moans from Caitlin, and what he'd just seen left him stupefied.

If this kind of thing happened to Caitlin every night, it was no wonder she was so stressed out and kept falling asleep in school.

He still didn't want to believe there was anything that couldn't be explained though. He buried his head under the duvet. The fluttering would be a bird trapped in the eaves. The banging was doors left open – and old timbers always groaned.

But the icy wind hurtling down the corridor, and the jammed door of the cellar, that was harder to get his head around… and, if there had been some old man down there, or something else making her shout those words, why wouldn't he have seen it? He wanted to believe she'd been dreaming, but – all the other things that had been going on, and the way they all stopped when the screaming stopped – there was no way he could match that with dreams.

Sleep only crept over him well into the night – and it was restless and spasmodic.

… And, when he woke, it had happened again.

All his drawers had been opened. The clothes he and Rudi had stacked were strewn over the floor. His wardrobe door was swinging and his letters and photos were scattered over the bed.

He didn't know what to do, and it was worse confronting it alone.

If he'd been with Rudi and Martin he might have contained all this; but he wasn't, and he really began to wonder if he could get through it without them.

The feeling only lasted a few seconds. After that the programs kicked in. Doing stuff – that was the way to tackle this kind of thing. He breathed deeply, calming the adrenalin, and then he began to retrieve his clothes – methodically folding them, re-hanging his shirts, gathering the letters and photos into a neat pile.

His travel bag was lying open by the window.

There was a key in one of the side pockets and, when he'd placed the bundle of papers in the case, he locked it, returning it to the corner of the wardrobe, and he put the key in his trousers pocket.

Rudi and Martin were in the bathroom when he went through, and Rudi looked enquiringly.

But Lloyd didn't want to say anything – not yet anyway. Rudi said something to Martin. Then they headed back to their own room.

Breakfast was the same anarchic chaos as everything else at Sarson Hall – only, this morning it was quelled by an oppressive tiredness.

Rudi was attempting to stir the lumps out of his porridge and he said, "Are you going to tell me what it was like?"

"Someone went through my things again," Lloyd said. "All my drawers was open and my stuff was everywhere."

"It couldn't have been Martin," said Rudi. "I'd have heard him. I was worried about you, stuck in that room on your own, and I hardly slept all night."

"I got through it, and I didn't reckon it was Martin anyway."

"Do you know who it was?"

Lloyd shook his head and shovelled some of the tepid porridge down his throat. He was beginning to suspect Justin might be right, and he didn't want to admit that, even to himself. Besides, how could you tell a guy like Rudi that you thought there was some weird force down there, brought on by a sick old house, and it was this that was messing with his stuff. In an effort to deflect Rudi's curiosity he steered away from the subject. "This stuff is like wallpaper paste, man," he said.

Rudi sniffed his bowl and laughed. "It even smells like wallpaper paste. Did anything else happen?"

"There was weird stuff going on all night," he admitted. "Worse than when I was in with you. Did you hear hailstones banging on the windows?"

Rudi shook his head.

"You didn't feel no shaking in the room?"

"No," Rudi said. "Did you?"

"Windows banging – hail and wind – the bed was shaking – I thought it might have been an earth tremor or something."

"That's weird," Rudi said. "Just thinking about it freaks me out." He shovelled in some porridge. "Me and Martin are going to see Dave. We're going to tell him we want you back with us. You shouldn't be left down there with stuff like that going on."

But Lloyd shook his head. "Dave won't agree to me coming back. He don't like me. I stand up to him see. That's why he put me down there in the first place. It was spite. If you say anything it might make things worse."

"I'll see what Martin thinks," Rudi said.

People were barging out now. The congealed gruel seemed to have heightened their aggression. They were supposedly getting stuff for school; but there was mayhem and the carers were ranting at everyone they saw.

As they were bundled through the door, Lloyd looked for Caitlin, but she wasn't there. He wondered whether he should check her out.

He hadn't mentioned Caitlin to Rudi. He could tell him his own personal experiences… but Caitlin… and the old man in the cellar… that was Caitlin's business and it was a bit like an intrusion to talk about that.

Caitlin did turn up for the minibus, and she looked as though she'd been put through a mincing machine. Her hair was wild and she had a pasty complexion. He could see her eyes, darkened with shadows and there was an expressionless pallor about them. As she sat in her corner of the bus she glared at the world, almost daring her surroundings to come near her.

He was beginning to feel sorry for her. He'd already decided, if there was something going on down in that cellar, it had to be stopped and the stuff he'd heard down there last night was seismic. It had rocked his brain, and it was seriously gnawing at his belief that all this was natural. He still wanted there to be explanations, but even the thought of natural explanations made him shudder. It was unthinkable that there was some old man down there, and if it wasn't a man, then, what made her cry out?

There were two things on his mind as they drove towards Brookley. One: he'd got to find out exactly what was going on with Caitlin, and, in order to do that, he'd have to convince her he was on her side. He knew she was a walking piece of malevolence... but... if stuff was happening to her, then it was down to him to stop it.

The second thing he had to do was get to Justin and talk it through with him. He'd go and find him after tea.

There were a couple of stormy geography periods before break where the teacher discovered Caitlin out for the count and decided to give her a bad time – but that was a big mistake, because Caitlin could respond to goading with more venom than an adder.

At break he searched her out.

She was moping by the bicycle racks, still looking as though she'd been in a fight with a polecat.

"What do you want?" she demanded... and he didn't know what to say. Starting a conversation with her was like plunging into sulphuric acid.

"You all right?" he said, and, immediately the scowl on her face deepened.

"That hasn't got nothing to do with you."

"Only, I noticed you wasn't at breakfast and I thought..."

"Yeah? Why was you looking for me at breakfast?"

For a moment he wondered why he was bothering. "It's just – well, I'm in the North Wing too, now... and..."

"You keep away from me then. You come near me and I'll gouge your eyes out."

This was hard and his lungs were on the brink of exploding. "Just shut up and give your ears a chance," he said. "It isn't that I fancy you or nothing. It's just there was stuff going on last night – weird stuff – noises and beds shaking and all that... and I just wondered..."

It was no use though. It was yesterday all over again.

She stepped back and her knees crumbled. Her eyes narrowed and some kind of fear distorted her face. "You're bent – telling me stuff about noises and that."

"I was just worried, that's all. I heard you sort of crying out... and you was shouting stuff."

"I wasn't shouting nothing, and if you say I was I'll stuff my fist down your throat so far it'll come out your backside."

The idea was so surreal he nearly laughed, but Caitlin wasn't laughing. She kicked out at him, and, desperate to get it all out in the open, he said, "You was sleepwalking too. You know that, don't you? You went down the cellar."

By now she was crouching, with her hands gripping her ears, and she was yelling, "Yeah, yeah," in an attempt to drown him out.

"It isn't that I'm trying to scare you nor nothing. I want to help. We got to stop what's going on down there."

But the chant just went on and he had to shout to get through to her.

"Who was the old man?" he said at last. But then she hit out with a vehemence that knocked him sideways and by now she was screaming some really foul stuff.

A load of kids had gathered and she barged through in an effort to get away but, as she did so, one of the politburo pushed into the crowd demanding what was going on. She looked accusingly at Lloyd. "What have you done to Caitlin, Lloyd Lewis?"

"I didn't do nothing," he said, but he was marched off to Mrs Cherry all the same and, by the time he got there, the combination of tiredness and injustice had wound him into just the right mood.

She was sitting behind her desk with her face like an over-ripe tomato.

"So, what's all this with you and Caitlin, young man?" she demanded.

He stuffed his hands into his pocket and gave a shrug. He knew that aggravated most teachers. "Nothing," he said.

"Caitlin doesn't rush across the playground screaming and blocking her ears for nothing."

"I was trying to help her, wasn't I? I got to share the same wing as her back at the home, and I could hear she wasn't sleeping too good. I heard her like, moaning all night, and I asked her what was wrong, that's all."

Mrs Cherry pursed her lips and simpered, "Oh. That's all, is it? A gentle enquiry into her well-being and she goes charging across the playground like someone shot out of a cannon."

He was amazed how many of these people turned to heavy sarcasm whenever they had a go at him. Dave was just the same. He gave another shrug, pushing his hands even deeper into his pockets.

"Well?" Mrs Cherry said.

"Well what?" He stared at the bulbous mole on her left cheek. He imagined it bursting – spurting pus across the room and he wondered if her face was red enough to light up at night. "I said did she know she'd been sleepwalking – and she was sleepwalking – because I saw her, didn't I?"

"Exactly as I thought," Mrs Cherry said. "You were winding her up."

"That isn't winding no one up, that's just showing concern. I wanted to know what was going on in her head to make her sleep walk."

"You wanted to frighten her," Mrs Cherry said. "You know Caitlin is fragile and you wanted to exploit that."

Lloyd stared at her. "If she's so fragile," he said. "What was the geography teacher – Mr Simms or whatever his name is – doing, getting at her all through geography, just because she went to sleep in his lesson. She needs that sleep, and she isn't getting none back at the home. If she's so fragile he should have left her alone – and I *was* worried about her – like I said."

Mrs Cherry gave an aggravating sniff and her eyes narrowed, embedding themselves into the fleshy depths of her face. "You… worried?" she said. "Don't give me that, Lloyd Lewis. Mr Trafford's told me about you. You're a troublemaker and you think Caitlin's an easy target. And it won't do. It won't do at all."

"Whatever," he said. "You believe what you want. I know what I was doing, and it don't make no difference what you think."

The red deepened. She was really wound up now. "Get your hands out of your pockets when you're talking to me," she snapped. "And do not use that insolent tone."

He slithered his hands out of his pockets, in one action that combined the movement with another massive shrug. "Is that it then?" he said.

"No, it is not 'it,'" Mrs Cherry said. She stood up, and her body was quivering. "You can take a detention this lunch time, and make sure you keep well out of Caitlin Jamieson's way from now on."

He gave another shrug. "If you say so, teacher," he said. "Is it all right if I go back to class now? I mean, I'm missing my education all this time and that's what I'm here for, isn't it – to be educated?"

"That's quite enough," she snapped. "I'll see you in detention class immediately after lunch." Then she heaved herself further over her desk, and pointed a finger. "And know this, Lloyd Lewis – I have you in my sights. Any more trouble and you'll be on the slippery path to exclusion. Is that clear?"

He shrugged again and, as he turned, he pushed his hands back into his pockets.

He waited until he was well outside the door though before he said, "Whatever."

She must have contacted Dave because, when they got back to Sarson Hall, Christine was on the steps waiting for him again. There was a look of malicious delight on her face, and she snapped out the words: "Lloyd Lewis" as he tumbled out of the minibus.

"What is it this time?" he said, and she gave him that in-the-know smirk that really irritated him.

"You'll find out soon enough."

She grabbed his arm, and he immediately shook her off. "Don't you touch me," he said. "You can be done for that kind of thing." He turned to the marauding crowd, searching out Rudi. "Rudi, you saw that, didn't you, man? You saw her with her hands all over me?"

All the kids jeered and, for a moment, Christine looked confused. Then she pushed him, propelling him down the corridor. "Don't be so ridiculous," she said. "And get down there to Dave's office without any more lip."

Dave was waiting with the same malevolent delight that Lloyd had seen on Christine's face.

"This seems to be getting a bit of a habit," he said.

"I haven't done nothing," said Lloyd.

But Dave was adopting the praying mantis pose, fingers touching, and he leaned back in his chair. "That's not how it appears according to Mrs Cherry. She said you had Caitlin in a state of hysteria at school today. And what is all this? She tells me you saw her sleepwalking. Is that right? I want to know what's going on down in that wing, boy."

Lloyd shook his head. Whatever was happening to Caitlin, Dave wouldn't do anything even if he told him. "That don't have nothing to do with you," he said.

He watched the colour on his face deepen, so that the rim of hair around his balding head seemed iridescent in contrast to the rest. "You will tell me, Lloyd Lewis," he said.

"It isn't my job to tell you. That's Caitlin's business. If she don't tell you, I don't tell you, okay?"

"Tell me, boy," he said again, and Lloyd looked at him.

"Like I said, it isn't my business to tell you."

He watched as Dave leaned back smugly in his chair. "Then I'm afraid I'm going to have to gate you," he said.

He had a little intercom on his desk and he pressed it. "Fetch Christine in, will you?" he said. "Tell her she's to take Lloyd Lewis to his room, and see he stays there."

But he had to see Justin. He needed to talk about last night, and if Dave gated him, then that wouldn't happen. In spite of himself he blurted out: "You can't do that." And the look on Dave's face made his fist itch.

"Oh, yes I can, Lloyd Lewis," he said. "You can stay in isolation until you decide to tell me what's going on."

"What about my dinner? The food here may be muck, but I need something. I got to live, man."

"Your dinner will be brought to you by Christine," said Dave.

"What if I need the toilet or something?"

"The carers will escort you to the bathroom — but I *will* know what is going on here."

"If I told you, you wouldn't do nothing. You never do."

But Dave was deaf to everything he was saying and there was no way he was telling Dave what he'd seen and heard last night.

Christine took him to his room, and it would be Christine who would monitor him. There was a sadistic relish in her voice as she told him that. Her enthusiasm for the task squashed any hope he had of giving her the slip, and that was a problem.

As she stalked back to the main building, he splayed out on the bed and he felt a jangling in his nerves.

Up until now gating had just meant he wouldn't be able to see Justin, but immediately, as the door shut, there was a shift. He'd forgotten the effect that room had on him and suddenly he was hit by the fact that he was stuck there to face the demons of the night.

He clambered off the bed and began to check his clothes. He wanted to see if there had been any more interference. Then he checked his letters and photos. But nothing had been touched, and he delved further into his travel case.

He'd got an iPod in there. He'd downloaded tracks, back in the other home.

He didn't listen to it often. He was normally too active to lie on the bed listening to music; but stuck in here he had to do something.

For a while he didn't touch it though. Instead he shuffled through his letters and photos.

Somehow, looking at the photos and reading and rereading the letters, took him away – back to the foster home with Jean and Bill. He must have been lying there for half an hour before he heard the resounding footsteps of Christine in the corridor.

She didn't come in. She just banged on the door and shouted, "Lloyd Lewis?"

When he answered, her footsteps retreated and he put the letters and photos to one side. Familiarity was taking the edge off the magic and, eventually, he leaned across and grabbed the iPod.

Outside the sky was weighed with clouds. He didn't think he'd seen a ray of sunshine since he'd been here. He'd have to put the light on soon, and he hoped it wouldn't short again. But first he keyed in some tracks and shut his eyes.

If he could just listen to the music and didn't breathe in the smell too deeply, he might just forget where he was.

The first track was an old Radiohead number, 'Paranoid Android.' He lay for a few minutes as the mood of the music swung and the song changed to the doleful falling notes of "rain down on me." Then he sat up and a fear crept into him. He could sense a faint distortion in the music, and steadily it grew, drowning the music out. Then, in the confusion of crackles, he heard other noises and they had nothing to do with the song. These noises touched him with a sheen of fear – because, what he heard on his iPod, coming distinctly through his headphones, was a demented cry – a wailing chant, a ritual of meaningless sounds – and, over this, clear and recognisable was a voice screaming, "Go away. Leave me alone. I hate you, old man."

It didn't stop, and its repetition beat on his brain, getting louder and louder. For a moment, he was frozen.

Then he tore the headphones away, hurling the iPod onto the floor, and he sat, rigid, his skin prickling. – There was a silence in the room that you could cut.

He didn't move again until Christine arrived with his dinner, and he was almost glad to see her.

He wasn't sure if he could eat – and yet, there might be some respite in filling his gut with food.

After Christine had taken his tray, he was desperate, and he didn't think she'd be back again for a good half hour. That would just about give him time to find Justin.

He could still catch him before he packed up and, almost before Christine's footsteps had faded, he heard what he hoped was Justin returning from the garden. He went to the door to check. Christine had closed the upstairs fire doors, so he crossed to the storeroom and he found Justin busy cleaning a spade on some sacking.

He looked up, surprised to see Lloyd. "I wasn't expecting you," he said.

"I got gated, didn't I? I'm supposed to be in my bedroom. It wasn't my fault though." He watched him take a corner of the hessian sack and begin polishing another spade.

"What's up, then?" he said.

"It's a long story, man. I've been put in one of them single rooms over the corridor. They done that last night because of me getting into that punch up with Martin."

"You're in this wing, sleeping?" said Justin.

"That's what I've got to talk to you about. There's stuff going on in here. I mean – last night – the bed was shaking. And all my things was on the floor again this morning. There was this wind blowing too, hailstones on the windows, and doors banging. I tried going to sleep with the light on – but that started spitting like it was shorting out."

As he was talking Justin wandered across to the wall. There were a couple of garden chairs there and he unfolded them. "Grab yourself a seat," he said.

The chair was damp and breathing an aroma of mildew. "I hope Christine don't check – not while I'm over here," said Lloyd.

"We'll keep our ears open. Now, tell me more about last night."

"All what I told you up till now was just for starters," he said. "The big thing was Caitlin." He looked hard into Justin's face.

"You won't say nothing though, will you? I mean – that's sort of private to Caitlin – until she says something herself."

"Sure," said Justin.

"Well, halfway through all what I already said, I heard this screaming. It was keeping me awake, man – so I had to sort it, didn't I? I went to see what was going on and – like – Caitlin wasn't in her room. All the noise was coming from down the cellar and she was shouting stuff, like – 'Go away,' and 'Leave me alone,' and 'I hate you, old man.'"

"Did you go down and see what was happening?" said Justin.

"I couldn't, could I? The door was jammed. I couldn't move it. And I didn't know what to do – whether to go to Dave or what – but then the shouting and everything stopped and she came up and it was like she was sleepwalking. She didn't see me. She walked straight past me and went back to her room."

"Have you told her about this?" Justin said.

"Yeah, at school today. But she wouldn't listen. She just ran off, screaming. That's why Dave gated me – because he said I was doing it to scare her, and I wouldn't tell him what it was all about."

"Why wouldn't you tell him?" said Justin.

"It's private, man. It's Caitlin's sort of – torment – and it's up to her to tell people. I mean, you can't go in like a bulldozer – not with personal stuff like that, 'specially to someone like Dave."

Justin was very thoughtful again. Lloyd could see something was on his mind. When he did speak, there was a kind of reluctance in his voice. "I know this may sound weird," he said. "But, like I said yesterday, my tutor at university is into this sort of stuff and, to me, it really does sound like paranormal activity – poltergeists and stuff."

"Polter *what?*" said Lloyd.

"Poltergeist," Justin said. He laughed. "It's a German word – for something that creates paranormal disturbances. I know you want to have rational explanations for all this, but I've got to be honest, it doesn't sound normal to me. I'm sure my professor wouldn't see it as normal. It's almost exactly like poltergeist activity. From what you've told me about Caitlin, she could be the cause of it. Sometimes it happens because someone is seriously unhappy. They can create the disturbances without realising it."

Lloyd shook his head. "That's weird, man," he said. "And it don't make no sense to me. I mean, that kind of stuff don't happen, does it? It's got to be something that I can get my head around."

"That's what I'd like to think too," Justin said. He stood and began folding his chair away. "But, say it isn't? Why don't you try getting your head around poltergeists even if they are supernatural? Go online. Google the word. Read what it says and see if it matches what's happening. Do it tomorrow and then tell me what you think. At least we'd know what we're dealing with then. I'll get back to my tutor – see what he says."

The idea of liaising with a professor at a university appealed to Lloyd. "That would be good, man. I'll get on the computer right now."

But Justin grinned. "You've been gated," he said.

"Tomorrow then," said Lloyd and he grabbed Justin's hand, shaking it again as if he was giving the friendship a stronger bond. "I'll see you, okay?"

He felt better now. He still didn't want to accept this stuff, but talking it through with Justin did help and, if it was something that wasn't normal, then, with Justin and the professor's help, he still just might be able to get his head around it. He'd Google poltergeists. If he understood what was going on, he stood a better chance of dealing with it.

When he went back to his room, though, he found, to his dismay, that Christine was there. She must have come back while he was with Justin. She was standing by the bed, arms folded, and her face was grim. "Where do you think you've been, Lloyd Lewis?" she snapped. "Dave said you weren't to leave your room."

"I heard this noise, didn't I?" he said. "Over in the storeroom. I thought someone was breaking in."

She grunted. "Never mind noise. You were told to stay put."

"This isn't a prison," he said. "And I'm telling you – I went over to see who it was. I wasn't going to wait for some guy to come in and murder me, was I?"

"And did you manage to apprehend the so-called killer?" Christine said.

"It was Justin – and we was talking. There isn't no law against that."

"There is when you've been gated," said Christine. "I'm going to report this to Dave, and don't think he'll take it lying down. You'll be gated for a few more days yet."

"Yeah, right," said Lloyd. He threw himself onto the bed.

"And now you're here, you stay here," she said.

It wasn't right. He doubted if it was even legal, and it meant he wouldn't get to the computer, nor see Justin tomorrow. He'd banked on half-hour breaks between Christine's checks, but she was cannier than that. She would come at random times just to catch him out, and the prospect of being stuck in this room weighed on him like a millstone. He wasn't going to be beaten, though. At the very least he'd get to the computer. He thought he might go down tonight when everyone was in bed. He was certain the night duty carers didn't patrol. If they did they would have known about Caitlin.

But the evening stretched into eternity. There weren't any disturbances to start with – but when night finally fell into its comatose depth, things did begin to happen. Doors started banging and there was the howling wind with the hailstones – and still not a cloud in the sky. And that was weird, because, ever since he'd been here the clouds had never broken. Tonight, though, and last night, when darkness came, the world seemed bathed in this eerie moonlight.

He couldn't sleep and, when he judged that everyone was in their rooms, he made the move. He crept out, grabbing his dressing gown and, as he went, he heard a click from Caitlin's door. She was groping down the stairs again and he could see she was in a trance of sleep. She would be heading for the cellar.

He tried calling her, but she didn't hear and he was helpless to do anything. The cellar door swung open, and he knew it would shut behind her well before he got there, and if last night was anything to go by, he wouldn't be able to shift it. The next half hour would be just one long explosion of tormented cries.

He turned back for the main building, to the computer room, and he felt ashamed, because there was a withering cowardice in him making him desperate to escape before Caitlin's first cries.

When he shut the fire door that linked the two buildings, though, it wasn't just Caitlin's cries that were gone. There was no wind and no hailstones. The temperature seemed to rise and it was as if most of the chaos was shut out. There were the groans of shallow sleep and he could hear floorboards creaking – and the uneasy restlessness he'd heard the first night... but the wildness of the North Wing wasn't there.

He stood for a moment at the head of the stairwell. Perhaps this *was* down to Caitlin. Perhaps Justin was right and she was creating the whole thing out of her own mind.

He shuddered.

It was hard to imagine craziness that could conjure up that kind of fury.

In the computer room there were three computers, one assigned to each wall. They were mounted on a running desk with a green swivel chair in front of each monitor. He booted up the computer nearest the door and waited for the circuits to find the Internet. Then he clicked on Google and typed in the word 'poltergeist.'

But as soon as he typed, something weird began to happen. The letters started dancing on the screen, shivering in and out of each other in a random order, tumbling around, only occasionally flashing up with the word he was trying to type. He clicked on search all the same and, straight away, the screen blanked so he could only catch glimpses of the results. Then the sound system began to crackle, and, even though he wasn't touching the mouse, the cursor leaped about the screen. Between flashes, for less time than an eyelid's blink, he saw a shape – a figure – an old man with a long tunic, with wild hair and a sort of woollen helmet. A white beard fell to his waist and the creature had eyes that pierced right through to Lloyd's soul. He only saw it for a split second at a time, but it left an image on his retina, and the image stayed shimmering. It was even clearer when he closed his eyes and it looked like something that had come from darkest history.

In a desperate bid to stop it he pushed the computer's control button, overriding the closedown procedure, and then, stunned into immobility, he stared at the blackened screen.

And, in his head, he could hear Caitlin's tormented cry – "Go away. Leave me alone. I hate you, old man."

He couldn't move.

It was as if the ancient creature had frozen his muscles. And the phrases rang in his head, over and over again, "Go away. Leave me alone. I hate you, old man."

CHAPTER 6

His mind was racing.

Caitlin's old man wasn't a living being. He was something dragged out of mediaeval history – a ghost – tortured by some past event, and it was this creature that was wreaking havoc on Sarson Hall.

If it hadn't been for what Justin had told him, the idea would have blown his brain. He was still stunned and the thought of a ghost appearing in front of him made him shudder, but natural or supernatural, he was still just as determined to have this thing sorted.

Where did it come from though and what could Lloyd do about it? Should the thing be exorcised?

From what he'd seen, the creature must have been from some time long ago, possibly before the Anglo-Saxons. He wasn't sure if something that far back could be Christian and, if not, there wouldn't be much point in getting a priest in. For some sun-worshipping Druid, calling on Jesus wasn't going to carry much punch.

But, if Justin was right and if he could believe his own eyes, he knew who his enemy was now, and that gave him a solid base for a campaign. This guy wasn't some joker, it wasn't some phenomenon brought on by a dysfunctional Caitlin. A spirit from the back of beyond had infiltrated the house.

His thoughts were occupying him so deeply that he lost all awareness of what was happening around him, the movements and groanings – and he certainly didn't sense the more regular creaks in the corridor outside.

He didn't hear the handle turn, or the sound of the door swinging on its hinges – and when he heard a rough voice snarl: "What you doing here, Lloyd Lewis?" he jumped.

Craig Donovan was standing there, his eyes narrowed and his face distorted by long-nurtured malevolence.

"Minding my own business," said Lloyd. "What's your excuse?"

Craig closed the door gently, easing himself into the room, and glared at him. "I'm minding my business too, runt," he said. "And you get this into your thick head. This computer room is my space at night. I do my thing here, so, your business *is* my business. Now, tell me what you're doing here."

As he was talking he came across and made a grab at Lloyd. There was no point in pitching into him either. It wouldn't be like the scrap with Martin. He tugged at his hand, struggling to release himself. "Get off" he said. "I can't say nothing, not while you're blocking my wind pipe."

Craig released his grip and smirked. "So long as we understand each other," he said. "Now – are you going to tell me what you're doing down here? 'Cause if you don't I'm going to knock you into next week. And I'll tell Dave I caught you in here when you should have been tucked up in your own little bed."

Lloyd stared at him defiantly. "Yeah?" he said. "You tell Dave you caught me in here and you've got to tell Dave you was in here too, so, what you going to do about that?"

"That's no sweat," said Craig. He sat down on one of the computer chairs, swivelling around. "I heard noises coming from the computer room, didn't I? The noises woke me up, see, and, being a good right-thinking person, I came down to find out what was going on – and I caught you in here. So – you telling me why you're in here or not?"

There was no way he could tell him the real reason. Craig wasn't the type to be impressed by poltergeists – and, if he did tell him, it would be all around the place that he was out of his skull.

What he said had to have filaments of truth though. The best lies were always based on half-truths. That way, parts of the story could be verified, and those parts that weren't true... well... most people couldn't be bothered to follow them up anyway.

"I got gated, didn't I?" he said.

"Yeah – I heard – winding Caitlin up at school. I tell you what, kid, you don't want to pick on Caitlin Jamieson. She'll get the better of you every time. It's like with me – you don't go messing with someone you can't beat."

"Yeah, okay," he said. "Anyway, I promised to e-mail a mate, and I couldn't get out, what with Christine patrolling and everything – so, when I figured they'd all be in bed I come down to do my e-mailing – That isn't no big deal, is it?"

"You reckon?" said Craig. "I tell you what, black boy. If Dave ever gets to hear you was out when you was gated, it'll be a big deal all right."

"And you're going to tell him?" Lloyd said.

"I might," said Craig. "If it suits me."

"Yeah, well, if you do…"

"If I do… what?" Craig leaned forward, pushing his face into Lloyd's.

"I haven't thought 'what' yet," Lloyd said.

"Well, don't bother. Because I don't plan on telling Dave – not yet – so long as you keep out of here from now on."

He almost sensed his release and got up, sidestepping Craig, preparing for a sharp exit. But that was premature. Craig grabbed him and held him with a calculated stare.

"If I don't say nothing though," he said. "That means you owe me – okay? There aren't no free lunches in here, and you got to learn that. Do you get what I'm saying?"

Lloyd shrugged. The idea of being under an obligation to Craig Donovan wasn't that great, but at least he could shelve it for the time being. There were more pressing things in his head.

"Whatever," he said, and eased himself out of the room, shutting the door quietly behind him.

Sometime in the future, Craig would want some kind of a favour. Then would be the time to sort him out. And he would sort him out. When the time came he'd let him know Lloyd McKenzie Lewis wasn't a pushover for anybody. There was no way he was going to be some kind of running boy for Craig Donavan.

He made his way back to the North Wing and, when he pushed through the fire doors, he could hear moans from Caitlin's bedroom. The ghost's appearance in the cellar seemed to have run its course or – maybe it hadn't happened. Perhaps the thing was too busy flashing up on the monitor down in the computer room.

He went back to his bedroom, but, as he opened the door, he stopped and stared.

His drawers and his wardrobe had been ransacked again and, this time, the poltergeist had really gone crazy. His bedclothes had been torn from his bed and his sheet was tied to the electric light flex. His case was hanging, unopened, from the base of the sheet, and it was swinging like some kind of corpse hanging from a gibbet.

For a while he just stood there, and it was almost impossible not to be swamped by it. What was he supposed to do? Clamber up and untangle his sheet, remake his bed, put his clothes back in the drawers and wardrobe, and then curl up like a baby and sleep the sleep of the innocent for the rest of the night?

The very idea of going into the room made him want to vomit.

If he was going to unravel that sheet he'd have to leave the door open and turn the passage light on. There was no way he was messing around with the flex while it was live – and it was quite likely the light would be on its shorting gig by now. He'd have to put his clothes away with just the sliver of light from the corridor.

Deliberately he began to undo the damage. At least the poltergeist hadn't been so vindictive as to tie the knot tightly. Unravelling the sheet from the flex was easy – and so was releasing his travel case.

He fumbled through the pockets of his trousers for the key so he could check for his letters and photos, and they were still safely stashed. It was as if the thing had done the sheet trick in a fit of pique because it couldn't get to his letters.

He locked the case again and put it back in the wardrobe along with his shirts and trousers. Then he tried the light, and it didn't spit, so he was able to close the door and begin folding the rest of his clothes.

When he'd made his bed, he pulled the duvet tight over his shoulders. But there wasn't a grain of sleep in him. He just lay there, staring at the bare walls.

He could hear the occasional wail from upstairs, and – in a way – there was a warped camaraderie about sharing this madness. It had changed his view of Caitlin. He wouldn't ever torment her about her moods and grumpiness again. The fact that she could put one foot in front of the other and present a feisty opposition was beginning to amaze him. She never let on about this stuff – not to anyone and he reckoned she had more spirit in her little finger than he had in his whole body. She'd been in this dump for weeks, and he was heading for the mad house after two days.

… But he wasn't heading for the mad house, was he?

It wasn't in his nature to head for the mad house.

He began to breathe deeply and steadily. Then he thought about Jean and Bill… and the days when he was a kid, living with them, and he thought about Justin. He'd find a way to get to him tomorrow, so they could start working out how to deal with all this stuff.

He'd tell Rudi about it too – and he'd tell him about Caitlin.

He carried on his steady breathing and let thoughts of Justin and Rudi, and Jean and Bill, swirl around his head. It was like a mental sedative and gradually, with superhuman effort, he slipped into a restive sleep.

The poltergeist, or whatever it was, must have spent itself for the night, because when he woke up in the morning, there were no more disruptions. His clothes were still stacked and the case was secure in the corner of the wardrobe.

He didn't wait for Christine. He went down to the bathroom. Then he dressed and marched unescorted into breakfast. In the confusion no one noticed or cared, although Rudi had seen he wasn't at dinner the previous evening.

"I got gated for doing Caitlin's head in, didn't I?" Lloyd said. "Christine brought my dinner in on a tray, and, no messing, she was guarding my cell like a Rottweiler."

Rudi laughed. "Me and Martin really are going to get you out of there," he said. He was stirring the globules out of his congealing porridge. There was a particularly obstinate glob and he tilted his bowl, pressing it against the side, squashing it like a recalcitrant pluke. Then he stared at the gluten-grey sludge and shovelled a spoonful into his mouth.

Lloyd patted him on the shoulder. "That shows real courage, man, and, if you can do it, so can I."

He shovelled a spoonful into his own mouth and looked around at the soured mayhem... it was time... he was going to tell Rudi what he'd found out.

"I got to see you lunchtime," he said. "In the computer room at school. I got something to show you. It's about the house, and the stuff what's going on here. I want to Google something Justin told me and I reckon it's going to blow your mind."

He kept his distance from Caitlin.

He was longing to ask her about the old man, but he knew it would be dicing with death and he could finish up being dragged up in front of the bulbous Mrs Cherry again... and her reptilian side-kick, Dave.

Caitlin kept watching him. She seemed frightened, and when he came to think of it, he could understand why. Delving into the sleepwalking and the old man must be like poking an open sore for her, and that wasn't the way to go about things.

At lunchtime he and Rudi went to the computer wing to investigate poltergeists. The idea that this stuff might be linked to the supernatural shook Rudi, but he had a level head on him. He could cope. And it was much as Justin had said. Poltergeists were paranormal disturbances – creating mayhem exactly like the stuff that was going on at Sarson Hall. Their manifestation was often brought about by the presence of a very disturbed or unhappy person – often a child.

Rudi thought of Caitlin, but Lloyd said: "This stuff was going on well before Caitlin – and it don't have to be caused by someone what's still alive."

They looked at the screen again. It said that poltergeists could be brought about by events from the past – paranormal echoes from an upheaval in history. "The house is really old," said Lloyd. "The North Wing especially. It goes back to Tudor times, Robin, my social worker said that, and… it could be something that happened even before Sarson Hall was built."

"We need to find out something about the history," said Rudi.

"Justin will know. He crashed out of university. He done history and archaeology. He knows loads of stuff."

"Could there be another reason why it's happening?" Rudi said, but the only other potential causes they could find on Google were described as "earth forces" – disruption of the natural forces of the earth.

"Would Justin know about them?"

Lloyd nodded. "If he don't, his tutor at university will. He's into that kind of stuff."

Rudi looked at the screen again.

"I think there's some kind of ghost," said Lloyd at last. "I tried Googling this stuff back at the home last night. I waited till Christine was out the way, and went down the computer room. And when I Googled, the screen went crazy and I kept seeing, like, this old guy flashing up. He had weird clothes on and his hair was grey. He'd got this long beard, like God – and he had a woollen helmet on."

Rudi breathed in sharply. "That is so creepy," he said.

"We got to put up some kind of a fight," said Lloyd. "I mean we can't just let the guy carry on like he is, and, if we can borrow some books on mediaeval history and stuff, we might find out when he hung out. That would be a start."

There wasn't much time after they'd finished with the computer, but they did manage to find a couple of books in the library, and their choice impressed the librarian. She wasn't used to kids from Sarson Hall taking out books that hinted of intellectual pursuits.

They hoped to look at the books that evening – but they reckoned without Christine and Dave.

Lloyd's favourite warden was waiting for him when they got back.

Rudi dug him in the ribs. "That's your woman," he whispered.

"Yeah, she really must fancy me," Lloyd said, but he was seething inside. "What you want this time?" he shouted. "I haven't done nothing. I didn't even speak to Caitlin."

"That's not the point, young man," Christine said. "You went out when you were gated and Dave isn't happy. I told you he wouldn't be."

Dave seemed to have forgotten about Caitlin, because the only topic for his rant this time was how Lloyd had left his room without an escort. And after the rant, he was frogmarched back to the room for another evening of incarceration, which really made him furious.

He'd planned for Rudi to come up and he needed to see Justin. It also hacked him off that Dave hadn't made a semblance of listening to his story about the suspected break-in.

But Dave never listened to anything, and it was clear that, whatever he and Justin did about the ghost, it would have to be done behind Dave's back. He would have to go to places and consult people – he'd have to break away from the restrictions of the home and risk Dave's fury on a permanent basis.

And... say they needed a priest to do some exorcising?

Smuggling a priest into Sarson Hall... that would be something.

He pictured some old guy in his black robes hiding himself behind bushes and darting from cover to cover, while the kids set up decoys to keep Dave and the carers out of his way.

But, in mid-dream, he shuddered, and a cold reality caught him.

This wasn't the stage for a farce.

He was stuck in this room and, last night, while he'd been out, some unknown force had messed with his drawers, with his clothes, with his travel case and his bedclothes. And when whatever-it-was got up to full momentum, it could shake the windows, create hailstones and gales, whip up pandemonium and there was nothing about it that made him want to fall about laughing.

The sky hung, grey and menacing, and, even though it was barely five o'clock, it was getting dark. Everywhere else in Britain would be celebrating spring, but here it might as well be January.

Christine banged on his door and stalked off down the corridor when she'd heard his growl of a response.

"I'll be back, Lloyd Lewis," she snapped. "So don't get any ideas about chasing burglars."

He risked the light and began to browse one of the books, but nothing even vaguely resembled the bearded figure he'd seen on the computer screen.

He was certain it couldn't have been something later than mediaeval times so, what came before the Middle Ages and before the Romans?

Was it the Dark Ages?

He shuddered.

Even the name sounded bad. No wonder the fury was so massive. It was something that had been festering from further back than Jesus. It was almost beyond him to grip something that went that far back.

He needed to get to Justin and describe this guy to him.

He leaned over and laid the book on the duvet. Nothing had happened to the light so far and, apart from the chilling clamminess and smell, there wasn't much that hinted at the paranormal.

Christine came back with his dinner and she seemed surprised to see history reference books on his bed.

"What's that you're reading?" she said, picking up one of the books and fingering through it.

"Nothing you'd understand. Them books have got words with more than four letters in. That's way above your head, that is."

She glared at him, but all she said was, "You make sure you get that food down you before I come back. I can't be waiting around for you – and I'll be back in fifteen minutes."

The dig had struck home though, because, when she came back, she snatched at his tray and said, "I got an A★ in English literature when I did my GCSEs so you can stop all that nonsense about four letter words."

"Yeah, right," he said. "And what grade did you get in the prison warden exam? Triple A★?"

He could see she was hard pushed not to hurl the tray at him and he felt a tinge of triumph. But she would watch his room like a hawk. There was no way he'd get to Justin.

There was half an idea forming in his head, though, and he knew, if he followed it through, it could be the most terrifying encounter of his life… but he was beginning to think he'd do it all the same.

He waited until everyone had gone to bed and, while he waited, he leafed through the books again, searching out the earliest people he could find; but they all seemed streets ahead of the apparition he'd seen on the computer.

Then the disruptions began.

As the doors in the main building slammed for the last time and night settled, his light began spitting. Winds started sweeping through the corridors with the melancholic song of a banshee. The sky began to clear for its nightly hailstone shower. For a while he just lay there, his book unread. Then he heard his wardrobe shift. It was as if some force was pushing it across the floor and, even though he'd endured this for two nights, it made his spine seize up.

When he judged that the duty carers had finished their surveillance he crept out of bed and slid into the corridor.

This time he didn't wait at his own door, or head back towards the main building. Instead he made his way up to Caitlin's room. He could hear her groaning. But he'd worked out from previous nights that, when she walked, she didn't know what was going on around her.

Tonight he was going to get to grips with whatever was going on down in that cellar. He was going to follow her and get down there with her. With luck she wouldn't even realise he was there.

He stood, shivering, waiting, until her door clicked and she emerged. She was in her own private trance again, treading out the path towards the stairs and, all the time, he stayed close at her heels.

The cellar door swung open as she got nearer, and still he stuck with her. Then he was through, following her towards the bowels of the house.

There was a resounding thud as the door slammed behind them and he gave an involuntary shudder, because this was the place where her "old man" had walked and, tonight, if he appeared again, he would be there to see it.

CHAPTER 7

He stood at the bottom of the stairs, and there was an icy clamminess in the air. There were whispers of sound, and groans – timbers tearing themselves apart. The electric light was on, although he couldn't remember either of them touching the switch, and the sensations down there were stifling.

He saw Caitlin move towards the back wall and then it began.

Whirlpools of dust – they seemed to wander at random; but, at the same time, there was an end – a focus.

He couldn't move. He was staring at the invisible point where they met, and they started growing, lifting rubbish from the cellar floor, tossing it roughly into the air, thrusting up leaves and bits of wood. And he could hear Caitlin's voice – nothing more than a whisper, but she was saying: "Don't you come, old man. You stay away. You stay like you are – flying dust."

The swirls spiralled as they merged, forming a living force field. Then they melted back into the wall, sucking out the loose plaster, and there was luminosity. It made him gasp because the merging spirals were morphing, taking on limbs. There was a long, ancient beard and shocks of wild hair. A body, and legs, – then a full image emerged, crouching inside the stones, and this was different from what he'd seen on the computer. This thing wasn't wearing the long cloak. It was naked to the waist, with just a chain of clashing stones hanging around its neck, and it was wearing rough breeches with some kind of crossed leather thongs on its legs.

For a moment it seemed carved into the stone, but its eyes were darting, searching the room and then groans and a spine-freezing rage echoed around the cellar. Out of the corner of his eyes, Lloyd saw Caitlin crouching, covering her ears, her face white with terror.

He wanted to go and shield her but he couldn't. The sight and the fury had made his muscles seize up, and even breathing was hard. He knew the whites of his eyes must be shining out of his face, and there was no logic in his thinking – just a primitive terror as the crouched figure burst into life.

Its eyes were flashing, its teeth gnashing and, wielding some kind of axe in its left hand, it leapt out from the wall. Its face was contorted with fury and Lloyd could see all of it directed at Caitlin.

It was darting at her, prancing on its feet, slashing the axe and, all the time, these unearthly sounds were coming from it, guttural noises that had no body to them, hissing, without any substance and they were echoing around the cellar.

Caitlin stayed crouched, but he could see she was retreating, creeping step by step away from the thing. Then she screamed – the same desperate words he'd heard from beyond the cellar door: "Go away old man. Leave me alone. I hate you. I hate you."

He still couldn't move and, all the time, the creature was leaping forward, pouncing, hissing out the hollow roar, and each time it got near to Caitlin it retreated, as if it was performing some kind of demonic dance. And it was Caitlin who was the only object of its attention. It was as if, for the ghost, Caitlin carried the evil of the world inside her.

Time and time again it leapt, scything with its axe; and with miniscule crouching movements, Caitlin retreated towards the steps.

At last Lloyd's senses began regrouping.

It seemed the ghost didn't know he was there. It hadn't looked at him. It hadn't even acknowledged his existence. It was just Caitlin.

At least it wasn't hurting her. It was acting more like a mad dog leaping about on its chain. All it did was hiss from a throat that had no larynx and, it seemed, its only motive was to scare her.

If he could draw its attention away it might deflect the fury and give her a chance to escape.

Summoning all his strength he filled his lungs, and bawled. "Leave her alone, stone man. You want to pick on someone, you try picking on me."

It was a wild challenge and he cowered, dreading what the ghost would do… And the thing heard. It had known he was there all the time, because it turned its eyes, and it was as if Lloyd was looking into the depths of history.

What came next, though, left him completely baffled.

The apparition acknowledged him with a nod, and then it made some sort of gesture with its left hand as if it was dismissing him – as if he wasn't important, and straight away it turned back to Caitlin, parrying with its axe and driving her further towards the cellar steps.

Caitlin didn't make any response when Lloyd shouted. She seemed to be so deep in her trance that she wasn't aware of anything except the ghost.

Then, as if it had suddenly burned itself out, the spectre melted back into the wall.

Lloyd saw the pale luminosity fade into the stones, and there was stillness as deep as frozen snow.

Caitlin didn't move straight away.

He felt really sorry for her. He couldn't understand why this thing had picked on her like it had.

He didn't go after her when she began her trance-like walk up the steps. It was best to let her get back to her room first. Besides, although he didn't want to admit it, what he'd seen had left him so transfixed he wasn't sure he could move.

His mind was teeming though – questions reeling without connecting.

Why did the ghost bully Caitlin? Because it *was* bullying her… and yet it wasn't interested in frightening him – even though the spirits and the poltergeists back in his room had made his life hell.

After a few minutes he thought it was time to go back up the stairs, but, as he made to move, his nerves froze and his limbs wouldn't budge. Then, as his instinct was telling him he must get out at all costs, he heard the door at the top of the stairs slam shut again.

The dim illumination of the forty-watt bulb began to stutter and he felt a cold sweat breaking out all over him.

This time the ghost had him in its sights and the swirls of dust began sweeping the floor, gyrating into pinnacles, darting silently towards their central point and, slowly the wall lit into the pale green luminescence he'd seen when Caitlin was there.

The creature had registered him, but obviously it only dealt with one person at a time... and now it was his turn.

He couldn't begin to describe the fear. His eyes were stretched and it was as if he'd become fossilised.

All he could do was stare at the crumbling cellar wall as, gradually, the dust and light mutated and became like an ancient wall painting.

This time though, there was more.

The thing was crouched, but it wasn't the bare-chested apparition that had raged at Caitlin. Now it was robed as it had been on the computer screen and it was wearing its woollen helmet. And in the wall, there were other objects.

Slowly, as the mutation continued, everything moved out into the room. The images hovered like holograms. And he could see what they were: pots – four of them – two patterned and two plain. They were simple, beautifully curved, and Lloyd couldn't understand. It didn't seem the ghost had any intention of terrorising him. When it saw him its first act was to lift its hand to its face and pull back its hair.

He peered into the darkness and he could make out a simple cylindrical ornament hanging from each ear. Then it pointed to its neck to show him the button holding the cloak together. After that it drew attention to its belt and Lloyd could see it, held together with what looked like a bone ring, or it could have been wood or metal... and, as he stared, he sensed the spectre was deliberately showing him these things.

To his shame he still couldn't move, and when it lifted its arm he wasn't sure if it was to show him the rectangular wrist guard or... it seemed to be beckoning. He wasn't convinced he wanted to go near it, even if he could have done; he was suspicious, and if he got too near...

Slowly it lifted its head and the strange, unearthly sound came again — only this time he sensed words.

He couldn't understand them. They were in some language the creature had known and used in his own time — but the sound — and the sight of the slow moving luminosity was the eeriest thing he'd ever seen and, instead of responding to the beckoning arm, as his limbs became free, he stepped backwards. He couldn't help it. The whole thing had his head reeling and his stomach was in turmoil.

He saw it shake its head and whisper the sounds all over again — and then it faded back into the wall... And that left Lloyd with a whole new sensation.

He was ashamed.

He'd had his chance. The ghost had shown him no hostility, and he'd backed away.

But — if he had stepped towards it, if he had gone to the wall, for all he knew, it might have grabbed him. It might have dragged him down into its own world of shadows and death.

On the other hand it just might have wanted to tell him something. It just might, for some reason, have wanted to create a link with him, and that idea left him gaping.

Whatever the ghost's plans though, he'd bottled out and now it was too late. He was left to wrestle with his own confusions and his own failure.

There was just the cold clamminess in the cellar now, and the smell of decay. The forty-watt bulb had settled and he knew, when he climbed the stairs, the cellar door would be open.

It wasn't the same as it had been for Caitlin. He was in complete control of his movements. There was no trance and he remembered every detail of what had happened.

He knew, the next day, he would have to keep his nose clean

If he messed up he would be in his room again, gated, and that would mean he couldn't sort things out with Justin.

And it was hard.

All day, at school, he was biting his lip. Some of the teachers were such morons, they begged for abuse, and years of practice made it almost impossible for him not to dish it out.

Mr Simms had a go at Caitlin again and he was almost on his feet before he remembered the threat hanging over him, but the biggest pressure for a flare up came when they got back to the home.

It was Friday afternoon, which meant even more of them were crowded into the dining room. They were being dished up with standard end-of-the-day treats. This time it was a mini Mars Bar with a mug of over-stewed tea or a glass of reconstituted orange – whichever their shell-shocked taste buds preferred.

Rudi wasn't there, and neither was Martin – but Craig Donovan was.

Lloyd had made a conscious effort to keep out of his way all day, because he knew that Craig had been eyeing him at breakfast. It wasn't so easy back here though and he could see Craig jostling towards him.

He was just about to consume his Mars Bar and over-ripe tea. He suspected that reconstituted orange would be so full of e-numbers that it might just push him over the edge. He had more confidence in his ability to deal with a hefty dose of tannin and caffeine.

He watched as Craig shoved across the room and he decided, if that guy had his sights on him, he'd better be told the truth now, because Lloyd wasn't going to take any rubbish from him.

Then he heard a voice wafting over the pandemonium. "Hey, you – black boy."

He'd said that in the computer room and Lloyd had let it pass, but he wasn't going to this time. "That's racist, man," he said.

He pushed a couple of kids out of the way so he could face Craig front on.

"Yeah, well? I am racist, aren't I? You going to make something of it?" Craig said. "And you is black, okay?"

It was all conducted at the highest volume. That's how it worked at Sarson Hall. Any abuse had to be heard by everyone.

"Yeah, all right," Lloyd said. "If you say so, pink boy."

The kids around sniggered and he was only a nanosecond away from a punch up – but, this time, Craig had designs for something else. "That's another one you owe me," he hissed. "You try getting mouthy with me and I'll take you apart."

He edged him into a corner where there was less chance of someone listening, and he lowered his voice. "Don't you forget it neither. That's twice you owe me – and owing me isn't going to be easy. When we get back to school Monday I got a job for you. And you're not saying 'no.'"

Lloyd knew he couldn't take him on. He would have to make some play at submission. "You going to tell me what this job is, or what?" he said. "So I can think about it."

Craig looked around and there was a furtive restraint in his voice. "It isn't no big deal," he said. "But you breathe a word about it and you're dead."

Lloyd nodded.

"Okay. I got this line running at school, yeah?" Craig said. "Kids – they aren't so smart – some of them, and I do their homework for them, right? Only, the teachers, they've got onto me. What I do is, I give these kids the answers to their homework and they give me a tenner. But I can't be seen to hand the stuff over, because of the teachers; they're watching me all the time. That's where you come in, black boy, because they won't suspect you. I give you the stuff for the kids in an envelope, right? Before school, then you do your bit at break time – give over the envelope and collect the money. You give the money to me when we get back. Okay? That isn't any big deal, is it? You keep your mouth shut though, or, like I said, you're finished."

Lloyd had expected something worse than running homework. "How will I know who to give the envelope to?" he said.

"Okay, listen. Monday at school, right? I'll show you the kid – but that's all. So no one's going to suspect nothing. Then, Tuesday I'll slip you the homework. You got to give it to the guy, quiet like – so no one sees you. Tell him it's homework from Craig – and he'll give you the money. Make sure there aren't any teachers around though."

Lloyd nodded, but he was beginning not to like it. The more he thought about it, the more certain he was that this wasn't homework.

"Okay," he said. "Because I owe you, and it isn't too much of a sweat. But it's only this one time."

He saw Craig's face harden and he shook his head slowly. "I told you kid, paying me off isn't that easy. If I ask you to do it a hundred times, then you'll do it a hundred times, right?"

It wasn't what Lloyd wanted to hear. He was certain now, there was something underhand going on, and he was cornered.

"You point the kid out to me Monday, and I'll see, because I do owe you one for down in the computer room. But don't push it. I got to be my own man."

"Yeah, well —" Craig said.

It was clear from his shrug that, for the time being, he was done with Lloyd, but Lloyd was uneasy. Whatever Craig was up to, it wasn't homework. He didn't have the brain cells to do his own homework, so how was he going to do it for other kids? And to make matters worse, Lloyd hadn't put up a fight. He'd been too afraid of getting gated again.

He looked around the room. He could have done with Rudi. If Rudi had been there, Craig wouldn't have cornered him. He downed the tea and mini Mars Bars and shoved through the crowd to get out and find him.

Rudi was wandering down the corridor from Dave's office with his hands in his pockets and he was looking pleased with himself.

"Me and Martin have been to see Dave," he said.

Lloyd glanced at him and frowned, because people didn't come back from seeing Dave looking like the cat that's just prized open the pilchard tin. "Yeah," he said. "What you go and see Dave for?"

"To get you back with us," Rudi said. "We told him he'd got you all wrong with the punch up and it was just a bit of fun that got out of hand. We said you were a good guy and we really liked you being in with us."

Lloyd had forgotten Rudi's mission to get him out of the North Wing, and it caught him wrong-footed.

A couple of days ago he would have been glad, but now he wasn't so sure. There was Caitlin. He didn't want to leave her at the mercy of the ghost. And his mind was set on sorting this out. Being back in the main building, sharing a room with Rudi and Martin, would cramp his style.

"What did Dave say?"

"Dave was Dave," Rudi said, "But we planted the idea in his head. If he doesn't do anything in the next few days, we'll go back."

"That's real nice, Rudi, man," Lloyd said. "But…"

He had to tell him. He already knew about the apparition on the computer monitor and the poltergeist. There was no reason not to tell him everything. He could see he was looking puzzled.

"What do you mean, 'But'?" he said. "You haven't got a problem being back with me and Martin, have you?"

Lloyd shook his head and grinned. "No way," he said. "You wanting me back, that's respect man, that's good, but – there's stuff going on in the North Wing that I got to tell you about, and I got to stay down there for a bit, on hand like, to see it through."

Rudi nodded and there was a glint of expectation in his eyes. "You going to tell me what it is then?" he said.

"No sweat. But you go and have your little Mars Bar first, and then we've got to find Justin, because, what I found out last night – well, we really need his help, him knowing all that history stuff."

The grey of the skies and sight of bare trees pierced Lloyd's senses as they stepped out of the main entrance.

No matter how often he walked into that expanse of abandonment, it always made him shudder. The curse of the ghost hung over everything, draining the life forces out of the place.

He pulled his jacket around him and told Rudi to do the same.

They found Justin at the back of the North Wing, turning over an unyielding bed of clay. Even the soil seemed contaminated with sterility. Justin leaned on his shovel and grinned.

"What's up?" he said. "You look like a couple of guys on a mission."

"We are, man," said Lloyd. "I got stuff to tell you what will blow your mind – and yours too, Rudi, and I got questions that need answers, because it's doing my head in."

Justin laughed. "No pressure then!" he said. He looked at his watch and then at the sky. "I think it's time I knocked off anyway. Digging over this clay is breaking my back." His hair fell loosely about his face. "Shall we go back to the storeroom? That way you can help me clean off these tools and give me the lowdown on what's doing your head in at the same time."

They trudged around the corner to the main entrance of the North Wing.

"I know it's cold outside," Lloyd said as they pushed through. "But I got to admit, this place still freaks me out – so – when we've finished polishing up your spades and stuff, do you think we could go back outside? I mean, I get enough of this place, having to sleep in here, isn't that right, Rudi? And I've been gated for the last two days."

Justin nodded. He grabbed some sacking and began working on one of the shovels. "Right, what's been doing your head in?" he said.

Lloyd told them – filling Rudi in with the bits he didn't know – about Caitlin's midnight walks and the ghost in the cellar.

"The guy had these crossed gaiter things on and he wasn't wearing nothing above his waist," he said. "And there was, like, this axe he was swinging. Then, when Caitlin had gone, he came back with them terracotta pots and stuff, and he had the cloak and helmet on."

"It sounds like some sort of Neolithic man," Justin said. "Or someone from the Bronze Age." He went to his rucksack in the corner and pulled out a writing pad he used to make notes about planting and gardening. "Do you think you could draw the pots? Because, if you could get them right, it might help identify him."

Lloyd took the pad. He was good at drawing, and sketching things was no problem.

"I'll draw the axe, too, and the guy showed me his necklace and earrings. I'll draw the belt, too, if you like."

He sketched quickly, with Rudi and Justin watching over his shoulder.

"You're really good at that," Rudi said.

"Yeah. It's one of my many talents. You got to run to keep up with me if you're talking about talents, man."

"You're not bad," Justin said with a grin. "And you've got a great eye for detail. That's definitely a pot from the Bronze Age – and the axe too. Draw the other pots and the ornaments."

Lloyd completed the sketches. He wasn't averse to adulation and he looked up, grinning. "That's a good likeness, that is. I'll sign it for you, if you want."

"An early Lewis. I'll frame it and wait till it makes my fortune," Justin said. He looked at the drawings. "Have you ever seen pots like these before – in a museum or something?"

Lloyd shook his head. "Couldn't find stuff like this, not even in the books we got out the library. Why?"

"Because, it looks like stuff from a tribe called the Beaker folk. They were really important," Justin said. He stacked the gardening tools in a corner of the room and draped them with the Hessian sacks. "We could go outside now if you want. We can chat in the grounds – go for a walk or something."

Lloyd was glad to be in the open air.

"There's still stuff I can't get my head round," he said.

They wandered off towards a cluster of trees at the back of the building.

"What do you mean?" said Rudi.

"Well, when Caitlin was in that cellar and the ghost was there, it was like it hated her. There was this weird hiss and the guy was terrorising her – but, when it come back and I was there on my own, it wasn't like that at all. It brought all them pots and stuff to show me – and it was like – trying to talk to me. It said things in this weird language too and it… well, sort of signed for me to come closer. That scared me, and I backed off – but it wasn't trying to frighten me."

Justin was thinking. "This may sound stupid," he said, "but – do you think it wasn't hostile to you because you're black?"

"What you saying, man? That sounds racist," said Lloyd, and Justin laughed.

"No. I mean, it may have identified Caitlin with Caucasians – and – whatever happened to it that was bad was done by white people. It might be linking her with that... and you, being Afro-Caribbean – and – this may sound even weirder but, presumably, this ghost has been around for a bit, and it knows about history – it may know your kind was oppressed by white people. It may feel some kind of kindred spirit."

"That's awesome," Rudi said.

"It's just an idea. It may be that it sees you as a sort of brother in oppression, and it's trying to communicate with you."

Lloyd didn't move. It made sense and suddenly all his desire to obliterate the ghost was turned on its head, and the thought took his breath way. "What would it want to communicate with me for?" he said.

"It could see you as an ally. It could reckon you might right a wrong for it," said Justin and now the thoughts were teeming in Lloyd's head. Righting a wrong for some guy who lived before Jesus; that was massive and it wasn't self-preservation any more. It was something way beyond his mind-set. He didn't think righting another guy's wrongs was anything he'd ever thought about, although there was Caitlin but... to do it for someone as old as this...

"I don't even know what bad thing it is what's doing the ghost's head in. So I don't see how I can put it right," he said.

"You've got us to help you," Rudi said.

But Justin sighed and sat on the stump of a nearby tree: "I don't know that I should be doing all this," he said suddenly.

"Why not, man?" Lloyd said. "You're the only guy here I can trust – apart from Rudi." He could feel a tinge of embarrassment colouring his face because there were deeply hidden confidences bashing on the door of his throat and they were bent on coming out. "You two are my best friends. I depend on you. If you can't do all this with me..." He tailed off and he saw Justin turn to look at him, slim, his long hair to his shoulders, straight and glinting.

"That's really nice," he said. "But, the trouble is, I'm staff here, aren't I? And it's like, I'm colluding with you… leading you into something – and it could be dangerous. I should be keeping you away from all this."

"Yeah, but, if that ghost wants me to do something – to right some wrong, like you said – then it wouldn't be right for me not to give it a go, would it? And I can't do that without you. I mean, you know about all this stuff and I'm – well – I'm leaning on you, man, and anyway, to me and Rudi, you aren't staff. I hate staff, but I don't hate you. No way. You're like a brother to me, isn't that right, Rudi?"

He could see Justin was touched, but it was still giving him grief.

"You got to help us," he persisted. "We don't know nothing about this stuff. You went to university… I mean – the Beaker folk – you said they was important. Me and Rudi, we don't know why they was important, do we, Rudi?"

Rudi shook his head and Justin smiled. "Okay," he said. "And thanks. That means a lot to me, that does."

"You going to tell us about the Beaker folk then?" said Lloyd.

Justin made room for the two of them on the stump. "You ever heard of stone circles?" he said. "Stonehenge and places like that?"

Lloyd nodded. "Yeah, 'course I have. You've heard of Stonehenge, Rudi, yeah? It's like where the Druids go to see the sun rise on the Summer Solstice."

Justin nodded. "The Beaker folk, they had a big hand in building those circles," he said, and Lloyd breathed in sharply.

"That old man?" he said. "He could have been one of the guys what built Stonehenge?"

"Or a henge like it," Justin said. "There's one much nearer. It's up at Brookley, although there isn't much of it left."

"That's so awesome," said Lloyd, and it was as if this creature terrorising Sarson Hall had suddenly taken on a new persona. It wasn't so much that he was getting to like the guy, but he was getting interested in him… and the ghost's manner with him last night, no way was it hostile, not like it had been with Caitlin.

He brought his knees up to his chin and looked at Justin. "The more I think, the more I reckon that ghost was trying to scare Caitlin off. It don't want her down there." He paused. "I mean, this may sound big headed, but... say it wants to tell me stuff and it don't want her around. Does that sound weird?"

Justin shook his head. "That was one of my thoughts while you were telling us about it. It was trying to talk to you. And it did wave you to come nearer."

Lloyd laughed. "I thought it was a trap, man. I thought, the minute I got within touching distance it would grab me and drag me off down to hell."

"Shouldn't you go down the cellar again?" Rudi said. "On your own. I know that's not a nice thought, but, if it's trying to tell you something, then you ought to give it another chance."

Lloyd sat back. "I suppose so. But..." He looked at Justin. "It isn't that easy, is it? Caitlin goes down every night – in this trance – it's like she's sleepwalking, and I don't see how I'm going to get down there without her."

Justin sighed. "This is the bit that worries me," he said. "I'm giving you advice and I don't know if it's the right advice. I don't even know if it's safe advice, but what I'd do is this: I'd try and stop Caitlin going down there. Wake her or something, guide her back to her room. Is there any way you can talk to her? Tell her what's going on, so she's prepared – you know, without blanking her out?"

"I could give it a try," Lloyd said. "Tomorrow's Saturday and there isn't any school. She wouldn't have Mrs Cherry to run to. And, back here, if me and Rudi got her on her own – I mean, Rudi, he would keep her calm. He's like, so well together, he could defuse a hurricane. Isn't that right, Rudi?"

Rudi laughed. "No, it isn't right," he said. "But I'll go and talk to Caitlin with you if you want."

"I think that's best," Justin said. "Tell her what happened last night and tell her you want to try and stop her going down the cellar – to protect her. I think you've got to warn her, because I read somewhere, the shock of waking someone out of sleepwalking could do real damage."

Lloyd got up and brushed a damp layer of leaves away. "So – what we going to do then?" he said.

"Talk to Caitlin tomorrow and then go down the cellar on your own on Saturday night – see if the ghost is really up for telling you something. I'll email my professor in London, because he'll be seriously interested in this." Justin eased himself off the tree stump and Lloyd looked at him. This triangle, he thought – him, Rudi and Justin – it was a great setup and it made him feel good. He hadn't felt this good since he'd come to Sarson Hall and it was a precious moment.

"But you won't be in this weekend. I mean, if I got some message, I got to be able to talk it through with you," he said.

"I'll come in," said Justin. "After lunch, Sunday. By then I'll have heard back from my professor."

They made their way back towards the hall.

A mist had come down and the irregular contours appeared almost spectral – peering out of the darkness and suddenly Lloyd shuddered.

"You won't let me down?" he said, and there was urgency in his voice. "I mean this sort of stuff is off the scale, man, and I'm depending on you. It's a massive challenge – 'specially when I see this place like it is now. I got to admit, sometimes I get real scared."

Justin put an arm on his shoulder. "I'm not going to let you down," he said. "And you don't have to do it, not if you don't want to. There's no pressure."

Lloyd stared at the menacing façade glowering through the mist and he stood still. "There is though," he said. "I got to do it. I don't know what 'it' is yet, but I never backed out of nothing yet, and there isn't no way I'm backing off now."

"You're a brave kid," said Justin. "And I want you to know, both of you – I'm really pleased you want me to help. And I don't know of two guys I'm more proud to call my friends."

"That's good, man," Lloyd said, although "good" did nothing to sum up the warmth that burned inside him. And slowly they made their way back towards the gloomy mass of Sarson Hall.

CHAPTER 8

Lloyd didn't go down to the cellar that night even though he was aware of Caitlin's movements. He could hear the mechanical sounds of her footsteps and he knew, in the cellar, the ghost would be terrorising her; but perhaps that was for the best. That way she would still remember the fear when he and Rudi tackled her in the morning.

There was the same pattern of disruption in the North Wing – hailstones, the wind, windows rattling, doors slamming, spitting light bulbs, and even though he understood so much more about it now and, even though he felt the anger might not be directed at him, it still unnerved him, and it made it hard for him to sleep.

Saturday was as grey as every other day, but the pattern in the home on Saturdays was different.

At weekends they ran a skeleton staff and it was the job of the kids to do the chores. There were duty rotas for laying tables; clearing up after meals; loading dishwashers; cleaning the showers and toilets; sweeping and mopping the floors, and it was all supervised by Dave's wife, Marion – and occasionally Christine. If there was some sort of crisis, which there frequently was, Dave would come ranting out of his office, while Marion and Christine would stand, arms folded, pert lipped, looking on with a sickening superiority.

As far as Lloyd was concerned, the rota worked out well because, after breakfast, he and Rudi were scheduled to clear the table with Caitlin and Martin.

Martin had some kind of bug again and he didn't show up for breakfast. In fact only about half of them did. The rest were in bed, either complaining of stomach pains and headaches or taking advantage of the weekend to malinger. Rudi said that was par for the course.

When the rest had wreaked their usual havoc in the dining room, just Caitlin, Lloyd and Rudi remained to pick up the bits. Dave, who had been summoned to a pitch battle involving pieces of stale baguette, was raving in a high-toned tirade somewhere near the television lounge and Marion had stalked off, arms folded, having laid down the law about clearing up properly and behaving like responsible human beings – which, she observed, would be a first for Sarson Hall.

Caitlin was unkempt as usual and her dark eyes peered from under her wild hair, but Lloyd felt there was more apprehension than aggression in the look.

She worked at the far end of the room, keeping as much distance between them as she could.

It was going to be hard and, for a while, they didn't speak – but this was the best opportunity they'd have all day and eventually Lloyd managed to work his way round so he could cut off her retreat. He glanced at Rudi, and straight away Caitlin leapt into defensive mode.

"What you two doing?" she demanded. She dropped a pile of bowls on the table and swung around, her eyes blazing. "You keep away from me, Lloyd Lewis. I know what your game is."

"I'm not near you," Lloyd said. "It's a good three metres."

"Yeah, but you're up to something, and I'll scratch ribbons out of your face if you start any funny business with me. I can take you on any time, you and your little sidekick."

"We're not wanting to do any funny stuff, honest Caitlin," Rudi said. "You've got me and Lloyd wrong. Lloyd's worried about you. We're dead genuine."

Her eyes were darting from one to the other and she was fingering the top of a chair, poised to make a break. "Yeah, I know about Lloyd Lewis," she said, looking at Rudi. "He's twisted. He just likes winding me up, and he isn't going to, because I'm not scared of nothing."

"We don't want to scare you," Lloyd said. "I know what's going on down in that cellar, don't I? And I want to stop it. That's what."

When he mentioned the cellar, her legs crumbled and she threw her hands to her ears, just as she had in the schoolyard. And she began that doleful chant, drowning him out.

They took a step closer, but her eyes were closed and the chant just droned on. Lloyd wondered why she hadn't made a dash for it, but it seemed the mention of the cellar had frozen her. All she could do was crouch and let out the droning noise.

"You got to face up to it, man," he said. "I'm not trying to scare you nor nothing. I just know what's going on down there. I been down there, and I seen it with my own eyes."

"Liar," she screamed – and the droning began again.

"Okay. Cop this then. There's a guy down there. He's got a beard and long hair – and it's really wild and he's got this necklace thing of stone around his neck. When you was down there, he was swinging his axe at you, right? The guy was stripped down to his waist with like, rough trousers and he had leather, crossed gaiters. You know I'm right, and it isn't to frighten you that I'm telling you."

He was battling with the drone and it reached such a pitch, he was afraid Dave would come in... but then it tailed off, and Caitlin opened her eyes. She stared at him, and he could see her eyes, dark brown, and their stillness was troubled, deep down. Her pupils were dark and her irises were stunning. It made him catch his breath. She had beautiful eyes and, beneath the flashes of defiance, they were breathtakingly sad.

"You're lying," she whispered. "You didn't see nothing."

"I did, man," he said. "The night before last I was down there with you, and I seen that ghost, jabbing at you with his axe."

"You couldn't have," she said. "I never seen you. I never went down the cellar, I..."

"You think you dreamt it all, but you didn't. Lloyd was there," Rudi said.

She turned to him. "Dreams is private. If I dreamt it, it's nobody's business but mine and I don't know how you come to know all this, Lloyd Lewis, but I don't want you telling me nothing more."

She wasn't moving and suddenly Lloyd grabbed her elbows, gripping so she couldn't free herself and he said, "Look straight in my face, Caitlin, because I'm telling you the truth. You didn't dream this stuff. It was happening. I seen it."

He'd had this gripping thing done to him when he was a kid, and he knew it worked. She turned and looked up, and her eyes reflected like the deepest of troubled waters. "You go down that cellar sleep-walking, like you was in a trance. I seen you, and the night before last I followed you down. You didn't see me, because you was asleep, right? But I seen the spirals of dust and I seen the ghost come out of them. I seen it leaping, trying to scare you. I would have grabbed you, to protect you like, but I was scared of waking you. What I'm telling you is, I been talking to the gardener guy, Justin. He's done archaeology and stuff and he thinks he knows who the ghost is. We're trying to break its power – make it go away."

He could feel the resistance in her arms relax, but her eyes didn't waver. All the time they just stared intently, unmoving and unblinking.

"It's right, what I'm saying, isn't it?" he said and she looked from him to Rudi.

"I seen that guy, yeah," she said. "But he don't scare me – and you tell anybody about this and you're dead."

"Stay looking at me, Caitlin, man," Lloyd said. "You're scared all right. I mean – I was scared and the guy wasn't even going for me. You was shouting, 'Go away. Leave me alone. I hate you, old man.' And you know what? I don't think it's right – the way it's picking on you. I want to stop it."

"Yeah?" she said. "You and whose army?"

"It don't seem to mind me, that's the weird thing."

He could see her wavering between submission and the shield of denial. "Well, what *you* planning to do about it then?" she said.

"This is why we had to talk to you," Rudi said. "So you're prepared."

"Yeah," said Lloyd. "It's like, tonight, I'm going to keep watch and when you do your sleep-walking, I'm going to stop you – I'm going

to turn you around and lead you back to your bedroom, and then
I'm going down the cellar on my own to face the guy."

"Yeah, right," Caitlin said.

"Thing is, Justin said, when you wake someone what's sleepwalking, the shock – it could be real bad, man – and I don't want
to frighten you. That's why we're telling you now – so you'll be
expecting it. What I want to do is get you back to your room still
sleeping – but if you do wake up, you'll be like – ready for it."

Caitlin looked from him to Rudi again. "And you reckon I won't
see him if you do that?" she said.

"Not if you don't follow me down the cellar. And when someone's
already down there, it's like, the door won't open for no one else."

"Don't you try no funny stuff," Caitlin said. "Because, you lay one
finger on me, Lloyd Lewis, and you won't have no eyes left."

"I'm only trying to stop the ghost doing your head in," he said.

"As long as you know, that's all." She pulled away and added: "And
don't you tell no one." Then she stalked off, leaving Rudi and Lloyd
to finish clearing the table.

They decided to go into Brookley that afternoon.

At weekends the older ones were allowed out. They had to take
their mobiles so Dave could contact them. They also had to be back
by six. No one was allowed out at night. Dave had set a curfew,
although everyone knew Craig Donovan went wherever he pleased
and at whatever time.

Lloyd and Rudi wanted to go to the library and find out about
the Beaker folk and they also wanted to find out stuff in the local
history section that might relate to the stones at Brookley.

Brookley was only a few miles from Sarson Hall and it was
a journey they made every day on the minibus. But travelling on
public transport and getting right into town put everything in a
different league. It was freedom. It was independent travel.

The town was a strange place – a mixture of old and new. On
the Sarson village side there were industrial and housing estates,
crowding in on the centre, but the centre itself was old, a mixture of

weathered eighteenth-century shops and houses, whose red bricks mingled with half-timbered buildings from Tudor times.

There were precincts and narrow cobbled lanes and the central concourse ran down a gentle hill. It opened onto a large square with an ancient market hall. The hall had a heavy slate roof supported by columns.

The library was at the back of the market hall in a narrow lane.

In any other part of the country, Brookley would be something of a tourist attraction. It was picturesque, but it was under the same spell as Sarson Hall – dank streets, a canopy of gloom cast by brooding clouds and, even though the freedom of rubbing shoulders with the general populace energised Lloyd, the people here had the same sour expression and the same dour faces as those of Sarson village.

They headed straight for the library.

The librarian was a middle-aged woman with glasses. She was severely dressed in navy cardigan and skirt, and she called them over as soon as they came in. Her hair was combed back, pinned tightly behind her head, and wisps of grey escaped around her face. She looked grim.

She didn't mince her words either. "You boys are from Sarson Hall, aren't you?" she snapped.

Rudi nodded. "We want to look in the history section."

The way she sniffed irritated Lloyd, but he bit his lip. If he started something now, they'd be chucked out.

"I don't want you making any trouble," she said. "We don't get children from Sarson Hall in here often, and when we do it isn't to search out history books. It's to make trouble."

"That's not what we're here for," Rudi said. "We want to find out about the Beaker folk." He gave her a disarming smile and Lloyd reckoned there was a big opening for him in the diplomatic service. "We want to discover what links the Beaker folk with this area, especially Brookley Henge – and we'd like to find out something about the henge, too. I don't suppose you could recommend any books?"

The woman's face didn't crack, but she waddled out from behind her desk and made for a corner of the library. She gesticulated with her head for them to follow. "There's a local history section and guide books, but you look at them where I can see you. No hiding behind bookshelves where you can make trouble," she said.

Under the influence of Rudi's diplomatic charms, though, she actually searched out a couple of books. "They're mostly local history," she said. "We haven't got a lot on the Beaker people – but there's a bit about Brookley Henge." She tottered back to a table near reception, still clutching the books, and she only dumped them when she got there. "Don't you move from here," she snapped and Rudi tried his charm offensive again.

"Thanks ever so much. You've been really helpful."

But the charm was merely greeted with a "Humph."

There was very little about the Beaker folk, just a caption under a black and white photo and it simply stated that the original stone circle was probably built in the Bronze Age by a settlement of the Beaker tribe.

The photo was of the henge, but it was puzzling. The so-called circle wasn't anything like a circle. It was just a collection of stones, some upright and some lying on their side.

The area seemed heavily abandoned and overgrown.

Rudi found another page related to Brookley Henge in the other book and it was a type of plan. The layout of the stones here was much clearer. "It's more like a crescent," he said.

By the plan was a street map and it showed a road running out of town, behind the market square, and the henge was only a little way up the road. Lloyd spanned it with his hand. "That don't look far," he said. "We should go up there. Check it out."

They took the books back to the librarian and Lloyd let Rudi do the talking. "Thank you so much for your help," he said. "We've finished with these now."

The librarian snatched the books with another disingenuous grunt, and Lloyd could see, in Rudi's eyes, that he wasn't done with her. He looked straight into her face, with the most disarming smile, and he put his hand out. "I'm really sorry," he said. "But I've just thought. Could we have that one back, just for a minute?"

It was the book with the street map. He thumbed through for the page. "We thought we'd go up to the henge and take a look for ourselves," he said. He pointed to the map, forcing her to engage. "It's that road, don't you think – the one behind the library? Could you possibly give us directions?"

The contortions on the woman's face nearly had Lloyd laughing out loud – but that would have ruined the effect. He turned away and stared at the door.

"I hope you're not planning to make mischief," she snapped. "Those stones up there are historic monuments and they're to be respected. Vandals have done enough damage up there already."

But the butter wouldn't have melted in Rudi's mouth and, from the corner of his eye, Lloyd saw the smile radiating at her again. "It's all right. You mustn't worry, ma'am, we're only interested in it as a historical monument. We've got a friend, you see. He's an archaeologist, and he's got us interested in the stones."

The librarian grunted. Her facial muscles were in battle – prejudice versus Rudi's charm – and neither side was winning. "Well. See you behave yourselves," she said.

"Yes, but how do we find the road?"

"Go out and turn right down the alley by the side of the library. It takes you into 'Back Row.' Turn left and then take the first right – and any damage reported up there, and I'll tell the police you were in here. The library's covered by CCTV so it won't take long to find you."

"You've got nothing to worry about," Rudi said. "We're just students of antiquities, and you've been most kind."

He handed the book back again and Lloyd dashed for the door. He couldn't contain himself any longer. "You're such a smooth operator, man," he said. "She couldn't handle that. It was awesome."

Rudi was grinning and his eyes sparkled, but he told Lloyd to hush his noise and they headed down the alley and up the hill, following a small side road. Almost immediately, they were out of town. There was a church and a low-walled cemetery and then they were between brackish fields and scrubland. The occasional skeletal tree prodded the sky, and it was bleak and raw.

About half a mile up the hill the hedge thickened and there was a gap leading into what looked like a stretch of moorland. They pushed through and just inside was a weather-beaten sign saying that this was Brookley Henge.

Their eyes swept across the desolation and it was as unloved and abandoned as anything they'd seen – but the stones were there, struggling out of the thicket – big, dark stones, just as they were in the photograph.

Lloyd was surprised at how large some of them were. They loomed up towards the sky while others lay uprooted in the clumps of gorse and bracken, and there was a rash of moss and lichen creeping over them. There were only six or seven big stones. And the place was so bleak it sent a shiver through him. It had a feel of abandonment, as if its spirit had been sucked out, and the stones lay in ruins like the rotting stumps of a ship's hull.

"It's like the place God forgot," he said, staring at the brooding megaliths.

"It's scary," said Rudi. "It's like – all the bleakness of the world is radiating from this one place."

"That's just what I was thinking, man. And it don't make no circle neither."

They wandered to where the stones gave way to bracken, following the line of the crescent. They didn't know what they were looking for but suddenly Lloyd stopped.

Where he was standing, buried in the cluster of scrub, there seemed to be a pit like the indentation in someone's gum where a tooth has been rooted out.

"Do you think there used to be another stone here?" he said. "A stone what someone took away?"

"If it is, there's another one here," Rudi said crouching behind a clump of gorse.

"And these pits follow the line," said Lloyd. "Like – it was a circle once and it's been ransacked."

They pushed on until the scrubland grew impenetrable, but, at roughly regular intervals, following the circumference, they found indentations – wounds in the earth where great stones had once been.

"Someone's been and smashed this place up," Lloyd said. He sat on a stump and he was thinking. "There's a feel about it, too – like the earth's grieving. It's all around you."

Rudi nodded. "Is that what's upsetting the ghost back at Sarson Hall, do you think?"

Lloyd shrugged. "The guy built the place didn't he? I mean, if I'd done all that and some moron had wrecked it, I'd be mad." He stood up. "We got to tell Justin when he comes in tomorrow. But... if it's this what's upsetting the guy, why's he down at Sarson Hall and not up here? And what are we meant to do about it – to calm him I mean. There isn't no stones we can put back."

He took a few steps away. Whether this had anything to do with Sarson Hall or not, there was something forlorn about the place. It was getting to his gut and, what was worse it made him feel useless. If this was the ghost's gripe, there was nothing he could do about it. "It's getting to me, man – this place. I don't see no point in hanging around," he said.

Rudi didn't argue, and neither of them said much on their way back to town.

That night, after the normal stormy period of fending off dysfunctional kids and enduring the ineffectual rantings of Dave and Marion, Lloyd was almost glad to get to bed. But there was an undercurrent of anxiety. The North Wing seemed poised. It was pulsing with potential disruption and the activities of the poltergeists were threatening just below the surface. And there was Caitlin. Although the ghost hadn't been hostile to Lloyd, he couldn't get out of his head the blind, terrorising fury it had shown to her. If it turned that kind of thing onto him, he didn't know what he'd do.

He knew he mustn't sleep, so he moved out into the corridor as soon as the final door had slammed in the main wing. He'd decided that balancing on two feet in a freezing passage was about the best way to guarantee staying awake – but the fury of pent-up rage burst onto the North Wing early, with all the usual manifestations of wind and weather. The house shook, the floorboards groaned. Hail and wind lashed at windows and the weird moonlight shone through with intimidating intensity.

Caitlin came out of her room, but the elemental wrath had made him nervous and he didn't have a clue what would happen when he tried to manoeuvre her back to bed.

He crept towards her quickly, aiming to get there before she reached the stairs and gently he put a hand on her shoulder. He made sure his grip was firm, and he eased her around, terrified he'd wake her, but as she reversed her course, there was no indication that he had. He didn't speak. He just propelled her down the corridor.

When he eased her back onto her bed, her eyes did open – not with the violent eruption of someone who'd been roughly woken, but with the half-closed look of subconsciousness, as if her mind and her limbs were still sedated.

The expression he saw under the hooded eyelids though, ripped through him. It was an unguarded look of gratitude, and there was a quiver of a smile on her lips. It made him catch his breath, because he wasn't expecting it.

Then he hurried to the stairs. He was frightened the cellar door would slam before he got there. He also wanted to get through, so the door would shut before Caitlin could follow him.

The door was swinging, but, as he descended, he heard it slam and that jarred in his heart, because now it was just him and the elemental fury. He'd taken a chance on the ghost being okay, but he couldn't be certain, and there were other things. Justin thought it might want to tell him something. But how would it communicate? It spoke this strange language that meant nothing to Lloyd.

He was really stepping into the unknown and he was nervous.

The ambient light from the forty-watt bulb was already shining on the walls, and, immediately as he reached the bottom of the stairs, the bulb started to spit.

Flicks of twisters began rising in the corner and he watched as they grew, darting in a random dance, searching out the centre point and merging, dissolving back into the wall. And all the time his body was urging them on, impatient to get the ghost out into the open, so he could know what kind of mood it was in.

Slowly the mirage took form and he saw it, crouched there in iridescent green, wearing the long robe and the woollen helmet he'd seen on the computer screen.

For a moment it didn't move, but, when it did, there was none of the demented dancing that it had shown to Caitlin. It just remained there, making a steady scan of the cellar until it saw that Lloyd was alone.

Then it pulled itself out of its foetal crouch and took a step towards him.

He couldn't help himself. He stepped back, but the spectre just shook its head and raised its hand to beckon him. The hoarse whispering that had sent shivers through him last time was there again, and it struggled in its throat to speak. But still, the words meant nothing.

When Lloyd had convinced himself there wasn't any danger, he took a few steps towards it, but, as he got nearer, his lungs filled with the reek of decaying earth. He struggled with his stomach, concentrating all his senses – and then the ghost did the strangest thing.

It lowered itself and drew a shape on the cellar floor. The shape was only there for a few seconds. Then it dissolved like a ripple in water.

But it was important because, immediately after it had drawn the shape, it straightened itself and pointed at Lloyd. Then it pointed at the drawing, and all the time it was nodding its head.

The shape was made of three lines forming a letter Y – the two open lines pointing at him and the single line pointing towards the ghost, and, each time it faded, it drew it again.

"What's it mean?" Lloyd said. "I don't get it. Is that a letter you're drawing? Have I got to do something that begins with the letter Y?"

It whispered a hoarse, guttural hiss, but Lloyd still couldn't understand.

It was clear it wanted him to know the Y thing was important though because it repeated the drawing so many times, each time pointing to it, then to Lloyd, and all the time its head was nodding.

Lloyd wanted to know more, but the apparition suddenly started retreating into the stones. It adopted the crouched stance, and the green luminosity faded. Then... it was a tornado of dust, swirling, shrinking and dying back into the cellar floor.

Above Lloyd's head the light returned to full strength while a stifling chill filled the air.

He didn't move. He had no idea what the ghost was telling him and all the time he was asking himself why a spectre would drag itself back through the ages of time to show an Afro-Caribbean kid the letter Y.

He knew that until he understood this, he wouldn't get any further, but he wasn't confident even Justin would have the answer to this one.

When he got back to his room, the poltergeist had been at work again, and that brought even more confusion because, this time, there wasn't any malice in its action.

His travel case was on the bed and it had succeeded in opening it.

His first instinct was to find his letters and photos, but not only was the bundle of papers still neatly stacked in the corner of the case, the case had been packed with clothes. There were a couple of pairs of socks, a neatly folded shirt, a pair of jeans, his toilet bag and a white T-shirt, all stowed more tidily than if he'd packed them himself.

The room was relatively calm too, and he was getting so used to these supernatural happenings that, after the initial shock, he was more curious than frightened.

There was still a cloying dankness filling the air and this bedroom certainly wasn't the kind of place to chill out in, but, as he sat on his bed, his mouth broadened into a grin.

Something had changed.

What had previously been the fury from hell was becoming friendlier, and he began to feel that, while the ghost had been trying to give him a message in the cellar, here, in his bedroom, the poltergeist had been doing something that might have been rated as a good deed... if he'd been planning a journey.

CHAPTER 9

It wasn't easy to get to sleep. His brain was in overdrive and the very act of closing his eyes was a struggle.

He tried the slow, deep breathing and the controlled relaxation, but still his brain was racing.

There were fragments of a pattern forming in his head.

He'd nailed down the ghost and he'd begun to sense the cause of all the trouble. His impetus had been given a massive boost by what had just happened, with the ghost and the poltergeist seeming to be so positive, and he was excited.

But he was confused.

It looked as if the reason for all the disruption was something that had happened way back in time, and he had this feeling about the stones at Brookley Henge. It was likely the ghost had been involved in building the henge and now it was eaten up with fury... but nothing was straightforward. He couldn't understand the Y shape – or the fact that the poltergeist had packed his travel case, or why the ghost's fury was directed at Caitlin.

He thought more about Caitlin, and then he stopped thinking about Caitlin because it was messing with his brain. He thought about the henge – being up there with Rudi. He thought about the bleak desolation, the devastation that had been left up there. He thought about the grim-faced librarian and the books. He visualised the travel case, packed, at the foot of his bed – and that blew his mind. He couldn't unpack the case though. There had to be a reason. He pictured the ghost crouching – drawing the signs in the dust – and he heard the unearthly whisper of its voice echoing in his head.

As night wore on, along with the voice came a procession – faces, places, the main street at Brookley falling away to the market square, the library – with books raining down from the shelves, and there was the librarian's face and, furtively moving behind everything, watching him like a jackal, was Craig Donovan. There was Rudi, and his face morphed to that of the wild-eyed ghost, and the whispering emptiness of the Beaker man's voice, and still there was Craig and sleep, unsettled sleep, wrestling with demons and ghosts; and Caitlin and Craig and Justin and Justin's eyes... and...

Morning came, breaking through his half-closed eyes and playing around his dampened eyelashes.

He dragged himself back towards consciousness.

Nothing in his dreams had made any sense and it all seemed to have settled in his head like sludge. Even opening his eyes was a decision too far, and thought fragments floated just beyond his reach.

But gradually they came together.

He stretched, and kicked the duvet to one side.

It was Sunday.

This afternoon Justin was coming over.

He'd be with Rudi all day and Rudi was a great guy.

It was all good. He could face the world.

When he pulled back the blinds, it would have been great if there'd been a flood of sunlight, but this was Sarson Hall and there were just bleak wastelands and acres of flat, grey sky.

He checked his travel case because, along with everything else, the packed case could have been a dream. But it *had* been packed. It was open at the foot of his bed with everything neatly stashed for a journey.

Carefully he pulled the zip, sealing the lid and locking it. Then he returned it to his wardrobe and headed for the main building.

The Sunday roster was different from Saturday's, although the groups were the same. Their group was scheduled to load the dishwashers in the kitchen.

He was curious about Caitlin. He wasn't sure she'd be there and, if she was, he wondered how she'd be after her first night not facing the ghost.

She wasn't down when he and Rudi settled for their toast and cornflakes, but she did come in not long after – and she had changed.

She'd showered. Her hair was still wet and hung loosely around her head – and her fringe was fluffed slightly with the dampness. It fell onto her forehead and made her face look, somehow softer.

She sat in her usual place, well away from him and Rudi. But something of the pallor had gone. Her movements were less lethargic and Lloyd noticed she wasn't so involved in the general spite.

She kept looking at him too – hooded glances where she didn't lift her head. He couldn't read the looks. They could have been suspicious or defensive and there was an ambivalence that unsettled him.

He knew they would have to face each other in the kitchen and he wasn't confident about that. His head told him he must raise the subject of last night because he wanted to steer her away from the cellar again tonight – to stop her having to face the terror of the ghost. Yet something inside him made him want to shy away from her. He was unnerved by the cloaked glances. And, with her loose hair and that sheen of moisture from the shower, and with her face so fresh from sleep – he wasn't comfortable inside his own skin any more.

He told Rudi about what had happened – about steering Caitlin back to her room, although he didn't mention the half-drowsy glance. He told him about the ghost's weird symbol and the packed case.

"That would do my head in," Rudi said. "And you stayed there all night – with a case packed by dead spirits?"

"Yeah, when you put it like that it's creepy – but I didn't think of it that way. I was just spooked because I couldn't figure why the poltergeist packed my travel bag. I mean, is it trying to tell me something, or what?"

He was avoiding Caitlin's glances, but doing that made him aware of someone else who was showing an unhealthy interest in him.

Craig Donovan was on the opposite side of the table, further down, and he was desperate to catch Lloyd's eye. That unsettled him more than Caitlin, because no way did he want a meet with Craig Donovan.

His best bet, he thought, was to stick with Rudi all morning. Craig wouldn't come near him, not with Rudi around.

At least he would be safe while they were in the kitchen. There was no danger of Craig muscling in there.

There was a routine when they set about stacking the dishwashers. They had to fill the sink with hot water while Marion checked it out. Then they had to collect the stacked crockery from the dining room, and rinse it before they loaded it into the dishwashers.

There were only the three of them. Martin had opted to miss breakfast again, and Caitlin was keeping her distance, shooting quick glances at Lloyd and then looking away. It was unsettling because Lloyd was so intensely aware of her hair, and the fringe, softening her face. It was disturbingly attractive and he was almost afraid to say anything to her – for fear of her reaction – and that was plain stupid. Only a few hours ago he'd been guiding her down the corridor back to her room and practically tucking her into bed… and she'd shown no hostility then. But he knew, with Caitlin, nothing could be taken for granted.

They made several trips from the dining room, while Marion supervised every move.

When the sinks were full and she'd dipped her hand into the water for the last time, she produced sets of rubber gloves, dumping them on the draining board, and grunting, "Put these on." Then she added: "And keep them on when you're loading the dishwasher. I don't want your nasty germs all over the plates."

"The dishwasher's meant to wash germs away, yeah? That's what it's for, isn't it?" Lloyd said. "And our germs aren't no nastier than nobody else's."

"Don't give me any backchat," Marion snapped. "And no messing around." Then she stalked into the dining room and she was in action almost immediately, bawling at some miscreant who was messing around under the table.

Lloyd heard Caitlin mutter: "Stupid cow," and he looked at her.

"You okay?" he said.

She was sliding plates into the sink and running a gloved hand over them to remove the larger chunks of breakfast residue and, as she looked down, her hair fell, brushing her cheek. In profile Lloyd noticed how long her eyelashes were. "Yeah, why?" she said. She didn't look up and she didn't stop working at the plates.

"You slept all right?" he said.

"Yeah."

He didn't feel comfortable and she wasn't making it easy. "You didn't see no ghost or nothing?"

Still she didn't look up but she stopped scouring the plates and stared at the water. Lloyd caught his breath because it was clear she was weighing her options.

"What you talking about – ghosts?" she said, still looking at the ripples swirling in the sink.

"Come off it, Caitlin," Rudi said. "You know very well what we're talking about. We went through all that yesterday."

"You shut your mouth and get on with stacking them dishes, Rudi Singh," she said. She flashed him a look and then returned her gaze to the sink.

"There isn't no need to talk to him like that," said Lloyd. "It's right what he said. You do know what we're talking about and we're not doing this to wind you up nor nothing. You was heading for the cellar again last night and I got you back to your room. You got to remember that."

She began rubbing at the plates more vigorously, and her face coloured up. "You don't talk about that, Lloyd Lewis. Not with him around. That's none of his business."

"He's my best friend," said Lloyd. "He isn't going to say nothing to no one."

"It's personal though."

"You got to trust me, man," he said. "And you got to trust Rudi. You didn't see no ghost last night?"

She carried on working and shook her head. "No – not last night."

"Well, that's okay. We're dead pleased, isn't that right, Rudi?"

"Yes, dead pleased," said Rudi.

Lloyd passed Caitlin the last of the cereal dishes. He wasn't overjoyed at her response. She was still prickly – but she wasn't in denial. He had to bring reality a step closer though. "You got to face up to it, Caitlin, man," he said. "There isn't nothing to say you won't go sleepwalking into that cellar again tonight nor tomorrow night."

She took the bowls and plunged them into the water. "You trying to scare me?" she said.

"No way. I just want you to know – I'm going to do what I done last night and, if you go for the cellar again, I'll steer you back. If I keep watch, you got nothing to be scared of."

She pushed the rinsed bowls towards Rudi and then looked at Lloyd for the first time, and that snagged his breath because there was a softness and the flicker of a smile, just like he'd seen last night. "That's okay, then," she said. She pulled off her gloves and laid them on the table. "You can do that Lloyd Lewis. But don't you go getting no ideas. You mess with me just once and it'll be the last time you mess with anyone. You got that?"

Lloyd laughed. "I just want to make sure the ghost don't get you, that's all."

"And don't neither of you tell no one about this," she said as she walked towards the kitchen door. "It's private and it isn't nobody's business – only ours."

When they'd finished their chores, Lloyd followed Rudi into the television lounge. He was determined to stick with him because of Craig Donovan, but it didn't work. Marion was there almost as soon as they emerged and she said Dave wanted to see Rudi in his office – and that meant, unless Lloyd went off to his bedroom, there was no cover from Craig.

He was puzzled as to why Dave wanted to see Rudi, because Rudi was the one guy in Sarson Hall that wasn't likely to get up Dave's nose.

Craig wasn't in the television lounge, but Lloyd knew it was one of his favourite haunts. It would only be a matter of time so he decided his bedroom, no matter how inhospitable, was the best option.

But it was too late. As he headed up the stairs he heard a voice over the general cacophony. "Hey – black boy."

He looked down. "I got a name, man," he said. "You use it if you want to talk to me."

Craig lunged up the stairs. "You trying to keep out of my way or what? You was deliberately avoiding me, breakfast time."

"Why would I want to look at you? You aren't that handsome."

"You won't be handsome neither if you try getting smart with me." He was right up to Lloyd now. "We got to arrange something for tomorrow."

Lloyd attempted to look blank. "What you mean, arrange something for tomorrow?" he said, and he saw Craig's eyes narrow.

"Don't put on that innocent stuff with me, Lloyd Lewis. You got a job to do for me, and no way are you forgetting that. I got to show you the kid you're delivering the homework to, remember?" He grabbed Lloyd by the arm and pulled him further up the stairs, leading him towards the fire door. "You got to come and find me, break time tomorrow, right?"

"That isn't going to be easy," Lloyd said. "Me and Rudi, we hang out together at break times. You don't want him to know about this homework stuff, do you?"

"You got to lose him, because if he finds out, you're finished. You find me, break time, and you make sure you don't have that Indian kid in tow. If you don't show up, I'll smash your bones, okay?"

It wasn't okay. None of it was okay, but Lloyd knew Craig had the upper hand. He was stronger and he was bigger, and the guy wouldn't have any qualms about messing him up. "If that's what's going to make you happy," he said. "I'll look you out tomorrow – but I'm not making no habit of it. You got to know that."

Craig stared at him. "You don't tell me what you are or what you aren't making no habit of," he said. "You do what I tell you, when I tell you – if you want to live."

"We got to see about that," Lloyd said. It was imperative he had the last word and he pushed past, heading downstairs so as not to give Craig the chance to answer – but he did catch a menacing snarl from the landing.

He could have done without Craig Donovan. He wanted to focus on the ghost – and Justin. But, at least, now he'd sorted tomorrow, he was certain he wouldn't be bothered for the rest of the day, and it wasn't long before Rudi came out of Dave's office.

Martin was with him and, when they saw Lloyd, Martin's pallid face half flinched into a smile. Rudi didn't look so pleased though.

"What you been up to?" Lloyd said. "You been naughty boys or what?"

"Dave wanted to see if we was still all right having you back in our room," said Martin, and that news made him stop dead.

"There isn't no way. You know that, Rudi, man. I told you."

Rudi shrugged. "We weren't given any choice. You've got to move out of that room. Dave needs it for someone else. If we didn't want you, he said he'd put you with Craig Donovan."

Martin was beginning to look confused. "Don't you want to move back? We smell or what?"

Lloyd shook his head. "It isn't that, man. It's complicated. I got to stay in the North Wing, that's all. I'm like, sorting something out down there. Rudi knows about it. Isn't that right, Rudi?"

"But you don't have any choice," Rudi said. "And Dave said you've got to go and see him now. I'll hang around till he's seen you if you like."

"That would be appreciated," Lloyd said. "I got stuff to tell you anyway. It's stuff we got to talk to Justin about."

He didn't knock. It was in his interest to get up Dave's nose today.

Dave was seated behind his desk and the cold blue eyes looked distinctly irritated. His chubby face simpered. "All right, Lloyd Lewis. Treat this like your own living room, why don't you? Anyone with a modicum of decency would have knocked and waited for some kind of response."

Lloyd gave the Gallic shrug. "I knew you wanted to see me. Rudi said, so what was the point of knocking and hanging around for you to say 'come in'?"

"A knock would show respect," Dave said and Lloyd stared at him.

"Yeah, respect. That's a tricky issue as far as you're concerned."

He saw Dave's mouth twist, but that was all. "I've been having a chat with Rudi and Martin," he said. "Apparently — for reasons that totally escape me, they want you back in their room."

Lloyd shrugged again, this time making certain his hands were deep into his pockets. "Yeah," he said. "That's cool. It shows respect that does — but — what would I want to go back with them for? I mean, I got my own room now, and I like that."

"I expect you do," Dave said. "But the general policy of the home is to put people together. It helps develop social skills. And, if Rudi and Martin do you the honour of requesting you back, I think you should have the good grace to accept."

"Grace hasn't got nothing to do with it," said Lloyd. "I like it where I am."

He wanted Dave to come out with some heated, tantrum-induced piece of malice like: "If that's how you want it, you stay in the North Wing," but he knew Dave wasn't that stupid. If staying in the North Wing was what Lloyd wanted, then there was no way he was going to let him.

"Well, leaving grace to one side, you've got very little choice," Dave said. "Next week I need that room for Daryl Johnson. You can pack your things this evening and, tomorrow, you can move back with Martin and Rudi. If you don't like that, I can always put you in with Craig Donovan. There's space in his room."

"Can't you put this Daryl Johnson in with Rudi and Martin — or you could try him with Craig Donovan. That would sort him out," Lloyd said. But he knew he'd lost — and he also knew losing was going to give him big problems.

Dave eased himself from his desk, which, Lloyd knew, was his pathetic way of signalling the cessation of battle. "Just put a sock in it, Lloyd Lewis, and get your stuff packed. You're back with Martin and Rudi and that's that. And any assaults on Martin and I'll try your own remedy – see if Craig Donovan can sort you out."

"He'd like to try," Lloyd said, with more feeling than he wanted to acknowledge. "But the way Craig sorts out guys wouldn't be that great, would it? Not that you'd want to know about that, Mr Trafford, sir. You got an ostrich mentality, that's your trouble."

He could see the colour spreading from Dave's face right up to his shiny, balding head. "Why is it, Lloyd Lewis," he snapped, "that you always manage to engender hostility – even when I'm imparting what, to any other boy, would be good news? Does this insolence come naturally, or is it the one skill you've managed to nurture in your tiny, puerile life?"

"If it's been nurtured, it's been nurtured by people like you, man," Lloyd said and, because he knew it really maddened Dave, he walked towards the door with his back to him and his hands plummeting the depths of his pockets. He even managed to heave his shoulders in the most phlegmatic of Gallic shrugs.

It was a round to Dave, though. He'd messed up Lloyd's plans, and that was another thing he'd have to talk over with Rudi and Justin. He might even have to bring Martin in on this one, because, when he was back in the main wing, he'd have to leave the bedroom every night so he could get down to Caitlin.

Justin was around the back of North Wing that afternoon. That's where they'd agreed to meet, and Lloyd's mind was so full he hardly knew where to start.

"There's things been happening all over the place," he said. "I seen the ghost again, and the poltergeist done stuff to my clothes and my suitcase, and me and Rudi, we've been up to look at Brookley Henge, and we got loads that needs talking about."

Justin was laughing. "Let's hope I can help some then," he said. "But, if I can't, we can always talk it over with my professor in London next weekend."

Lloyd's eyes widened. "We going to London next weekend?" he said.

"I emailed the professor and he phoned me last night. I told him what was going on and he's dead keen to meet you. I've got to get Dave's permission, but that shouldn't be a problem."

Lloyd looked slightly abashed. "I wouldn't be so sure about that," he said. "I just been winding the guy up and he don't like me a lot."

"He'll be okay," Justin said. "When I tell him Professor Appleyard at the Institute of Education wants to see you, he'll be really pleased. I'll say you've got an interest in archaeology and you've been doing things up at Brookley Henge."

"Is that what the guy's called? Appleyard?" said Lloyd.

"Yes, James Appleyard. He's great. You'll like him."

They walked across to the boundary wall and Justin found an old tree stump where they sat. "Now, tell me about Brookley Henge," he said.

"It's a wreck up there, man," said Lloyd. "If the ghost guy did build it, no wonder he's mad. There isn't no proper stone circle no more. It's just a kind of crescent and half the stones have been knocked over. It was a stone circle once though. We followed the line and there was – like – dents in the ground where the stones used to be. We couldn't get all the way round because it was too overgrown but there was a circle there once, definite. Someone's been up there and messed it all up."

"Recently, do you think?" Justin said, and Lloyd shook his head.

"Them dents is old. They been there for years, isn't that right, Rudi?"

Rudi nodded. "Could be hundreds of years," he said.

"Were the stones left lying around in other places?"

"That's the weird thing," said Lloyd. "We looked for them, but there wasn't no sign of them. Someone's been up and took the lot."

Justin thought for a moment. "We need to talk to Professor Appleyard before we come to any big conclusions," he said, and suddenly Lloyd's eyes lit up.

"I know what that poltergeist was doing, now. You're right about us having to go to see this professor guy. That's what the poltergeist was telling me. I told you it had been messing with my stuff. Well, what it done was, it packed my travel bag – shirts, socks, everything, all folded away neater than I could do."

Rudi breathed in sharply. "And is that right, Justin. Would we need to take clothes? Are we staying overnight?"

Even Justin looked taken aback. "At the Appleyards'?" he said. "Yes. They did suggest it. They thought you'd like to see something of London while you were up there. Jenny Appleyard, the professor's wife, suggested that."

"We got to do it." Lloyd said. "You been to London haven't you, Rudi?"

Rudi shook his head.

"There's great places up there. I been – two or three times."

"I'll see Dave tomorrow," Justin said. "Then I'll get back to the Appleyards." He glanced at Lloyd and grinned. "And I think you should give baiting Dave a miss for the time-being. If you get on the wrong side of him again, he isn't likely to let you go."

Lloyd laughed. "I got the message. I'll give the guy a quiet time, till after next week."

"That's fixed then," said Justin. "Now, tell me what happened with Caitlin, and down the cellar with the ghost."

Lloyd told him how he'd steered Caitlin back to bed and then about the ghost and the symbol he kept writing in the dust.

"It was like a Y shape," he said. "And it must be important. I mean, he kept writing it down and every time it faded he done it again, and he was pointing to me, like I had to go with this thing. But I don't get it. I mean, the letter Y. Is it the start of a word or what?"

"I don't see how it could be," Justin said. "The Bronze Age people didn't do writing, certainly not using the Roman alphabet. That didn't come in for years." He leaned over and grabbed a small twig, drawing the shape in the ground. "Was the symbol like this?"

"That's the thing," Lloyd said. "Only – the ghost kept drawing it the other way round, like the single line was pointing to him."

Justin redrew the symbol and frowned. "It doesn't make a lot of sense to me. I suppose it could be some sort of map, indicating three places – Sarson Hall – the henge – and some other place, but... it could be one of a hundred things." He drew the shape again, staring at it. "It could be a symbol; something significant to the Beaker folk, or – if we could link it with all the stuff we know – the Beaker history, the stones, things we use to understand the culture of the henges..." He stopped suddenly and looked at Lloyd. "He drew the two prongs pointing at you?" he said, and Lloyd nodded.

"Every time. And he pointed at me, like I had to do something with the Y thing."

"An arrow – pointing you forward? But forward to where?"

"This sounds a bit weird, but, it was more like he wanted me to kind of use the Y," Lloyd said.

Justin looked at the drawing in the ground again, and under his breath he muttered, "A divining rod?"

"A what?" said Lloyd.

"A divining rod. There are things called ley lines that are linked with stone circles. They can be detected with something called a divining rod."

"Ley lines?"

Justin grinned. "They're amazing things. They run underground – like magnetic rivers and they're all over the world, going from one ancient monument to the next. People like the Aborigines and the Japanese knew about them way back. The Japanese called them 'Dragon Currents.' It could be the Beaker folk knew about them too, because these ley lines link up with all the stone circles and megaliths across Europe. The Y thing could be a divining rod. Ley lines might be important to the ghost."

"Can they do anything, these ley lines?" Lloyd said.

"You bet they can. In Ireland they say if you build a house on a ley line, it will destroy it or at least put a curse on it forever. They're like – channels for supernatural forces and mystical currents."

"That's awesome, man," Lloyd said. "And they're really there, under the ground and they can be detected by this divining rod thing?"

Justin nodded.

"But what is a divining rod?" said Rudi.

"There are people – dowsers – who have the ability to sense where there's stuff hidden underground. They do it with divining rods – if there's water or oil, they can sense it. That's what they're used for, mainly, but some dowsers can detect ley lines." He looked at Lloyd and Rudi again. "Some of the divining rods look like a letter Y. These days they're often made of metal – but they can be made out of wood." He got up and scoured the ground. "Like this," he said, picking up a twig. "This is hazel. That's the type of wood they use for divining."

"How does it work then?" said Lloyd.

Justin gave a sheepish grin. "There's no way I can do it, but I'll mime for you. It goes something like this."

He held the two prongs of the twig in his hands and stretched his arms out so the probing single prong was horizontal to the ground. "If there's water – or some other mineral or force under the ground, then the rod will bend – a bit like this."

He manipulated it with his fingers and the rod nosed gently towards the ground.

"You're doing that with your fingers," Lloyd laughed. "That's a con."

"I told you I couldn't do it," said Justin. "Not many people can."

Lloyd grabbed at the stick. "Let's have a go. Like this, you mean?"

He walked slowly around, moving away from the hedge towards a mound in the scrub where the ground seemed to form a hillock. He was holding the twig loosely as he'd seen Justin do, with his thumbs keeping it level and, as he got near the mound, it twisted downwards and Justin started laughing.

"That's even better than I did," he said.

But Lloyd's eyes were wide. There were sensations in his arms, and a tingling that carried right through to his hands and the tips of his fingers. "It isn't me what's doing it, man," he whispered. "That's the twig. It's doing it on its own. Look, I'm hardly touching it."

They stared.

"It's just lying in my hand."

The hazel twig pivoted gently, nosing towards the ground. He passed it over the hill several times and each time, it bowed, quivering.

It was as if there were forces under the earth operating through him. As if he was a conduit, guiding them through to the divining rod and it was the forces that were making the rod bend.

He could hardly believe what was happening.

CHAPTER 10

No one moved, and Lloyd could feel the excitement bubbling inside him.

Justin was looking at him and his eyes were probing. "You can dowse," he said.

He looked at the hazel twig. "Looks like it, don't it?"

"And the ghost knew that," said Rudi. "That's why he was showing you the Y sign."

"And if he wanted you to dowse, there has to be a reason." Justin said. He came across to the hillock where Lloyd was standing and Lloyd looked at the hump of earth.

"What's in there, then?" he said. "What's made the twig bend like that?"

"It could be some archaeological remains. It could be water."

"That's weird," said Lloyd. "What about them ley lines you said about? Could it be some of them?"

But Justin shook his head. "I don't think so. Ley lines run in set paths across the country. You don't get random bits of ley line. It's more likely to be a well or something."

"I don't see why the ghost would want me to dowse for a well," Lloyd said. "Wells haven't got nothing to do with it."

"I don't know that much about dowsing," said Justin. "We'll have to ask the professor." He grinned. "He'll be really impressed you can dowse."

Lloyd liked that. This Professor Appleyard was top man at a university. Impressing someone like him was good. He looked at the dowsing rod and laughed. "I reckon I'm really impressed myself, to be honest."

They tried again and watched the rod bend as Lloyd stood over the hillock. Then they moved around the trees and the bare patches of waste, but everywhere except the hillock seemed barren until they got close to the North Wing. Then the rod started moving again – just twitching to begin with, but, as they got nearer, he could feel the power in his arms, and the twig bent itself in his hand. It was almost brutal and his instinct was to hold the two prongs so the rod wouldn't fly out of his grip.

"See that, man?" he whispered. "Whatever I'm picking up here, there's loads of it – and it's got to have something to do with the ghost if it's doing it around here."

"Say we went down the cellar," Rudi said. "That's where the ghost is. If all this is linked with him, there should be more forces down there."

They made their way down the dimly lit stairwell and it didn't matter how many times Lloyd went down there, it always sent a shudder through him. The place had an atmosphere and it could be cut like cheese. Even now he could sense the spirits waiting, and the whole feel of the place stunned him to silence.

"Are you going to try with that twig?" Rudi whispered, and Lloyd walked across to the wall. He had the hazel branch in his hand – and, already, he could feel it moving. There were vibrations tingling in his fingertips and, when he looked at it, it was writhing like a snake. There could be no doubt. The forces buried around the cellar were massive.

But there was no continuous line, apart from along the wall.

When they were back outside they tried to piece it all together.

"We've got so many bits of information," Justin said. "There is definitely something down in the cellar that can be detected by dowsing. It could be anything though, water, even badly insulated electric cables, and then there's that mound in the garden, and forces coming from the wall."

"And I bet it's just the North Wing," Lloyd said suddenly. "If we tried the main building, I bet we don't find nothing."

"Why?" said Rudi.

"Because the North Wing is where all the aggro is. There isn't so much going on in the main wing. That's more like a kind of echo.

It's like bangs and creaks and grumpy kids. There's a bit of poltergeist activity, but it don't blow your head like it does in the North Wing."

They headed for the main Georgian building and Lloyd held out the dowsing rod again. There were quivers, and spasmodic twitches, but, compared to what had gone on around the Tudor wing, this was more like nervous ticks.

"It's like I said, all the ghost's grief and that is in the old building. I could sense that the first time I seen it." They sat on the wooden bench by the wall and looked out across the bleak grounds. Then he said, "Shouldn't we try it up the henge? I mean, we figured this stuff could be connected with Brookley Henge and if it's connected with them ley lines you said are up there then we ought to test it out. I mean, rivers of force underground, that's awesome, man and, if the ghost wants me to dowse, it's got to be for ley lines. The guy isn't going to be interested in no wells and stuff and, like you said, it could be the ley lines what's giving him grief."

"We could go up there tomorrow when you get back from school," said Justin. "I'll clear it with Dave when I tell him about the professor and him wanting us up in London."

Lloyd grinned. "If Dave's going to give us the go-ahead for London and Brookley Henge," he said, "I got to be a saint for the rest of the week. And I don't know I got the kind of goodness in me. I mean, it's hard, sucking up to morons."

Justin laughed. "You've got plenty of goodness in you, Lloyd Lewis, and sucking up to morons isn't goodness. That's expediency. What you've got to develop is diplomacy. You've got plenty of goodness."

Lloyd looked up at him. "Do you reckon?" he said. "I never thought of me having no goodness. No one ever said so – but, this expediency stuff – I got to give that a try." He glanced at a grinning Rudi and then back to Justin. "Is that how Rudi goes? Because that guy's got diplomacy coming out of his ears."

Justin nodded. "Yep, that's how Rudi goes – diplomacy and charm – and really that's the only thing that separates you two.

You're both really decent kids, but Rudi manages to keep his feet out of his mouth, while you spend most of the time with yours stuffed right in it."

Lloyd laughed. "That's true, man," he said. "That's exactly what I do and I got to give this diplomacy a go. I mean, it's amazing. I seen Rudi do it. You should have seen him with that crabby librarian down in Brookley. He had her so charmed up…"

"It would keep you out of a lot of trouble," Justin said.

It was going to take more than diplomacy, though. Lloyd knew that. He had to keep Caitlin away from the cellar and he had to get down there himself – not such a problem from his bedroom in the North Wing, but serious grief if he was going to be operating from Rudi and Martin's room.

Then there was Craig Donovan. Something had to be done about him but, at the moment, he didn't know what, and, what with discovering he was a dowser and the trip to London and everything…

It was his last night in the North Wing too.

Marion dug out his suitcase so he could pack and, later, he managed to steer Caitlin away from the cellar.

He went down there on his own, but he wasn't sure the ghost was going to show. For ages there was just the ice-cold atmosphere and a thick silence. Then he saw the spirals.

They wandered aimlessly to start with and they weren't moving towards any specific point but then they came back, forming a pattern of movements towards the centre of the wall and, slowly, the crouching spectre appeared. Tonight it was cross-gartered, with the bare chest and baggy breeches, but it didn't move. It stayed crouched, gripping its axe, and staring out of fiery eyes.

There were hissing sighs, and they tore the air like dead breath. But the creature never spoke.

Lloyd tried talking to it, but, with the rank air and the stagnation all around him, nothing came out except a stifled croak, and the smell of decay was so strong, taking in breath to talk was enough to make him want to gag.

He wasn't sure why the ghost was there and, eventually, with a hollow sigh, the creature lifted its hand and then faded back into the wall.

Next morning, having deposited his cases back in the main wing, Lloyd's prime concern was losing Rudi so he could meet up with Craig Donovan.

He decided to tackle the matter head on.

"I got a bit of business to sort out," he said. "And I got to be on my own. The guy I'm dealing with don't want no one else around."

Rudi looked anxious. "It isn't going to get you into trouble, is it?" he said.

Lloyd wasn't comfortable. He screwed his face up. "I tell you what," he said. "The minute there's trouble, I'll get it sorted, right? It's just a bit personal, that's all. I got to do something for this guy, and I got to do stuff for him tomorrow too. I'll catch up with you real quick after – just five minutes it'll take. Then I got to tell you about last night."

Rudi wandered off, but Lloyd could see he wasn't happy and he didn't like that. Rudi was top man and he didn't want to give him grief.

It wasn't so easy finding Craig either, not with the masses conglomerating around the grounds, but strategic thinking led him to the bicycle racks. Somehow, all the dodgy kids assembled there and, if they weren't there, they'd be at the back of the boiler house.

Craig was by the bicycle racks. He was away from the rest and he nodded when he saw Lloyd.

"I was beginning to think you wasn't going to show," he said. "Which would have meant your life was over."

Lloyd grinned. "It isn't that easy, is it? Not locating one guy out of the thousands hanging round this place. I mean it's hard, even when the guy's as ugly as you are."

Craig led him across to the boiler house, which didn't surprise Lloyd. "This guy who I'm doing the homework for," Craig said. "He's usually around here. And that's where he'll be tomorrow, but you got to be careful. You don't go near him if there's any teachers around. You got to understand that. And make sure no one sees you give him the envelope or take the tenner off him."

Lloyd thought Craig must think he was stupid. No kid in their right mind would believe you had to do all this just to pass over a bit of homework and, when they finally located the guy, he was certain.

The kid was a good six feet tall. He had short blond hair – not quite a number one, but heading that way, and he had to be in the sixth form, or at least year eleven, and the idea of a half-formed brain cell like Craig Donovan doing this guy's homework was like an amoeba teaching Einstein.

"You're sure it's homework you're giving him?" he said. "That guy's year eleven or twelve at least."

"He's big for his age," Craig said. "And he's as thick as two planks. It's no sweat doing stuff for him – and it's none of your business anyway. All you got to do is deliver the stuff."

He knew there wasn't any point in pushing it. Like he'd said to Rudi, if it got out of hand, he'd sort it. For the time-being he just wanted to keep Craig off his back.

"I'll give you the homework before we go in the morning," Craig said. "Down the shower room, just before we get on the bus – and that's where you can hand over the tenner when we get back. Kids don't go down there, not if they can help it. That's a good place to meet."

With everything fixed, Lloyd searched out Rudi and, for the rest of the day, he kept well out of Craig's way. He made a special effort to keep clear of other trouble too. He had to practise this diplomacy stuff. He noticed Caitlin giving him the occasional furtive glance. She seemed to have an even fresher complexion today and it was clear she'd showered and washed her hair again. She wasn't dozing off in lessons either and she seemed sharper. She even got involved in classes, especially with Miss Webb, and he couldn't resist saying something to her, just to see how she'd react.

Caitlin didn't give much, but she seemed happier, and when he told her he'd been moved back with Rudi and Martin, she even made a joke.

"I'll sleep even better knowing that, won't I?" she said. "I mean, I won't be lying in fear, thinking you might creep in on me while I'm sleeping."

Lloyd laughed. "In your dreams, man. I got better things to do with my life than creep in on you."

"Yeah?" she said. And there was a tantalising challenge in her voice. He liked that.

"I'm going to get down the North Wing, though, every night, just to keep an eye out, in case you go off on your sleepwalking gig again."

"Don't go getting caught then," she said, and it was as if the barriers were down. There was no way she was ever going to get stuck into to a real conversation, but… it was okay… this thing with Caitlin.

He knew he'd have to tell Martin about it, because, as soon as the carers had gone to ground, he'd have to leave the bedroom and it would be no use telling the guy he was going to the toilet. You couldn't be in the toilet for the best part of an hour, not even after eating the food they dished up at Sarson Hall, and he'd have to go down to the North Wing every night till this was sorted, or until Dave moved Caitlin back into the main wing.

He didn't know how he was going to play it with the ghost either. He'd have to visit the cellar – every night probably – to keep it sweet, and he'd have to be double sure he didn't get caught, certainly up until the weekend.

That evening he and Rudi went to find Justin.

He was around the back of the North Wing, digging over another barren patch of earth masquerading as a flowerbed. When he saw them, he straightened himself, levering up on his spade and his face lit into that smile again. The thing about Justin's smile, Lloyd thought, was that with some people their mouth smiled while the rest of their face stayed dark. With Justin, all of his features smiled.

It was as if his whole body was smiling – even his hair danced when he smiled.

"You ready for a trip to Brookley Henge?" he said.

"We going now?" Lloyd asked.

"Yep." Justin laid his spade to one side.

"What about dinner?" said Rudi.

"Dave said I could get you fish and chips in Brookley." And that made Lloyd's eyes widen.

"How you swing that, man? You got something on Dave or what? That's like giving us a treat and Dave don't do treats."

"I must have, mustn't I?" Justin laughed. "Because he said it was okay for you to go to London this weekend, too."

"That is so amazing," Lloyd said. "You got to be some sort of a genius."

They stacked the tools back in the North Wing. "You'll need a jacket," said Justin and he pulled his anorak around him. He had an old, clapped-out van and in the back there were pieces of sacking wrapped neatly around a pile of digging implements. Lloyd noticed that they were all immaculately clean.

"That your university training?" he said. "Taking care of all them tools?"

Justin grinned. "Old habits die hard."

"They shouldn't be old habits. That's what you should be doing. It's a waste, you hanging around here when you could be doing big things with your studies and stuff."

They clambered into the van. "How do you know we're not doing big things here, with you, a fully equipped dowser? And we will be working with the professor from now on. It's a bit like university."

"That's true, man," Lloyd said. "With you and the professor and everything."

"Is that what you'd like to do then?" said Justin.

"If I had the brains. And I wouldn't drop out like you done neither."

Justin eased the van down the drive and he was grinning again. "I don't reckon you would," he said "And don't you do yourself down, Lloyd Lewis. You've got the brains, no sweat."

The henge was bleak and grey, just as it had been the last time they were there. It was a weird place, and the weirdness wasn't just the look of it, although that was bad enough – random stones blackened with age, rising from other stones that were lying like dead corpses. It made Lloyd shudder just to see them. But it wasn't just how the place looked. It *was* the fact that the stones seemed so much like dead corpses. It was as if this was some kind of ancient battlefield, and the overgrowth of brambles and bracken added to this feeling. Most of all, though, it was the ambience. The forces of life had been drained from the place. There were no birds, no insects and, up here, on a barely used minor road, there wasn't even a passing car to suggest life. Sunlight never touched the place – and the abandonment could be felt.

They didn't say a lot. They just wandered around, as if their thought patterns needed to adjust.

Rudi was the first to speak. He'd gone out on a limb, away into the bracken and he'd found one of the scars.

"What do you think, Justin?" he said. "Would there have been a stone here?"

Justin and Lloyd fought their way through and Justin paced around, feeling the indentation with his foot. Lloyd could see a faraway look in his eye, and a kind of warmth. It was as if he was into his own comfort zone.

"You should be doing this fulltime, man," he said. "Places like this was what you was made for. Any fool could see that, couldn't they, Rudi?"

Rudi nodded and Justin laughed. "Would you like to rephrase that?" he said.

Lloyd grinned. "No way, man. He knows what I mean."

"You're right, though," Justin said. He sighed and looked away into the distance. "Right on both counts, I think – about me and archaeology – and about this imprint. This has definitely been left by a Standing Stone."

"There's loads more. They're all around the place," Lloyd said.

They forced their way deeper into the bracken, pushing through the scrubland and at last Justin stopped and stared around him.

"Like you said, this would have been a complete circle once – and you're right about it being ransacked. There's no sign of the missing stones. Most likely people took them to build hedges and stuff."

While he was talking, Lloyd had wandered away towards the centre and suddenly he stopped. "There's another pit in here," he said. He crouched into the scrub. "It shouldn't be, should it? I mean, this isn't part of no circle."

Justin scrambled over to where he was crouching. Then he walked further into the growth and stopped. "There's another one here," he said.

"What's that mean?" said Lloyd. "Was there two circles?"

"It looks like it. It looks like this place was a double henge, and that's weird because no documentation has ever claimed that." He grinned. "You've made a bit of an archaeological discovery, Lloyd Lewis. Because being a double henge makes it an important site."

They followed the course of the inner-circle and found other indentations. Some were so faint it needed imagination just to identify them, and Lloyd was beginning to feel impatient.

"Isn't it about time I done some dowsing?" he said. "I mean, that's what we're up here for."

Justin laughed. "Sorry. But what with you finding this other ring and everything – we'll have to get a proper archaeological investigation going. We'll get Professor Appleyard on to that when we go to London."

They pushed back towards the half-wrecked stones, and Justin fetched the hazel twig from the van. When he came back he had a compass too, and an ordnance survey map. They laid the map out and searched for Stonehenge. Then he worked out the bearings with the compass. "A ley line would run directly from here to there," he said.

They went out beyond the stones and Lloyd's senses were buzzing. If this worked out, he was about to experience the most ancient of primordial forces right through his body and that was mind-blowing. Justin pointed out the direction of Stonehenge and he began to wander around, holding the divining rod in front of him. He'd moved beyond the stones now, because the stones themselves were giving him sensations, a bit like the mound and the North Wing. He needed to find a new force but, for a while, nothing happened. Then the rod twitched and, as he moved west, the sensations grew. "I got something," he shouted. "It's like – I'm going into a path and the further in I get, the stronger it is."

The rod was quivering, and there couldn't be any doubt. He'd hit on some force and, to him, it was like dynamite.

Justin held him still. He was looking closely at his compass. "You want to go south," he said. "If you can track a force in that direction, then we've got a ley line." He looked at Rudi and his eyes were sparkling. "Fantastic, isn't it?"

"Awesome," said Rudi.

They watched as Lloyd followed the route. And the dowsing rod twitched and shivered. The ley line was heading straight off towards Stonehenge. Its force rippled through him right to his fingertips and it was magical. He carried on following it until the hedge blocked his way – and there was no break. The line was strong, and it was a force that was as ancient as the world.

"It's like – I'm touching creation, man," he whispered. "That's the most amazing thing I've ever done."

"It's massive," Justin said. "I've never seen anything like it. I can't wait to see James Appleyard's face when we tell him on Saturday."

But Lloyd had moved away from the hedge and out of the force field. He was looking across to the other side of the henge. "What about over there?" he said. "Where would it go if I went over there?"

"Avebury, I think," said Justin.

"Shouldn't I try the line to Avebury then?" said Lloyd. "See where the forces go from here. And I got to pick up readings away from the stones. I mean, it's like, them stones, or where they used to be, is creating a kind of interference. If I could get in that field over there…"

They went back onto the road. The growth in the field was more controlled, as if a farmer had been grazing animals, or he'd cut the grass and Lloyd could wander without having to contend with scrub and bracken; but it took him a long time to get any sort of response. He could see Rudi and Justin watching, and there was a look of mingled anticipation and apprehension on their faces.

Eventually he wandered back towards the stone circle and, near the hedge, he picked up a few flickers. Then he moved north, following the line he thought would lead towards Avebury and the movement in the twig became stronger – but suddenly, with a shudder, it fell limp.

He tried again, retracing his steps and going off in a slightly different direction. But the same thing happened, a flicker, then a surge, and then... nothing.

"What's wrong?" Justin said.

"Come over here and you'll see. I picked something up, look." He went back to the power force and showed them. "But when I move away it drops off."

"Perhaps this isn't the ley line. Perhaps that runs from somewhere else. Go up and down the field. See if you can pick up an area of force in a different location," Justin said.

Lloyd wandered from one side of the field to the other, with the divining rod thrust out in front of him, and there were surges, near the hedge and further away, but no continuous line. It was all random patches.

"It's like all the force has been broken up," he said.

"But that doesn't make sense," Justin said. "The henges link ley lines across the country. We've got a line coming from Stonehenge. There's got to be one going off towards Avebury."

Lloyd tried again, combing the field from top to bottom, but none of the surges ever seemed to link, and, by now, it was beginning to get dark.

They went back into the henge and sat on one of the flattened stones. "None of it fits," Justin said at last.

"Do you think Professor Appleyard would know why it's happening?" Rudi said.

"I'll have to give him a call, because I can't figure it out," said Justin.

But there was an idea forming in Lloyd's head. "I know this may sound stupid," he said, mulling over the words. "And I don't know much about all this stuff – not like the professor and all that, but – say these stone circles are like guiding pointers for the ley lines. It's like they direct them from one stone circle to the next – like joining up the dots. Do you get what I'm saying?"

Justin looked at him. "Yes… go on."

"Well, say – because some guys wrecked the stones and made off with them – say this place has been trashed so much, it's kind of lost its power to do the guiding so now there isn't no line running from here to Avebury. Say – by ripping out all them stones, they smashed the system. That would be why there are just bits of broken power all over the field."

"I've heard about that," Justin said. "Disrupted ley lines, and I've heard people say they can cause the most violent of paranormal disturbances."

"Would that be why all this weird stuff is going on back at the home?" said Rudi.

Lloyd leaned forward, gripping his hand around the divining rod. "The thing I don't understand," he said. "And I said this before, isn't that right, Rudi? If the disruption stuff is caused by what's going on up here, then why is the Beaker guy and all the poltergeists running riot down Sarson Hall? I mean, that's a good four miles away, and Sarson Hall isn't even on no line."

He turned the hazel branch over in his hand. "It still don't make sense, do it? I mean, that's the trouble with all this stuff. None of it fits together. It's like – it ought to fit – it ought to be simple – but it isn't. And that's doing my head in."

CHAPTER 11

When they'd finished at Brookley, it was back to the main wing, and sharing a bedroom with Martin.

They needed to prepare him for Lloyd's excursions to the North Wing but he was already in bed, flat on his back with his duvet dragged around his neck. He was staring at the ceiling and his loose curls were splayed out across the pillow. His head and his hair were all they could see, and there was very little expression on his face. He did give the slightest glimmer of a quizzical grimace when Lloyd began to explain what was going on.

"I got to go back down the North Wing, when the kids have stopped mucking around and the carers are out the way," said Lloyd.

"Why you going down there?" The muffled voice came from beneath the duvet. "You got something going with Caitlin Jamieson or what?"

Lloyd laughed. "It isn't got nothing to do with Caitlin Jamieson."

They tried explaining what had happened with the ghost and the poltergeist, and about the ley lines and Brookley Henge, but Martin just slid into a whole new realm of boredom.

"You know what, Lloyd Lewis?" he said. "You got problems. I forgot about you and all this curse stuff. If I'd remembered, I wouldn't have said nothing to Dave about you coming back in here. It's boring if you want to know, and either you're round the twist – or you really have got something going with Caitlin Jamieson and you're using this for cover."

Rudi said about the divining but his reaction to that was even more dismissive.

"You got to think I came down on a sunbeam, mate," he said. "You two's as bad as one another, and it's all rubbish, so give it a rest."

"Well, I got to go out," Lloyd said. "So I can get down the cellar to see the ghost, and I'll be gone for a good hour. And it's likely I'll have to do it every night, so you better get used to it."

"Whatever," Martin said. He pulled the folds of duvet right over him. "You got stuff going with Caitlin Jamieson, that's what you've got."

Getting out wasn't going to be a problem. It was obvious Martin didn't care either way, but Lloyd was worried that he would start spreading stuff about him and Caitlin, and that would cause real trouble, especially if Dave got to hear. "It hasn't got nothing to do with Caitlin," he said again, but by this time Martin had sunk even deeper into oblivion.

"Whatever," he mumbled again.

After Rudi had settled, Lloyd lay, staring at the ceiling, listening to the raging mayhem outside.

He'd forgotten the chaos that went on in the main building. He could hear Dave bawling from his office – and Christine close by. There were kids yelling back at her and there were crashes as though chairs were being chucked. It was like World War III out there. He wondered if they'd ever settle, but, eventually, for some reason, the steam ran out, the lights went off and night closed in. After that there were just the creaks and groans of the house, and the restive disruption of uneasy sleep.

He waited until he thought the carers would be back in the common room. Then he slipped out of bed and into the corridor.

He had to grope his way, finding his feet in the darkness. But then, in a confusion of light, someone snapped a switch and Christine's voice rang out: "Where do you think you're off to, Lloyd Lewis?"

He swung around and his brain groped for a story – but his attempt at claiming he was heading for the toilet failed miserably. The toilets were behind her at the other end of the corridor – as she pointed out with considerable enthusiasm.

"I lost my sense of direction, didn't I?" he said. "It's only the second night I been in this wing, remember?"

Christine's face looked mean and pinched and he knew all this was going to be hard, especially if she was on the prowl every night.

Back in bed, he could hear his heart thumping. If he wasn't down in the old building soon, he'd be too late. Caitlin would be in the cellar and there would be nothing he could do about it. He couldn't make another move, though, not until he was sure Christine had gone.

Eventually, he slipped out of bed and pulled the door open again, just the narrowest slit and he peered into the corridor. There was nothing except sooty blackness out there, and his eyes adjusted. Then he eased himself into the passage hardly daring to breathe. Every creak and groan could be Christine on the stairs again. But there was nothing and, this time, he made it to the fire doors.

On the other side was a different world – the howling wind, the sheer blasts of ice. There were bangs and clashes, and hailstones, and there was that clear, cold moonlight. Before he opened the doors he'd been certain the sky had been heavy with clouds, and that was the weirdest thing. He gave a momentary thought to the new kid, Daryl Johnson. That guy must be scared rigid. But then something else grabbed at his attention.

Caitlin was already out and she was treading, step-by-step, towards the cellar.

He moved down the corridor, as light-footed as he could, slipping sideways so he could ease past her on the stairs, and he put his hands on her shoulders. Then, carefully, he manoeuvred her so she was facing back towards her bedroom, and he set about raising her, one foot at a time, towards the upstairs corridor.

He must have had the knack because she didn't seem startled. It was hard, though, getting her to reverse the downward motion. She kept putting her foot forward, feeling for a drop, and when her leg came against a rising step, she stopped. He had to lift her legs physically and it took three or four steps before she got anything like a rhythm going.

Eventually, though, her body mechanisms clicked and he was able to guide her back to her bedroom.

She slid under the duvet and the half open eyes hinted her relief. So did the semi-smile. There was a sigh that floated out of deep sleep and it sent a shiver through him and suddenly, because he couldn't resist it, he leaned forward and stroked her hair. It was soft, and fell gently through his fingers. Then, out of sleep, her hand emerged and, for a moment, she held him, keeping his hand pressed against her head, and her face looked up in the clear moonlight and she gave him that look again.

It was like, something big was happening, and he wasn't sure what it was.

He eased his hand away, because he knew that was the right thing to do. She was half asleep and he was wide-awake and that was wrong. Besides, he had to get down to the cellar and be back before Christine got wind he was out of bed again.

There was a whole turbulence of feelings inside him, though, and these were different from the feelings he was used to. Normally he got through by analysing stuff, but this time he was almost content to let the bewilderment lie – to have it remain curled contentedly in his gut.

He could hear the cellar door banging. It was open, waiting for him and, although there was still a lot of apprehension, there was also an excitement. If he could manage to make his voice work, he'd got stuff to tell the ghost. He'd followed its guidance and now he could dowse. He knew about the fractured ley lines. He knew about the sabotage inflicted on the ghost's systems, and, he knew the old Beaker man had been key to his discovering all this stuff.

All the regular things happened. The cellar door slammed, the light-bulb crackled, the atmosphere was thick with cold, but the ghost didn't show. There were a few random twisters – wisps darting around by the wall, and there was the silence of the dead, but nothing transformed into any kind of spirit. The spirals dropped back and, for a while, he stood waiting, hoping the dust would kick up again. But there was nothing, and disappointment crept over him. The ghost wasn't going to show. In his frustration, he kicked at the piles of dust on the floor. He'd hoped the creature would have wanted to hear about his dowsing, and he wanted it to come up with some more signs – pointers to the next step. He was afraid he might not see it again until after they'd been to London and, as he made his way back to the main wing, he felt a wave of discontent.

There was no trace of Christine on the landing and Martin was moaning in his sleep. Even Rudi was sleeping.

He slid into bed. He wasn't sure about tonight. He didn't see that there was any way forwards, not if the ghost didn't show. In fact, it hardly seemed worth going down to the North Wing at all.

But… there was Caitlin.

Caitlin was never going to give up sleepwalking into the Beaker man's lair and Lloyd was certain, if it was her that went down to the cellar, the ghost would be back in full force, terrorising her. And that meant he'd have to do this every night, just to keep her safe.

Next day was delivery day. Lloyd was reluctant to drag himself out of bed, and there was still the fixation from Martin about Caitlin.

"Go on your trip last night, then?" he said. "Good, was it?"

He ignored the inference. "You come up with me and Rudi to see Justin tonight," he said. "Talk to him if you don't believe me, and while you're up there, I'll show you the dowsing."

Martin yawned. "Tricks with sticks," he said, and this time Lloyd didn't respond. He knew he had to keep out of trouble. He just grabbed his toilet things and headed to the showers.

He'd have to go down there again after breakfast so he could get the envelope from Craig, and that didn't sit easily with him.

There wasn't anything right about what Craig was doing and he'd have to get it sorted, but it couldn't be this week. He had to keep his head down at least until they got back from London.

At breakfast he couldn't help looking in Caitlin's direction. He half-expected a scowl, because of what he'd done with her hair. She was very quiet. Her head was down and she seemed to be concentrating on her food, but, as he looked, he caught her giving him a half-glance, her eyes peering through the falling fringe, and when she saw him looking, there was that semi-smile that sent a shiver down him.

After breakfast he found Craig pacing around by the showers. He had the envelope in his hand and it wasn't very big. If that was homework, there wasn't much of it – not ten pounds worth for sure.

"Where you been, black boy?" he said. "You got to be smarter than that, picking this stuff up. If one of the carers came down – me hanging around with this in my hand, how do you think that would look?"

"I had to get my stuff from the bedroom didn't I? Else I wouldn't have had nowhere to put the envelope, and how do you think that would look – pink boy?"

He stuffed the envelope in his holdall and headed for the minibus.

At break he knew Rudi was bothered, but he made himself scarce all the same. They arranged to meet up by the main entrance just as they had the previous day. Then Lloyd searched out the blond guy with the skinhead haircut. He was around by the boiler house and the operation went without a hitch. But he didn't feel good about it.

"You Craig's new runner?" the blond kid said, and the guy was looking as shifty as a weasel. "There aren't any teachers around, are there?"

Lloyd pulled the envelope out of his back pocket. He'd transferred it from the holdall as soon as they were released from class. "Not that I seen," he said. "You the guy what Craig's done the homework for?"

He could see the boy couldn't get hold of that. Then a light dawned and he gave Lloyd a patronising look. "Is that what he's calling it, now?" he said.

It was just as Lloyd thought. This didn't have anything to do with homework. It was dodgy and it was all wrong.

But there was nothing he could do. He took the money and headed back to Rudi, shoving the two five pound notes in his back pocket. He was careful that none of the teachers were around; but he was convinced this needed sorting as quickly as possible.

There wasn't a lot to tell Justin when they got back from school, but Lloyd wanted to see him, partly so Justin could talk to Martin, and it wasn't easy prising Martin out of the television lounge.

"What is it with you?" he said. "I'm not interested in all your weird stuff. I don't even know this Justin guy. I mean, all this stuff with sticks – what do you call it, divining or whatever – it isn't nothing to do with me."

It took physical force to shift him, with Rudi and Lloyd tugging an arm each. But they did eventually extricate him from his chair.

Justin was raking dead leaves for a bonfire, and he straightened when he saw them, brushing his hair away from his face.

"Who's this, then?" he said.

"He's our roommate, Martin. We told you about him," said Lloyd.

Justin leaned on the rake and held out his hand. "How you doing, Martin?"

Martin grunted and wiped his hand on the back of his jeans. He gave Justin a limp handshake, and he still had the expression of displacement on his face, confused and out of his own biosphere.

"We brought him so you could explain what's going on in the North Wing, and so Lloyd can show him the dowsing," Rudi said.

"He don't believe us, see," said Lloyd, shoving Martin gently in the mid-riff. "And he's got this idea that when I go down to the old building at night, I'm going down there to see Caitlin."

Justin laughed. "Bit of a doubter, then, Martin?"

"Well… what would you think?" he said.

Justin smiled. "I don't think Caitlin features that much, and what he says about the stuff going on in the North Wing has got me convinced. I know you're going to find that tough to take, but what Lloyd's told me, what he's seen… well, the guy couldn't have made it up."

"Yeah, right," said Martin.

He was still hunched, and he didn't give much impression of being all that interested.

"Can I show him the dowsing?" Lloyd said and Justin laughed.

"It's your thing. You can show who you like."

He fetched the twig, but when Lloyd took it over to the raised ground and it began moving, all Martin did was sniff. "It's like I said – tricks with sticks," he said.

"You couldn't do it," said Lloyd. He thrust the hazel twig towards him, but Martin just shoved his hands in his pockets and began to slouch back towards the main entrance.

"It's nothing but bilge," he said. "You got that gardener guy took in, but it isn't going to happen with me."

Justin put an arm loosely around Lloyd's shoulder. "The world is full of sceptics," he said. "And I don't think you're ever going to convince that guy."

"I will, too," Lloyd said. "I'll drag him down the North Wing tonight. Let him see what goes on down there. That will sort him out."

Martin was no more pleased to be dragged down to the North Wing than he was to be prised away from the television lounge. But Lloyd wouldn't give in.

He made sure Christine wasn't around and then they slipped off towards the fire doors.

The icy blast caught them as soon as the doors were opened, ripping down the corridor, and there were bangs and ear-splitting groans. Moonlight was shafting through the window and there were hailstones like golf balls. There was a crash from Daryl's room downstairs and it sounded as if his wardrobe had gone over. And the whole place shook.

Suddenly Martin gripped at Lloyd's arm and Lloyd could see his face was white and his mouth gaping.

He nodded. He'd made his point and Martin hissed through clenched teeth: "I'm getting out of this."

Then he was off, barging through the fire doors, and he shifted faster than Lloyd had ever seen him shift.

It gave him some sort of satisfaction as he eased down the corridor towards Caitlin's door, but later, down in the cellar, the spirals were all that happened again. It was as if the Beaker man was too weary to put in an appearance.

After breakfast the next morning, he was heading upstairs for his holdall when he heard a very familiar and very irritating call. "Hey, black boy."

Craig was standing below him in the hall, staring, his face brazen. "I got another bit of homework for you to deliver, okay?"

It was starting to rattle him, all this stuff from Craig. "Look, pink boy," he said. "I done stuff for you already this week and I told you, I'm not your runner. I got other things to be thinking about. You give the guy the homework yourself."

But Craig had him pinned against the banister in seconds. His face was within an inch of Lloyd's and it was sallow and greasy, with hints of red eruptions. Lloyd leaned away. He was very conscious that Craig was stronger and bigger than he was and, at that moment, this corner of the stairs was seriously lacking in surveillance. "You listen to me, black boy," Craig hissed. "If I say you deliver homework, you deliver homework, okay? No questions or I'll splash your little black face all over the wall."

It was in Lloyd's head to knee him, but he couldn't. It would put the skids on their trip to London. His only chance to retain some dignity was to agree, but with as much bad grace as he could.

"Just get your spotty head out of my face, man. And quit calling me black boy, will you? What you got? Some sort of fixation on black guys?"

He had to move quickly because he knew what was coming and he pulled his head to one side just as Craig's fist shot past his ear. "You watch your mouth," he hissed, but Lloyd had already wriggled free and was making it upstairs to his room. He turned on the landing and glared back.

"Right. You listen to me," he said – and he had the advantage now, because he was standing above Craig, looking down on him.

"I got big things on this week, and I don't want nobody rocking no boats. So I'll deliver your stuff, this once. But you got to start showing respect, man. I got black skin, all right. You got pink skin. Inside there isn't no difference, and you got to get that sorted in your head. Okay?"

"You just deliver the envelope," Craig said. "That's all I care about. Meet me same place as you did last time, this break, and I'll show you the kid – and make sure you lose the Indian guy."

He swung around and headed for the main door, while Lloyd fetched his stuff from the bedroom.

Martin was taking the day off school again, and when he pushed through, he couldn't help noticing a new respect in the half-bleary eyes. He was banging out some tune on his iPhone, but when Lloyd came in he pulled the headphones off. "You having trouble with Craig Donovan?" he said.

Lloyd grinned. "Nothing I can't handle. I got to talk to Justin about him, but don't bother yourself. I got him in my sights and he hasn't got much time left."

Martin nodded, this time not in the rhythm of the iPhone, and said, "That's okay, then – but if you need back-up, you come to me, okay? That guy is one big pain in the backside." He looked around and then, as if some fibre of urgency was struggling to break out, he added: "I got to say this, before you go. We got to talk, about last night. I mean, that stuff down the North Wing. I didn't have no idea. It's mind-blowing down there and you got to fill me in."

"No problem," Lloyd said. "When we get back from school you come with me and Rudi. We meet up with Justin most nights to talk about this stuff, and he's well clued in."

Martin retreated to his iPhone, sinking back into his pillow, and Lloyd was relieved. It would make it a lot easier to keep an eye on Caitlin and get down to the cellar every night if Martin understood what was going on.

When Craig pointed the boy out at break, it left no doubts in Lloyd's mind. This kid was definitely sixth form. He had long, straight hair, parted in the middle. It didn't have any of the bounce that Justin's had, and the guy had a mean look on his face. But he wasn't wearing school uniform and there was no way he was going to stump up ten pounds for the privilege of letting a unicellular blob like Craig Donovan touch his homework.

He told the others about it that evening and Justin gave a worried nod, as if he understood what Craig was in to straight away.

"You don't know what's going on, do you?" he said. "And I don't think I'm telling you, either. The less you know about it the better, but you've got to go and see Dave."

The way he said it made Lloyd look up sharply, and then Martin nodded, which didn't help, because he said, "I know what he's in to," and straight away Justin hushed him up.

"Trouble is," Lloyd said, "Craig Donovan's got a line on me. If I tell Dave anything, there's going to be trouble for me as well as Craig, and that will mess with the trip on Saturday."

"Is it likely Craig will ask you to do it again?" Justin said.

Lloyd nodded. "He's got me doing it twice this week already."

"Okay. Do it this time, but make sure you don't get caught. Then, if he asks you again next week after we've been to London, go to Dave. Once you've reported it, you're in the clear, and that's the main thing for the time being."

Now he was certain there was something bad going on and, next day, it made him doubly nervous. It was like delivering a primed grenade and, what was worse, as he made it towards the bike rack, he was collared by Miss Webb. She wanted him to do extra maths because she thought he was good enough to be fast tracked, and that was okay. It meant Justin might be right about him and university. But... this break... with a primed bomb in his back pocket and with Craig and the sixth form kid waiting, it all came at the very worst of times. He was like a cat on fire, and she hung on to him, too. It was nearly the end of break when he got away and he only just made it to the lanky-haired kid.

The guy was looking seriously stressed.

"Where the hell you been?" he said.

"I got collared by Miss Webb, didn't I?"

"She didn't find the stuff on you?" The boy's eyes were darting around and his hand was out, twitching.

"No," said Lloyd. He pulled the envelope out and shoved it into the boy's hand. "Craig told me this was homework and I can't get my head around that. I mean, how has a pea-brain like him got the skill to do homework for a guy like you?"

The sixth-form kid shoved the envelope in his pocket and pushed a ten-pound note into Lloyd's hand. And all the time his eyes were darting. "That's for me to know and you to find out," he said. "Now get lost before anyone sees you."

That night, when he gave Craig the ten pounds, he told him. "I got collared by Miss Webb, didn't I?" he said. "I couldn't get away neither and I only just made it before the end of break."

"You didn't let her see no envelope, did you?" Craig said.

"It was in my back pocket. But it was risky. You got to find some other way of delivering this homework stuff. I mean, she was on for me to do extra maths, and that means I got to get coached in break, don't it? I'm not going to be around to do this stuff."

"That's your problem, black boy," Craig said as he shambled off. "You try wriggling out of this, and I'll see you're in it so deep with Dave Trafford you won't come up for air. So forget it."

Lloyd braced himself. After London, he'd blow Craig Donovan open. He'd got Justin's backing now. Next time he got an envelope, he'd go to Dave. He'd tell him the reason why he was down in the computer room if necessary – and if Dave did gate him – what difference would that make? With the professor guy interested in all this stuff, there'd be too many people on Dave's back for him to do any real damage.

He could hardly wait for Saturday. There was only one thing that bothered him – and that was Caitlin. He wasn't going to be there Saturday night and that would mean she would be free to wander again.

He thought Martin could go down and stop her. He knew about the North Wing now – and about Brookley Henge and the displaced ley lines, but when he saw Caitlin at break, she wouldn't even listen to the idea. "Don't you tell Martin Doyle nothing," she said. "I told you already, it's got nothing to do with nobody but us."

"Yeah, but you don't want to go down the cellar no more, facing that ghost. And with me being in London, there's no way I can stop you," Lloyd said.

He could see she was scared. Her hands were twitching to go up to her ears again and, already, her feet were doing the little dance.

"You don't talk about that stuff," she said, and it was in a half-whisper, as if the idea had paralysed her throat.

"But you got to face it, Caitlin, man. If I'm not there – someone's got to stop you – and Martin knows about the North Wing."

This time her hands did go up to her ears. "You're not telling him," she said and it was almost a yell of fear.

It scared him. He looked around the grounds because no way did he want some teacher muscling in.

"Well, what are we going to do?" he said.

She stood there looking lost. It was hard not to put an arm around her, because this was freaking her out.

"I don't know," she said.

"I could try and talk to the ghost," said Lloyd. "The trouble is, he don't show up no more. It's just dust swirls when I go down."

"Couldn't you not go to London?" Caitlin said – but that was a non-starter.

"This London trip is big, man. The only thing I can do is go down the cellar and hope the ghost shows up, and if it does, I'll tell it about you."

It didn't have a lot going for it, but it was the only plan he had and, on Friday night, when he went down to the cellar, the swirls seemed to have more urgency. Eventually they did materialise into the Beaker man. It didn't move out from the wall but its echoing sighs and hisses filled the room and this time Lloyd succeeded in talking.

He told it everything: about the stone circles and the destruction up at the henge; about the dowsing and the fractured ley lines;

about the forces he'd picked up around the North Wing and in the cellar. He even told it about the professor up in London and their visit. He couldn't be certain it made any sense, but the sighs and echoes did follow a pattern, sometimes slow and even like the last gasps of the dying, and then more animated, as if it was trying to tell Lloyd something. There were even a few attempted words, and the more excited passages of breathing seemed to fit with stuff about destruction and broken ley lines, and the North Wing. It also got quite excited when he mentioned the mound – and that puzzled Lloyd.

When he got to the subject of Caitlin, though, and explained about this kid sleepwalking into the cellar, and how he'd steered her back to her room, and how she was likely to show up instead of him tomorrow night, there was nothing but the slow laboured breathing, and he couldn't be certain it understood or took in a word.

Caitlin would go down the cellar tomorrow for sure – and doubts kept him awake for most of the night.

CHAPTER 12

Tiredness didn't get in the way of his excitement the next morning, though.

He and Rudi were wrapped in their own world at breakfast and the pandemonium raging around them hardly made any impact at all.

"It'll be great, man," Lloyd said. "'Specially for you, seeing as you haven't been to London before. It's dead good."

"How is it that you've been?" Rudi said.

"Me and Lee Peddar – we used to ride the trains. The other home was right by the station. It wasn't no trouble."

Rudi looked at him. "But the money for the fares? Did you get that with your paper round?"

"There wasn't no barrier at the station was there? It was easy. We just got on the train. It didn't cost nothing."

"But that's illegal. It's like stealing."

"No it isn't," Lloyd said. "I mean, the train's going to London anyway. It don't cost nothing extra to take me and Lee."

"If you got caught though."

"We didn't. That was the fun of it."

Justin was waiting with his van when they'd finished breakfast. They took the travel case, still packed from last week. There was room for Rudi's stuff too. For Lloyd, this was the fulfilment of a dream. His travel case, him going somewhere on a train, it was magic and it was official, with tickets and reserved seats and an authenticity that put it in a different league from riding the trains with Lee Peddar.

They left the van at the car park by Didcot Parkway station. They had window seats and Lloyd let Rudi face the engine.

"It's good in London," he said. "It's like, to get around, you got these trains that go under the ground. You go hundreds of feet down and you need escalators and stuff."

Rudi grinned and gazed out of the window. The clouds were thinning and a faint haze of shadow was etching the fields.

"And it's like, when you get near Paddington there's these railway lines, miles across – like a whole field of them, and Paddington's massive, isn't that right, Justin? And the streets, man, down Oxford Circus – there's so many people, you got to push your way through – people shopping in big-brand stores. You got taxicabs – there's hundreds of them – and buses! I mean, you got to see it, man."

"I have," Rudi said. "I've seen it on films and TV. I know all about the Underground and cabs and that."

"But it isn't the same. It isn't like seeing if for real, is it Justin?"

Justin had his broadest smile on and his eyes were dancing. "You're like a little kid, Lloyd Lewis," he said, and Lloyd sat back in his seat.

"Well, it's good, going to London. I always wanted to do travelling. That's why I got the travel case." He watched the wooded hills of the Thames valley slide past, and then he looked across at Rudi again. "This train's doing a hundred and twenty-five miles an hour. Do you realise that? That's over two miles a minute. That's more than twice as fast as your old van would go, top speed, down a hill with the wind behind it, isn't that right, Justin?"

Justin grinned again and, for a while, Lloyd didn't say anything more. He just watched the landscape mutate towards the conurbation of Reading while the clouds continued thinning and the shadows became more distinct.

He did manage to point out the vastness of Reading station – just in case Rudi hadn't noticed, and then he explained that Paddington was even bigger. "It's like it's all covered with this massive glass canopy, with steel girders," he said.

As they shot through Ealing Broadway, he pointed out the Underground. Rudi was beaming, but he didn't say anything. Lloyd decided he was probably too overwhelmed, so he sank back in his seat to drink in the unfolding vastness.

By the time they reached Paddington, the sun was out at full strength and, for the first time in a fortnight, he saw the sky a cloudless blue.

Going on the tube to Russell Square meant a whole new commentary, working the ticket machines, how to tread on and off the escalators without putting your life in jeopardy. Then there was the joy of going up the escalator that goes down when there weren't too many people around. He was a talking encyclopaedia about cleaning the tunnels, about the rodent population, about which lines were deepest, and how, in the war, they used tube stations as air-raid shelters. It was all dished in Rudi's direction on account of Rudi not having been to London before, and he didn't take any notice of Rudi's gentle insistence that he already knew about the Underground.

The professor had suggested they meet in the foyer of the British Museum. He thought that would be more impressive than his office at the university… and he wasn't wrong.

"What about that?" Lloyd said as they walked into the massive edifice. "That's sick, Rudi, man."

He stood there, taking in the white central precinct, the pillars and the huge glass roof and Rudi grinned.

"Yeah, sick," he said, and Lloyd dug him in the ribs.

Justin was searching out the professor, and they headed around the plaza, defining the central shopping-enclosure.

James Appleyard was sitting at a table in the food hall, and he wasn't a bit like a professor. He was slim and had dark hair and he was really casual looking.

His handshake was firm. "Lloyd, Rudi, how marvellous to meet you," he said, and close up he didn't look much older than thirty. His clothes were trendy, and the guy had gelled his hair.

"You're dead young for a professor, man," Lloyd said. "I reckoned you'd be some kind of grizzled-up old guy with a long beard and glasses. You look good, don't he, Rudi? I mean, I thought professors wore old scruffy suits and had beer guts."

Professor Appleyard laughed and his eyes were dancing. "I do have glasses," he said. "Little half-rimmed jobs so I can peer over the top at my students. They tell me it gives me gravitas."

Then he turned to Justin and Lloyd saw his eyes soften. "Justin," he said. He threw his arms around him as if they were long-lost brothers. "It's been too long, mate."

Justin was hugging him back and in no way did it look like they were a professor and his renegade student.

The professor organised drinks and a snack. "Coke? Would that suit?" he said "And they do these wicked triple-chocolate muffins."

"That would be great," Lloyd said. "Isn't that right, Rudi?"

Rudi nodded and Lloyd sensed he was still overawed. The professor was a real knockout. He wasn't like Dave and the carers, or the social-workers. He didn't have any of their patronising twaddle.

When they'd settled, he asked about their journey and the home, and then he asked about the supernatural things that were going on. It was easy to talk to him. Lloyd had been afraid he'd be a bit awestruck, but, with no disrespect, talking to this guy was like talking to a mate.

"The ghost is one of the Beaker people," he said. "Justin figured that out from the drawings I done, and it was weird because one time when the guy turned up he had all these artefacts, like he wanted to help me identify him."

"Really?" the professor said. "That's amazing."

Hanging from the back of his chair was a sort of man-bag and he delved into it, pulling out a notepad. "Do you think you could still remember? Could you sketch the artefacts for me now?"

"No sweat. I could do the ghost too if you like. I seen the guy so many times, I know him off by heart." He sketched out the ghost in both guises, cloaked and with the cross-gaiters, and he drew the artefacts, while the others watched.

Justin glanced at the professor. "Brilliant, isn't he?"

"Absolutely amazing," said the professor. "These are so detailed I could use them in a textbook." Lloyd could tell he wasn't blagging either – and that made him feel really good. He put a hand on Lloyd's shoulder and looked him straight in the eyes. He had soft eyes – hazel coloured, warm. "These drawings are stunning, Lloyd," he said.

Lloyd leaned back, admiring his own efforts. "Thanks, professor, man," he said. "That's respect, that is. I appreciate that."

"You don't have to call me professor, either," he said. "James will do."

"You don't mind us calling you that?"

"Not at all. It makes me feel younger having young guys calling me James. Now, tell me about the haunting. Justin says you have a theory."

He took a bite into his triple-chocolate muffin and followed that with a swig of Coke. "It isn't nothing really," he said. "I bet it'll sound rubbish to you, but what I figured is this: this ghost – he was the one what built Brookley Henge, right? And when we went up there with Justin we found like these dents in the ground where a double henge use to be – and that means, when he built it, it was important, okay? The thing is, it got vandalised – like some guys have been up there and taken all the stones. So, for starters, the ghost isn't that pleased."

The professor nodded. "Yep. I wouldn't be that pleased either."

"But there's more, isn't there? This ghost, I reckon it wants me to do something about it. I mean, it figured I could do dowsing. It made this sign and Justin worked out it was a divining rod."

Professor Appleyard leaned back in his chair. "And can you?"

"Yeah, it's dead good."

"I don't suppose you could tell me what it feels like, this divining?"

Lloyd looked at him, because he figured the guy was seriously on the right wavelength. "That is one big sensation, man. I mean, when you walk across say, a ley line, it's like the power comes through your nerve-endings. Like it's speaking to all the muscles in your body and the feelings, they fill you up like the oldest forces in the earth inside you – the forces of creation going through you, direct to the rod."

The professor nodded. "That's so amazing," he said.

"Yeah, well… and this is the rubbish bit. When we went up to Brookley Henge to trace the ley line, Justin figured it would go off south to Stonehenge, which it did… and then it was supposed to go north to Avebury. But it didn't do that. We kept getting like these bits of force all broken up, scattered all over the field – and I figured that… and I know this is rubbish… but… well… say the stone circles was set out like sign posts – like links in the chain and, over time they kind of developed a power over the forces – like they focused them – from one henge to the next and, when the circle was messed up, then the directing power was lost so, instead of running in a straight line, the forces all got scattered – like they got no guidance no more and don't know where to go."

"Fragmented ley lines," Justin said, and the professor nodded.

"That's quite a theory – and you've got some good evidence to support it. It would certainly explain the paranormal activity."

"Yeah, but… what I don't get is this. Why is all the activity going on down in Sarson Hall. I mean, that's miles clear of Brookley Henge, and it isn't even in the path of the ley lines."

"What did you say the home was called?" the professor said.

"Sarson Hall," said Lloyd. He spelt it out and, as he was doing this, Justin sat back on his chair and gave a sort of gasp.

"That never occurred to me," he said, looking straight at the professor. "And that would explain a lot."

"What would explain a lot?" said Lloyd.

But the professor just grinned. "Just a little hypothesis," he said. "If it's okay with you, I'd like to come back with you tomorrow and take a look at this Sarson Hall."

"Yeah, but what is it with this hypo thing?"

The professor wouldn't give, though, and there was a hint of mischief in his eyes. "It's just an idea. But I may be barking up the wrong tree, so wait till we get back tomorrow and, if what I'm thinking is right, then I'll tell you. It's one of these annoying things about academics. They like to be certain before they say something." He looked at Justin, his eyes twinkling. "Isn't that right, Justin?"

Justin laughed. "It certainly is, Professor James."

But Lloyd was already on another tack. He was watching the chemistry with the professor and Justin, and he said: "With this guy as your professor, man, how come you dropped out of university? I mean, you two, it's like you talk the same talk."

James gave the loudest laugh of the day and he clapped Lloyd on the shoulder. "That's exactly what I've been telling him, Lloyd," he said. "And don't you give up either. With a bit of luck, we'll get through to him in the end."

"I mean, it's obvious," Lloyd said. "I reckon the guy's crazy, hanging around down Sarson Hall when he could be up here doing all this. If it was me, no way would I swap this for gardening down that dump."

"Would you like to be doing all this?" Professor Appleyard asked.

"If I had the brains, yeah, that would be awesome. You'd like that too, wouldn't you, Rudi?"

Rudi grinned. "If I could afford it," he said, and Professor Appleyard laughed again.

"That's not a big thing, Rudi, man," said Lloyd. "The education what you get – that's the important thing."

Professor Appleyard was still laughing. "It would be nice if a few of my students had that attitude, eh Justin?" And Justin had that smile on his face.

"Yes," he said. "But Lloyd's a one-off. Besides, he's still young enough to have ideals."

"If I had the brains, I'd still want the same thing when I was your age. That's certain, that is," said Lloyd.

The professor leaned back. "You've got the brains, Lloyd, I've no doubts about that," he said. Then he looked at Rudi. "And you too, Rudi, I shouldn't wonder."

They went into the Egyptian Hall after that and it was mind-blowing.

Then they took the tube to Kentish Town, and caught a bus to Highgate village where the professor lived. They left the travel bag and Justin's holdall there.

"Are we still in London?" Lloyd asked, as they made their way back to the bus. "Because your house, it's got this garden, and it's like, country, isn't that right Rudi? I mean it's all fields and woods and stuff over the road."

"That's Hampstead Heath," said the professor. "We'll go over there tomorrow if you like – take a picnic, and a ball to kick about."

They took the tube to Waterloo and came out through a labyrinth of paths and roads, meandering under brick archways and over crossings, until they saw a concrete building, which the professor said was the Royal Festival Hall. They went down the side and out onto the Thames Embankment, and it was magic.

The London Eye was just downriver, and over on the other bank was Big Ben and the Houses of Parliament. "It's just like you see in pictures, isn't it, Rudi? What do you think of all this now, man?"

Rudi's eyes were sparkling. "Brilliant," he said, and seeing his mate so blown out made Lloyd feel really good.

The professor's wife, Jenny, was waiting for them in the foyer of the Festival Hall and she was really nice – small, slim, with dark curly hair. It bounced around her face. She gave Justin a hug just like the professor had. Then she shook Rudi and Lloyd by the hand, and her face seemed ready to break into a smile at any excuse.

They went into a restaurant down by the side of the Festival Hall, and that was awesome, because it was built into a railway arch and the brickwork of the arch was part of the restaurant.

"Are there trains up there?" Lloyd said.

"All the time," Jenny laughed. "Amazing, isn't it?" She looked around. "I love this place. It was my idea to bring you here."

After they'd eaten, they crossed over Hungerford Bridge and took a boat down the Thames. They passed some fantastic places – the Globe, the Tower of London, St Paul's Cathedral and the Tate Modern and, when they got to Greenwich, they disembarked and had a tour around the O2. And that was like a massive domed tent with a town inside. There were shops and restaurants and exhibition centres. They even had a multiplex cinema – and this huge arena where top groups had gigs.

Then they went back to Charing Cross and up the London Eye, finishing in McDonalds, and all the time they talked and laughed and joked, and the professor pulled Lloyd's leg because he kept saying: "Isn't that right, Rudi?"

And all the time, Lloyd's brain was wrestling with the avalanche of good feelings. Being with James and Jenny – it was a little microcosm, and it was as near to…

Rudi was the one who forced his brain to face what he'd been fighting. They were settling into bed that night, and he said: "I suppose this is what it's like all the time for other kids." And immediately Lloyd sat up.

"What you saying, man?"

"Well, being a family. Doing stuff together with people that are there for you. Having a good time, like today."

"The professor and Jenny aren't there for us," Lloyd said.

"I'm not saying that. It's just…"

But Lloyd turned, resting his elbow on the pillow, with his hand supporting his head, and he stared Rudi straight in the eyes. "Look, Rudi, mate," he said. "We got to face up to this. They're nice people, okay? But that's all. The professor's up for this ghost thing back at the home, and that's great. And they want to give us a good time, right? But by Monday, we'll be out of their heads. We're kids that haven't got no family, and that isn't going to change. It's no good you thinking about parents and brothers and sisters and all that stuff. That's got to be dead stupid, because, you start thinking that, you start getting your hopes up and then, these people have gone – they're out of your lives, and you got kicked in the teeth. And there isn't going to be no one around to pick up the pieces neither. That'll be down to you, so don't go there. Believe me, I know. I've been there. I got the T-shirt."

Rudi didn't say anything for a minute, but then he sighed – and there was a hitch in his voice. "I guess you're right," he said. "… But it's hard."

"It *is* hard," said Lloyd. "That's why you can never trust people, not even the professor and Jenny." He paused, and then chuckled, flinging himself back on the bed. "They're okay though. And while the professor's doing this ghost stuff it'll be great. We got to make the most of it, isn't that right?"

Next morning after breakfast they went across to Hampstead Heath. Jenny cooked an amazing breakfast – sausages and bacon, eggs, mushrooms, beans and fried bread. She joked to James that, as far as he was concerned, it was a one-off, because she wasn't having some pot-bellied overweight jelly for a husband and, from tomorrow, he'd be back to fruit and muesli. She packed a picnic basket with coffee, baguettes, salad, ham – and all kinds of other stuff for the Heath. Lloyd and Rudi took the basket and, in spite of what he'd said to Rudi last night, Lloyd was having a massive tussle with his head.

This *was* what other kids did in proper families, and it was hard because his brain kept trying to run around the idea of James and Jenny, fantastic people, intelligent, great house – treating him and Rudi like kids with no hang-ups. Justin was like one of the family too, almost like a big brother. The ideas were there, banging at the back of Lloyd's mind, oozing into the cracks and crevices, and it was Bill and Jean all over again. But James Appleyard had young guys going through his hands all the time and probably some of them came back at weekends. They were at university for a few years, and that was that – a new lot in and the last lot gone. That was what he did for a living. Justin was part of it, or had been, and Justin understood. In a way Lloyd and Rudi were part of it too, now, because it was Sarson Hall he was really interested in. He was a professor of archaeology. That was his life.

Somehow though, it was more difficult with him and Jenny than it had been with other people. With others Lloyd could put up barriers – shield himself... but with James and Jenny, he couldn't, and that meant there was nothing to hide behind. They were laughing, teasing him and Rudi about the weight of the basket, pointing out bits of London they could see from the Heath, stopping and splaying out on the grass in the warm sunshine, kicking a ball about. It wasn't like with the carers and the social-workers in any way.

James and Justin weren't that rubbish at football either.

"You're dead athletic, man, for a professor," Lloyd said. He wrestled the ball away from James and he was panting. "Even after you ate all them sausages – you're still fit."

James laughed and darted the ball away, dribbling it faster than Lloyd could run, and skimming it across to Justin.

Jenny was laughing, sitting by the basket on a car rug. "He'll run rings around you, Lloyd," she shouted. "He's merciless. One thing you'll learn about James, he's got to win at everything – no matter what and no matter who he's playing with."

Lloyd threw himself on the grass beside her and grinned. "Give me five minutes to get my breath back, okay?" he said. "Just five minutes. Then I'll show him what football's all about."

They walked some more after that and talked about Sarson Hall and all the stuff Lloyd had discovered. James had loads of questions. Some of them were quite difficult. It made Lloyd think in ways he hadn't thought before, and Justin started laughing. "He thinks he's doing a tutorial, Lloyd," he said.

James was laughing too. "This is nothing like a tutorial. Students in my tutorials don't have answers. You leave him alone. He's playing a blinder."

"Yeah," Lloyd said. "A bit of tough talk, that shows respect, man."

After lunch they set off back to Sarson Hall.

Before they left, Jenny kissed Lloyd and Rudi and she gave Justin a hug, like she did when they met on the South Bank.

But the party was over.

As they headed back from London, it seemed they were driving out of sunshine into thick fog again. The blue of the sky faded to flat greyness and the chill of winter closed over the landscape. They were in another world, another season, another age.

James diverted to Didcot to pick up Justin's van, and then they headed for Sarson Hall, and it was as bleak as an Arctic winter.

Somehow, being away from it had softened Lloyd. He'd forgotten how all-powerful and menacing this place was, and, when he saw it again, he shuddered.

Even James noticed.

He stood on the gravel forecourt and looked around, whistling between his teeth. "It's got the feel of steel about it, this place, hasn't it?" he said.

They headed for Dave's office and it was interesting to watch Dave face up to the professor.

He leaned back in his chair and smiled, his little row of teeth gritted in his jaws. "Professor Appleyard," he said. "We weren't expecting you. I hope these two haven't created havoc in your homestead."

"On the contrary," James said. "Two more charming, intelligent boys I have yet to meet."

Lloyd watched Dave's eyebrows arch. "We do try to teach them the niceties of social behaviour," he said, and Lloyd's fists itched to smack him one.

"They've been an absolute delight. Don't worry Mr Trafford, I certainly haven't come here to complain. They've been filling me in on some of the amazing phenomena that have been manifesting themselves around Sarson Hall."

Dave smiled a weak, sickly smile that camouflaged the bile. "I'm not sure you should take too much notice of the fertile imaginations of two teenagers," he said.

But James shook his head. "I don't think this has much to do with imagination, Mr Trafford. It smacks of authenticity to me, and Justin has verified a lot of it. That's why I'm here."

Lloyd could see the colour welling up around Dave's neck, just like it did when he wound him up. But the smile was cemented onto his face. "I've heard Lloyd's theories about curses and the supernatural," he said.

"There are other things, though," said James. "From what he's told me, I suspect there's some ancient link between this place and the henge up at Brookley. What I'd like to do, if I have your permission, is to take a look at the Tudor wing and then go with the boys up to Brookley Henge."

Dave didn't want it to happen. Lloyd could see that, but the guy was a blagger. All this rubbish about teaching them social etiquette – there was no way he dared get into opposition with the professor. "That would be fine," he said. "It's our policy at Sarson Hall to encourage the young people to take an interest in academic pursuits. But I'd appreciate it if they kept their findings to themselves. Some of the young people here are emotionally very fragile, you understand, and prone to hysteria."

"I'm sure you can rely on them," James said. "But there's material around here that interests me very much. The boys have found out a lot. With Justin's help they've done some very creditable fieldwork. You should be proud of them."

It was hard not to start falling about laughing because asking Dave to be proud of him was like asking the guy to swallow a cup of cold sick.

Dave got up, like he always did when he wanted to dismiss the assembled company. "It's nothing more than we expect," he said. "And we'd like the boys back by six if you could manage it, for their dinner, you understand?"

"Absolutely," said James. "Nothing must come between boys and their stomachs, isn't that right, Lloyd?"

"It's not just a matter of their stomachs, Professor Appleyard," Dave said. "It's what keeps this place running – respect for house rules." And that was such a load of garbage Lloyd had to grip one fist with his other hand. That bloated face was just asking for a smack.

They went out onto the forecourt and around to the North Wing and, as soon as James saw it, he stopped and nodded, looking at Justin, "As I suspected," he said. Then he ran his finger over the stone. "The clue is in the name, you see, Justin."

Justin grinned. "It's a bit obvious now you've pointed it out." he said.

"So, what do you think is going on here?" the professor asked. It was as if they were doing their own private tutorial, and Lloyd was listening with a hunger to be part of it.

"The Tudors ransacked Brookley Henge?" Justin said.

"That's my guess."

"Broke up the stones and brought them here?"

"Either that or they brought them whole and broke them up on site." And Lloyd's eyes widened.

"You saying this place was built out of stones from Brookley Henge?" he said.

"That's my thesis, Lloyd," said James. "The clue is in the name of the hall, you see."

"How come?" said Lloyd, and Justin grinned.

"Sarson Hall," he said. "Sarson is a derivative of *sarsen* – that's the stone the Beaker people used for the larger monoliths down at Stonehenge. It's a local stone and it's highly likely they used it for Brookley Henge too."

"We'll know for certain when we go up there," James said. "But, if this place was built out of stone taken from the henge, that could explain the paranormal disruption."

"That's amazing, man," Lloyd said. "It's like they practically shifted the henge off its site, away from the course of the ley lines, and that's why there's readings all around here. Some of the forces came with them."

"Show him," Rudi said. "Get the divining rod and show him what it's like."

Justin fetched the hazel twig and Lloyd took it. He held it loosely, gradually getting closer to the wall of the North Wing and it began quivering. It grew stronger as they got nearer and he heard James gasp.

"That is absolutely astounding, Lloyd," he said.

"You want to see it down the cellar, man. It twists like a snake down there."

James was almost knocked over by the oppressive atmosphere in the cellar. "This place makes my flesh creep," he said.

Justin glanced at the wall and raised a questioning eyebrow and James nodded. "Sarsen stone, no doubt," he said. "And my guess is, we'll find exactly the same stone up at the henge."

Lloyd showed them the strength of force in the cellar, and it blew James's mind. "And all this is coming through you into the rod?" he said. "Can I hold it?"

He handed it over, but, with James holding it, it just lay inert. A twig plucked from a hedgerow and he shook his head and handed it back. "It's been a privilege," he said. "I shall never forget this."

Lloyd grinned. "It's nothing special. It's like I was born with the power, and I didn't know – not until the ghost showed me."

They drove out to the henge, and the professor wandered around for a while. It was bleak and abandoned and, when he'd done his survey, Lloyd showed him how he'd found the ley line back towards Stonehenge and then he searched the field running north again and it was clear the lines had been broken towards Avebury.

James confirmed the stones up at the henge were sarsen stone – and that gave Lloyd a whole new line to think about.

The Tudors must have ransacked the place way back. Over four hundred years ago they'd built Sarson Hall with the stones from up here. That was why this supernatural chaos was raging back there now. At last, it was beginning to make sense.

CHAPTER 13

Lloyd and Rudi sat on one of the upended stones.

The professor was wandering around with Justin. They were looking at where the inner circle used to be. They were deep in talk, and Lloyd was thinking as he watched them – layers of thought.

At the top of his consciousness were ideas about the disrupted ley lines, and the stones from Brookley Henge, plundered and used to build Sarson Hall. But lower down, where his thoughts were more random and harder to define, nebulous ideas flitted around, evasive thoughts that were out of his control, and, in these, he wanted to be talking to the professor like Justin, about his own big hypothesis, thrashing out his own ideas. And, sliding among the half-defined dreams was Jenny, and the house in Highgate village and Hampstead Heath – picnics and football, laughing and... He struggled to blank those thoughts, trying to concentrate on the henge and the ley lines.

James came and sat beside him. "There was certainly a double henge here," he said. "Justin tells me you spotted that."

"Yeah, you could tell where the stones had been. It's like someone's massacred the place. Didn't the Tudors have no respect for ancient monuments?"

The professor laughed. "That's a fairly recent development in the human psyche. And there isn't much of it around even now."

Lloyd wriggled into a more comfortable position. "While you was out there," he said, "I've been trying to get my head around all this and I think I got a new idea. It's like – I been trying to fit all the pieces together."

James looked at him, and it was weird how Lloyd could read people's looks. When Dave looked at him, his eyes showed that supercilious arrogance, and with Justin it was like, warmth – a kind of welcoming embrace, but with the professor it was different. The look was more… interest and… respect.

"That's exactly what you should be doing," he said. "I'm still trying to take it in, but you've been living with this for the past two weeks. You'll have more of an idea where the pieces fit."

"Not till you said about Sarson Hall being made out of stones from up here, I didn't," Lloyd said. "But now I've got, like, this theory."

Justin eased them up so he could sit on the stone as well.

"It's tied up with the other theory, the one I told you before – how these stone circles sort of direct the ley lines. It's like, they're power points. Do you see what I'm saying?"

James nodded.

"Well, say these power points work like magnets – because there are forces like that in the earth, isn't that right? I mean, Earth is like one big magnet, isn't it?"

"Absolutely," James said.

"Well, what I been thinking is this. We got this ley line, right? Running up from Stonehenge, no problem. But, then, there isn't no line running on to Avebury – and I couldn't figure why. I mean, there are some stones here. The magnet wouldn't be so strong, but it's still here."

James leaned forward. He looked at the ground and he was nodding.

"Well this is my theory, right? Because the stones was shipped over to Sarson Hall – en masse like, it's like – the main magnet has moved, and now there are these two forces working on the ley lines, the one up here and the one down at Sarson Hall."

"There are three, really," James said. "Because we've still got Avebury, don't forget."

"I didn't think of that. But – well – if that's three forces, it's like the ley line don't know where to go no more, and that's how it's got broken up. I mean, it's all in pieces in that field next to the henge, isn't that right, Justin? And it's all in pieces around Sarson Hall. I bet we could find bits of it all the way from here to the hall if we tried, all messed up."

"And possibly running all the way to Avebury?" James said.

"What do you reckon, Rudi?" said Lloyd.

Rudi grinned. "I reckon you're a genius," he said, and they laughed. But the professor was still mulling over the theory.

"What can we do about it, then?" he said suddenly.

Lloyd sat up. "You asking me, man?"

"Of course I'm asking you. It's you that's come up with the idea. I can't think of a more capable guy to work on a solution, can you?"

Justin looked at Lloyd and he had his warmest smile on. "And I'm telling you, Lloyd – that, coming from the professor, is just about the biggest compliment you could ever hope for."

"Is that right?" said Lloyd. "Do you rate me, then?"

James gave an enigmatic shrug. "Justin knows me better than most," he said. "You just get your head around the solution – like you did the theory. And we're here to help you – me, Justin, Rudi. But it's you that's got the links with the paranormal, and you're the one who can divine ley lines. We've got to accede to you."

It was almost too much. It was pushing him into isolation and, if he was honest, all he wanted now was to be one in a team. "That's a big ask, man," he said. "It's not doing me no favours neither. I know I do stuff independent like – but – I need help with this."

"We'll be around, don't worry," James said. "I told you, we'll support you every which way. All I want you to do is carry on developing your theories, keep thinking things through just like you've been doing."

They made their way back to the car, leaving the stones stark against the darkening sky and, all of a sudden, Lloyd shivered. The full grimness of Sarson Hall had grabbed him again.

When they got back the bleak edifice was there, imposing itself, a monolith in its own right, blocking out the last dregs of daylight, and, in spite of the weekend, with its dazzling sunshine and the fun of being with James and Jenny, he was now held in the grip of the place again.

Caitlin was waiting, sitting on the step and, even in the gloom, he could see the tell-tale hollows around her eyes and the distress of sleeplessness. Under the mop of hair her face looked pale and bloodless – and he knew he had to get to her.

James stood beside the car, looking around at the grounds and he rubbed his hands uneasily. At last he said, "Well, guys, I think I must make tracks. Tutorials and lectures in the morning, and a big consultation with a Ph.D. student." He was holding out his hand and Lloyd took it. Suddenly he was in awe of this guy, and he had this uneasy feeling that James was slipping through his grasp. He was going back to London and his Ph.D. students and Lloyd couldn't compete with that... but he needn't have worried. As he took the professor's hand, James suddenly pulled him towards him wrapping him in a huge hug, just like he'd done with Justin up at the British Museum. He did the same with Rudi too, and then he said, "It's been really fantastic, boys. I hope we'll be seeing lots more of you."

He hugged Justin then. "Keep in touch," he said. "And see to it you get these boys back up to London as soon as you can."

The doubts melted. It was going to be okay.

"It might be an idea to make a trek next weekend," he added. "Between here and Brookley Henge – see if Lloyd's fragmented ley line theory works. Could you manage that, do you think?"

Justin nodded. "I'll let you know how it goes."

"See you do," James said, and then he grinned. "I'd best go and pay my respects to your Housefather... remind me?" He looked at Justin.

"Dave Trafford."

"Ah, yes, Mr Trafford," said James. "Now boys, let me know what happens next weekend." He put an arm around Lloyd again and smiled. "And you keep up the good work, young man. You're doing amazing things here." Then he bounced up the steps, past Caitlin, and he waved.

"Thanks again, Mister," Lloyd said, and Rudi's voice chimed in.

"Yes, thanks."

Justin was moving towards his van. "See you tomorrow?" he said. And it was all disintegrating – but there was new stuff for Lloyd to be working on… and there were memories. No way would those memories ever melt away.

First, though, there was Caitlin.

"I got to talk to her," he said. "And full respect to you, Rudi, man, but it's best I do it on my own. You know what she's like."

Rudi nodded. "That's okay. I'll go up and unpack the case, shall I?" And Lloyd gave him a probing stare, but he was grinning.

"You know what it means if I say yes to that?" he said. "It means I must trust you like I never trusted no one. Because that travel case is real special."

"So?" Rudi said, grinning back. "Shall I unpack it?"

"As long as you keep your thieving hands off my jazzy boxers."

Rudi skipped up the steps and Lloyd headed for Caitlin, but when he sat down, she hardly moved.

"You okay?" he said.

She clasped her chin into her cupped hands. "You got to be down there tonight," she said. "You got to stop me doing that sleepwalking stuff."

"Did the ghost give you a bad time?"

She shook her head. "I kept myself awake all night, didn't I?" There was a flat weariness in her voice. "I tried reading – and I was pacing up and down. I never got in bed once. I listened to my iPhone and I barricaded my door with chairs and my wardrobe."

"You shifted that wardrobe? All on your own?"

"I thought, if I did that and I started sleepwalking – with all that stuff in front of the door, I couldn't get out."

"That's real rough, man," he said, and he put a hand over hers. It wasn't an instinctive move. It demanded even more courage than he'd needed to face the ghost. He was afraid she'd pull away – but she didn't. Instead she turned her hand gently under his and let her fingers close around his hand and she was staring blankly across to the skeletal trees.

A surge of blood sent him dizzy when she gripped his hand, and there was a moment's confusion. He didn't know what to say.

"You haven't got no more worries," he mumbled at last, and his voice caught in his throat. "I'll be there like – tonight and every night from now on."

She turned and looked at him. She had long, curling eyelashes. He'd noticed them before, but the impact was stronger this evening. "You're not a bad kid, Lloyd Lewis," she said and then, with a movement that was as ephemeral as the touch of a bird's wing, she brushed his cheek with her lips and, at the same second, released her grip. Then she stood up and slipped back into the house.

For a few minutes, he didn't move.

There were so many things in his head – so many things that were happening to him – all new and all at once… but still nothing was straightforward.

He kept a low profile for the rest of the evening. He and Rudi told Martin about London and James and Jenny Appleyard, but it all seemed to flow over him again. Friday night had been a wake-up call, but Saturday and Sunday seemed to have reinstated his apathy, and there was only a laconic half interest.

They went down to the television lounge, but Craig Donovan had the controls and Lloyd noticed he was trying to catch his eye. He carefully avoided looking at him, and when he went to bed, he was certain Craig would be there in the morning, and that was a big distraction.

The events of the weekend had fallen around him like an avalanche – getting involved with the professor, the trip to London, finding out why the ghost was parading around Sarson Hall instead of up at Brookley, coming up with his new theory, being told by James to get it sorted… and that was the hardest bit. He'd hoped for guidance from the professor, but at least he'd still have Justin. That was the one constant in his life – Justin and Rudi.

He'd have Justin's support with Craig Donovan, too.

He was certain Craig had another kid lined up. The guy had been turning himself inside out to catch Lloyd's eye in the television lounge. He was beginning to suspect what Craig was up to as well – and it repelled him.

As he lay there, the delinquency that raged beyond the bedroom door burnt itself out and, once again, only the embers of chaos were left – groans of uneasy sleep, creaking floors, unnatural banging in the rooms, the sickly stench, and after the uneasy peace had fully instated itself, he crept into the passage.

The elements in the North Wing were in riot again, but, this time, he understood why. The building had displaced the earth's forces and the earth was rising up in protest.

At the end of the passage, in the eerie moonlight, he saw Caitlin.

It was something of a routine now, steering her back to bed, but it was also something he was strangely comfortable with. In fact, he liked doing it. He liked holding her shoulders and guiding her. He liked the gentle motion of manoeuvring her onto her bed and pulling the duvet over her. He liked running his fingers through her hair, seeing the half-hooded glances. He looked forward to it, because it always left him with an inexplicable contentment.

This time he bent down and brushed his lips against hers and, as he did so, he sensed a slight flutter – just the hint of movement from her lips.

The ghost didn't show again, and, once more, that disappointed him. He'd broken so much new ground and he wanted to tell the Beaker man. In a way, its absence reinforced his dilemma. James Appleyard wasn't giving him any guidance and now, neither was the ghost – and, next morning, his worst fears about Craig Donovan were confirmed.

All through breakfast he could sense his eyes boring into him and, as they were leaving, he forced himself to face up to the fact, and he looked directly back.

Craig jerked his head towards the stairs and made for the landing.

"You're getting the hang of this," he said.

"I knew you was trying to catch my eye last night," said Lloyd. "You got more homework?"

"Yeah, tomorrow."

Lloyd nodded. "That's no problem," he said. "But I been thinking. I reckon it would be easier if you gave me the envelope tonight. I can keep it in my bag, no sweat. I mean, Rudi and Martin aren't going to see it in there, are they? And it would be less hassle than trying to get down the showers in the morning. There's too much stuff going on in the morning and you know what Christine's like. She goes crazy when we turn up late, and, if we both keep turning up together, she's going to start making connections."

"That's good thinking," Craig said. "If that's okay with you – keeping the stuff in your room – and you're sure the other kids won't get hold of it?"

"No way, man," Lloyd said. "I'll put it right down the bottom of my bag."

Craig's grey eyes were still cold. There was a lot of malice there, and he was staring too hard into Lloyd's face.

"You carry on like this, black boy, and it won't be long before we start working as a team," he said. "I could start cutting you in if you do this stuff right."

"No sweat," Lloyd said. "Give me the stuff down the shower room – soon as we get back, okay? I'll keep my bag with me so I can stash it."

He began to retreat towards the stairs and Craig waited. He'd clearly taken on board what Lloyd had said about them being seen together.

"Meet me, break, so I can show you the kid," he said.

It nagged at the back of Lloyd's head all day though, because he wasn't certain he could rely on Dave.

But he was going through with it. No way was he going to spend the rest of his life being Craig Donovan's errand boy and he wasn't going to get involved with the kind of stuff the guy was in to, either.

From now on it was going to be "The Lloyd Lewis Show." He'd decided that. If he didn't take control – of Craig, and the ghost – then, no one else would. That was certain.

He picked up the envelope after school and made a big show of putting it at the bottom of his bag.

There was no hint of suspicion either. It looked as if Craig was warming to him – but Craig was down there below the average slug, and this thing had to be stopped.

He took the bag to his bedroom and retrieved the envelope. Then, shoving it into his back pocket, he went into the grounds to find Justin.

Justin was by the mound, and he was staring at it. "Did you say the ghost seemed to react when you mentioned this hill?" he said.

"Yeah. He sort of mouthed off this load of stuff and it was like he got quite emotional about it."

Justin scuffed with his foot. "There's something in there," he said. "We'll have to take a look some time."

"Could we make it tomorrow?" said Lloyd. "Because I got other stuff in my head right now. I got to do another delivery for Craig Donovan. I got the envelope." He pulled it out and shoved it in Justin's direction.

Justin lay the spade down and took it and his face darkened. He turned it over, running his hand across its surface. Then he put it to his ear and shook it. "Do you know what this is?" he said.

They wandered over to a felled tree trunk and sat down. "I think I got an idea," said Lloyd.

"I think it's cannabis. He's dealing," Justin said.

"That's what I thought. And it's stuff like that what killed my mother."

He handed the envelope back.

"Aren't you going to open it?" he said, but Justin shook his head.

"You've got to take it to Dave unopened. If it's open when Dave gets it, Craig will say you planted the stuff."

"What have I got to do?" Lloyd stared at the envelope. "It don't feel like there's anything bulky in there."

"It'll be taped to paper – spread thinly – but I'm certain that's what it is. You just go and see Dave – tell him what's going on. Say you're suspicious about the envelope. I mean, you know Craig isn't doing kids' homework, so there's got to be something else. Play the innocent though. Don't let on you suspect that it's drugs. Let Dave find that out for himself."

"Say he asks how I come to be doing this stuff for Craig?"

"Well, how did you?" Justin said.

"He caught me late one night in the computer room, didn't he? I was Googling poltergeists – like you said. He told me he'd report me to Dave, and I'd already been gated – so I couldn't risk it."

"You could explain that to Dave," Justin said. "Or you could just say Craig threatened to work you over."

"I got to think about it," Lloyd said suddenly. He pocketed the envelope, but Justin shook his head.

"You've got to go now. You've got to stop him before he gets you any more involved."

Dave didn't seem overjoyed to see him. He stared through his rimless glasses and there was no hint of welcome.

"What is it, Lloyd Lewis?" he said.

"I got to talk to you about something, haven't I?" Lloyd said.

Dave sighed, pointedly closing his eyes. "Not more rubbish about your ghost, I hope," he said.

"It hasn't got nothing to do with the ghost," Lloyd said. "This is other stuff, and you got to do something about it."

"Someone messing with your beloved travel case again?"

"No way, man." Dave was really riling him. "It's about Craig Donovan. There's stuff going on at school that you got to know about."

"And you're going to tell me, I suppose." It was said in that semi-sarcastic way.

"Yeah, right, I'm going to tell you, because the guy's got me involved, hasn't he?"

He pulled the envelope from his pocket and smacked it onto the desk. "This stuff is Craig claiming to do some guy's homework for him. He's got me delivering it because he said teachers are on to him – so he can't deliver it himself. The other kids pay him a tenner for what's in this envelope and no way is it homework."

Dave didn't touch the envelope and he hardly moved – only to purse his fingers like a praying mantis and rest his elbows on the desk. He had that superior stare on his face and his eyes were blinking.

"So, you want me to stop Craig Donovan doing kids' homework for them? You want me to stop him displaying a bit of entrepreneurial initiative – stop him making a few pounds on the side, is that right?" he said.

"It isn't homework, man," Lloyd said. "No way could Craig do these guys' homework."

"Why not? You've got special insight into Craig's IQ, have you? You have special access to his academic records?"

"You know very well I haven't," said Lloyd. "And I don't need no special access neither. The guy's brain is less developed than an earthworm's."

"Well, I don't think it's that underdeveloped, is it, Lloyd Lewis? After all, he's managed to make a few pounds using his own initiative and he's coerced you into assisting him."

It was becoming very clear Dave wasn't going to do anything and he was already homing onto the sticky subject of Lloyd's involvement.

"You open the envelope and see what kind of homework he's doing, then," he said, but Dave's steely glare didn't waver.

"I most certainly will not," he said. "That's a private matter, between the boy concerned and Craig. It's none of my business and it's certainly none of yours." He leaned forward, pushing his mitred hands ahead of him so his face was fairly well filling Lloyd's face. "Now, understand this," he said. "Since you've been here, you've been bent on trouble. You've picked quarrels with Martin, you've been tormenting Caitlin Jamieson, you've come up with this ridiculous story about ghosts and you've even duped a professor from London into getting involved, and now you're having a go at Craig Donovan, to say nothing of your persistent petulance, and I'm warning you, Lloyd Lewis, I've just about had it with you. Drop it, okay? And I suggest you keep a very low profile from now on."

"So, you aren't going to do nothing?" Lloyd asked.

"The boy's just showing a bit of initiative," snapped Dave. "Why should I interfere? And, as I've told you before, I don't take instruction on how to run this place from a thirteen-year-old kid. Now get back out there and keep your nose out of trouble, because I've just about had my fill, understand?"

Lloyd got up. He was almost rigid with fury and his hands were itching to smack that smug face, but – he'd got to remember what Justin had said about diplomacy. "Suit yourself," he said. He did put his hands in his pockets, though, and he did give the most enormous Gallic shrug – and, as he walked out, he had to make one parting shot. "But I've told you. You remember that and, if it turns out Craig Donovan is up to something, it isn't down to me, okay?"

"Get out," Dave said, and his face was red from the neck up. On another occasion Lloyd would have felt good about that. This time, though, it was serious. He headed for the garden to see Justin again – but Justin's van had already gone and that left him abandoned, and his mind was whirling.

He was dealing with a real concoction of feelings this time and none of them were under his control.

He'd half-suspected Dave wouldn't back him, but common sense had persuaded him that he'd have to. This was big stuff, dealing in drugs, and somewhere up the line there would be another guy, even more deeply involved than Craig, and he shuddered, because, as soon as he thought of that, he thought of a whole chain of people, going right up to top-grade criminals. He was in the chain too… and he'd stay that way until he could do something to smash open Craig Donovan's activities.

He could hardly cope with the anger he felt for Dave. Either the guy was part of the chain himself or he was the biggest wimp in the universe.

He was disappointed with Justin, too. With something as big as this, he'd have expected him to hang around. And now he'd got all this stuff in his head and no one to turn to and he had to offload somewhere.

There was only one guy left, and that was Rudi.

He found him in the bedroom, reading. He looked up when Lloyd came in. "You okay?" he said and Lloyd threw himself on his bed.

"Yeah, if being in it up to the top of your head is okay," he said.

Rudi put the book to one side and eased himself into a sitting position. "What's up?"

"Craig gave me this envelope, didn't he?" Lloyd said. "I took it to Justin and he said I was to go to Dave."

"Yes?" Rudi said.

"Well that guy's so wet he's waterlogged. Either that or he's in on the whole thing."

"Why? Justin never said what he thought Craig was doing."

"He reckons he's dealing. He reckons it's cannabis in the envelope."

"And you told Dave that?"

"Not exactly. I told him about the homework, though, and all that great lump of gelatine could come up with was, if Craig says he's doing homework – that's what he's doing, and doing kids' homework for a bit of pocket money is good. The guy tried telling me Craig was some sort of an entrepreneur."

Rudi's face twisted in disbelief. "That's crazy," he said. "And he didn't even look in the envelope?"

"No way, and I can't get my head around what drives Dave sometimes. It's like the guy won't do nothing about anything."

"He just wants an easy life," Rudi said, lying back on the bed.

"He don't like nobody rocking his boat, neither. It's like – the guy's hiding from every bit of strife that ever comes up."

"Is he afraid of Craig, do you think?" Rudi said. "Craig does just what he likes and no one says anything. He goes off into town, he's got control over the TV downstairs and the computer room. He's got scams running in the home and, when Dave goes on about some kid doing all the pranks and stuff in here, I think he's got Craig down for that too. That's why he won't do anything about it."

Lloyd fingered the envelope. "I was thinking that," he said. "But it don't help with this cannabis stuff, do it?"

"Let's have a look," Rudi said.

Lloyd passed over the envelope and Rudi ran his finger across it. "I can feel a sort of lump," he said. "In the corner – like a raised bit. Would that be the cannabis?"

Lloyd felt it and there was certainly something. It had been concealed – most likely folded into the paper and taped, like Justin had said. He shook his head.

"What am I meant to do with it?" he said.

"You have to talk to Justin."

"Yeah, but Justin's gone AWOL and I got to deliver this tomorrow."

"You'll have to deliver it, then" Rudi said. "And tell Justin tomorrow night. If you don't give it to the guy tomorrow, Craig will know something's up."

Lloyd didn't want to do it but he couldn't see any other way. And, the next morning, he found the boy Craig had earmarked and he offloaded the envelope.

But now he was certain what was inside and that made him really edgy. He was always conscious of the potential for a teacher to be watching, even though he made doubly sure the coast was clear. And even if there wasn't a teacher, there could be another kid; someone suspicious of what was going on, some hyperactive creep that would report it to Mrs Cherry.

There wasn't going to be another delivery. He was certain of that. He'd do something next time – even if he had to go to the police himself.

It had become top priority. He'd have to talk it over with Justin – and that annoyed him. Time with Justin was precious and there were more important things to do.

He wanted to get inside that hill, and he wanted to put his theory about the broken ley lines to the test. But events had taken over; getting Craig Donovan sorted was top of the list. Until he'd sorted him, he felt everything else was on hold.

CHAPTER 14

Straight after their mini treats that night, Lloyd and Rudi searched out Justin. He was down by the front entrance, sweeping leaves, and when he saw them, he grinned. But Lloyd wasn't smiling.

"You never waited, last night," he said.

He leaned on his brush and shook his head. "I couldn't. I meant to say. I had a videoconference with the professor – on Skype. I had to get home."

"Only it didn't work with Dave. He wouldn't believe me. He reckons Craig's some sort of entrepreneur. He said he really is doing kids' homework and I got to encourage him."

"He didn't look in the envelope?" Justin said.

Lloyd shook his head.

"He had to deliver the stuff this break time," said Rudi.

"I was really stressed, too," said Lloyd. "I mean, I knew what was in the envelope this time, didn't I? And – if I'd got caught, I'd have been right in it."

"You'd better bring the next envelope to me," Justin said. "And we'll take it to Dave together."

He gave them a reassuring smile and straightaway Lloyd felt easier. Just seeing the guy generated a sort of safety zone.

"You going to tell us about the video conference, then?" he said.

Justin grinned again. "Later, maybe. So, are we going to look at the mound and do some dowsing, or what?"

"Find out about force patches coming away from Sarson Hall?" Lloyd said, and Justin nodded.

"It's no good having a theory if you don't do anything to prove it."

Rudi and Lloyd laughed. "You sounded just like the professor then," Lloyd said.

They headed back to the North Wing and put the gardening tools away. Then they collected the dowsing rod from the van.

Lloyd felt instinctively that there wouldn't be any fractured forces around the south and west of the ground, or the east. Brookley Henge ran northwest of Sarson Hall and, if his theory was right, all the patches would follow the line between the hall and Brookley. And around the northwest he found patches straightaway. They were just like the one's he'd discovered in the field by Brookley Henge, faint at times, hardly raising a flicker in the dowsing rod. Some of them were stronger, but they were all broken, like shards, scattered around the grounds.

He trawled the front and back of the main wing too, and the west side, but, as he'd suspected, there was nothing there – and Justin looked pleased. "If we can trace patches all the way to Brookley Henge on Saturday, it looks as if your theory's right," he said. They sat on the felled log by the mound. "Do you want to do a dig now?"

Lloyd nodded. "That would be good."

"We'll have to be careful though, and we can only scrape the surface," Justin said. "If it's a genuine archaeological site, we'll have to do a proper dig, with other archaeologists and stuff."

They collected spades and trowels from the North Wing. Then Justin showed them how to remove the turfs, cutting squares with the spades and gently levering the sods away, working on a small area at a time.

"Is that how proper archaeologists do it?" Lloyd said, and Justin grinned.

"You are a proper archaeologist. I mean, James is seriously impressed with you two."

There was an anomaly in Lloyd's thinking as they set about the mound. In spite of the grief that gripped this place, sometimes he had feelings here that were bigger than anything he'd felt before. Things were happening to him, big things, and he was beginning to feel that no matter what the next three or four years threw at him, he could see a life beyond homes and social-workers. He was starting to know where he was going. And, as he cut away at the turf, he felt good.

Rudi was working at a piece of turf too, and the guy was puffing like an old steam engine.

"You're so unfit, man," Lloyd said, leaning on his spade and Justin laughed.

"Never mind – a couple of weeks doing this and he'll have muscles as big as... bees' knees." He laid a couple of pieces of turf together and showed them how to stack them.

Then he demonstrated removing the topsoil, scraping gently, a layer at a time.

"You do that so, if there's some big relic down there, you don't do no damage to it, is that right?" Lloyd said.

They worked carefully, removing the soil and mesh of decaying roots until Lloyd's trowel hit something hard.

"Gently," Justin said. "Clean it with your hands now – just the top dirt."

But it was only a jagged piece of stone, and there were more, lying together as if they'd been dumped. Justin picked one up and looked at it more closely.

"It's sarsen stone," he said. "Most likely these are the trimmings from when they built the hall."

"This pile been here since Tudor times?" Lloyd said.

"It looks like it. It looks as if this was an old stone dump. It would explain why you sensed it with the hazel twig; but I can't understand why the ghost would be so interested."

"Are you sure it was this hill the ghost got excited about?" Rudi said.

"Yeah. It was every time I said about it... but, like Justin said, it don't make no sense – a load of old stones. There must be something else down there."

"I doubt it," said Justin. "That pile was made by the Tudor masons. It's got nothing to do with the Beaker folk and it would be a crazy coincidence if they just happened to dump their trimmings exactly where there were Bronze Age relics."

Lloyd got up and leant his spade against the hill. "If there's nothing down there except them stones, then the stones got to fit into the pattern somewhere," he said. "And I don't see how."

There wasn't any visit from the Beaker man that night, which meant Lloyd was still on his own with his theories and his new discovery.

He was certain the pile of stones, or something buried beneath them, was important. He tried working through everything he knew, searching for a hint that would link it all, but there was nothing. All he had was a random list of facts and theories.

The pile of trimmings though… something in his instincts told him they were the key; the Beaker man had reacted so strongly when he talked about the mound.

It played around his head so much he couldn't sleep and, that night, he seemed even more aware of the groans around him.

Caitlin eyed him at breakfast the next morning.

When he'd steered her back to her bedroom, he'd sort of kissed her lips again. It wasn't just a light brush this time either. It wasn't passionate or anything, but it was a real kiss and, even though she was in her trance, she seemed to respond. It was odd though because when they were both awake they reverted to cautious glances and half smiles.

It was a strange relationship – more a kind of drifting, as if they were floating towards each other on a tide. But he was happy with that. There was a sort of tranquillity about it that was different from anything else going on at Sarson Hall.

Miss Webb took him to Mrs Cherry at lunchtime to talk about the fast-tracking and they sorted a timetable. He still couldn't fathom Mrs Cherry and he had to think hard about what Justin had said – about diplomacy – because, when Miss Webb told her she felt he had a flare for maths, Mrs Cherry just stared and said: "Lloyd Lewis? Are you sure, Miss Webb?" His tongue was itching to tell her where she got off. To appease himself he just sat there glaring at her, imagining himself squashing that mole on her face.

That evening they went off to find Justin and he was looking pleased with himself.

"I had a phone call from James last night," he said. "He and Jenny are coming over this weekend to do the dowsing trail with us. James is really keen; I told him about the stones. He said we were probably right about them being trimmings from building the hall."

"Did he say why they was important?" Lloyd said. "Because I'm thinking they're the key to the whole thing – only I can't see how."

"Ask him on Saturday," Justin said. "He might have a few ideas. He's cleared it with Dave for the weekend so we don't have to go and see him."

The ghost still didn't put in any appearances and, for the next few days, things were fairly quiet. That is until Thursday morning, when Craig caught up with him on the stairs again.

"I got something for you tomorrow, black boy," he said. "You meet me, break, and I'll show you who you got to deliver to."

It was almost as if he'd dropped the pretence, and this assumption that Lloyd was totally under his control annoyed him.

"You telling me or asking me, pink boy?" he said.

"Don't make no difference. You just be round by the bikes, break time, and I'll give you the envelope down the showers after school."

"I'll think about it," Lloyd said, but when he said that, Craig grabbed his collar and the look in his eyes said everything. He was lethal, and if Lloyd challenged him, there'd be no restraint.

"Okay – I thought about it," he said, grinning, and the malice faded.

But that evening, as soon as he'd got the envelope, he went to find Justin. He'd told Rudi what was going to happen and he explained that, for his own safety, he didn't want him involved. Rudi had protested, but Lloyd was insistent.

Justin was out by the hillock, raking leaves again.

"I got another envelope," Lloyd said. "And we got to make Dave do something about this one, because Craig Donovan is really getting out of order. It's like the guy thinks I'm in his pocket."

Justin wiped his hands on his trousers and carefully slit open the envelope.

There was a piece of folded paper inside. It didn't have any writing on it; straightaway Lloyd knew the homework thing was a sham. But he'd always known that.

Justin was careful, opening the paper.

Inside was a neatly folded piece of tissue, probably from a toilet roll, and it was sellotaped. Justin didn't touch it. He just lifted it to his nose and sniffed. Then he folded it again and slipped it back into the envelope. "Cannabis," he said. "Like I thought."

When they got to Dave's office, he knocked and waited. If it had been Lloyd he would have barged in, but that was because Lloyd still hadn't got his head around this diplomacy stuff.

The usual pert "enter" came, and straightaway he could see Dave wasn't pleased. "What do you want?" he snapped.

Justin took the envelope and placed it on the table. Then he looked straight into Dave's eyes and said, "I think you should take a look at this, Dave."

Dave picked the envelope up and looked from Justin to Lloyd. "Is this the homework Craig's doing for some kids?" he said. "I told Lloyd to let it rest; it's a bit unethical, but the boy's showing initiative and I want to encourage that."

"Take a look in the envelope," Justin said again.

It was clear Dave didn't want to. For a moment he just sat there, his pale eyes staring. Then he sighed and leaned forward, easing out the folded paper. When he saw the tissue sellotaped to the inside, he just went red from the neck up and looked at Justin. "Do we know what this is?" he said, and there was a kind of catch in his voice.

"Don't touch it," said Justin. "You don't want to get fingerprints on it, but I've had a sniff. It's cannabis. I'd know that smell anywhere."

Dave stared at the paper and he was drumming his fingers on the desktop. His face was still bright red. Even the bald patch was red and his eyes glinted behind his rimless glasses.

At last he got up. "Well, we'd better get Craig Donovan in here, then, hadn't we? Find out what it's all about."

"What are you going to do about it?" Justin asked, and straight away Dave sat back in his chair again, looking up, and his fingers touched the tip of his lips, making that gothic bridge. "I think it's better to keep it in house, don't you?" he said. "I mean, if we can nip this thing in the bud – gate him for a couple of weeks, let him know we're on to him… and we'll watch him like a hawk from now on. I dare say the boy will have learned his lesson. And… I mean, the reputation of Sarson Hall – if this was to get out, the press will be down here like vultures, and all that media coverage…"

Lloyd looked at Justin, and Justin's face was set. He was shaking his head all the time Dave was talking and that was a relief to Lloyd because, if nothing big was done, he knew he'd get it. Craig was like a mafia boss around here.

"No way can you do that, Dave," Justin said. "He's supplying drugs to kids in school, and he'll be part of a chain. That's a big offence. You brush this under the carpet and it'll make you an accessory. Either you call the police now, or we'll have to take this into Brookley Police Station ourselves."

Dave was fiery red by now and his mouth was twitching. "But our reputation – Sarson Hall – the other kids," he said.

"Never mind the reputation. Craig is breaking the law and he's coercing Lloyd into working with him. And I'm not letting that happen. Call the police."

Lloyd's stomach was churning. It was like a scene out of a film. He watched Dave's hand creep across to pick up the telephone. He pressed a button on the intercom, and his voice was clipped. "Get the police, will you?" he said. "Tell them we seem to have issues with drugs… tell them it's urgent." He put the phone down and glared. "Well, should we get Craig Donovan in now? Confront him?"

"Not till the police get here," Justin said. "You get him in here now and he'll concoct some story before they arrive."

He sat in one of the chairs opposite Dave's desk and looked up at Lloyd. And, for the first time, he smiled.

"Grab a pew," he said. "And don't look so scared. You've done great."

"I don't know so much about that," Dave said. There was a malicious smirk on his face. "He's been delivering the stuff for Craig. It seems to me he's pretty much involved."

"That's rubbish," said Justin. "The kid was bullied into delivering the stuff and he reported it, twice – three times actually, because he came to me last week, and I told him to report it to you. You told him there wasn't any harm in it, so the guy came back to me. There's nothing wrong with what he's done. He deserves a medal."

Dave was tapping the fingers of his mitred hand, and he had that supercilious look. They didn't say anything more. They just sat there, waiting until voices outside told them the police had arrived. Two uniformed officers came in, a man and a woman – and the change in Dave took Lloyd's breath away.

He was up shaking their hands as soon as they were inside the door and he was telling them about Craig, and how Lloyd had been suspicious, and how, in line with the policies of the home, Lloyd had brought his suspicions to the attention of one of the staff, the gardener here. There was an envelope Lloyd was being cajoled into delivering, and they'd found a suspicious package in it. They didn't know what it was – Dave suspected cannabis, but rather than open it, he immediately called the police.

Lloyd's eyes were wide, but Justin just gave a half-grin and shook his head.

"Have any of you touched the package?" the female officer said.

"No – at least, I haven't. You didn't touch it, did you, Lloyd?" Dave said.

"You know very well we didn't touch it, man. We was the ones what told you not to," Lloyd said, and Dave looked at the police with a simpering ingratiation.

"Very streetwise, some of these boys," he said.

He told the secretary to fetch Craig and the tension grew.

When Craig came in, Lloyd watched him to read the expression on his face, and it was fascinating. He could see the guy was thinking on his feet. He took in the sight – Dave, the open envelope, Justin and Lloyd, and the two police-officers; the first thing on his face was blind panic, but then another look at Lloyd and there was a sudden adjustment. He contrived to look surprised and innocent, and he said, "You want to see me? Lloyd Lewis, is it? He got himself in trouble?"

It didn't surprise Lloyd, but it scared him because he knew what line Craig was going to take.

"Do you know anything about this envelope?" the female officer said.

"Don't think so," Craig said. He made a grab at it, but the male officer stopped him.

"We don't want you touching it now, do we, young man? Your fingerprints will be all over it if you do that."

Craig caught Lloyd's eye and, with his finger, he quickly drew a line across his throat. "No. I never seen that envelope in my life," he said. "What is it? Something Lloyd Lewis brought in?"

"We suspect that it's cannabis," the female officer said. "Stuff being distributed at school?"

Craig shook his head, the innocent look on his face again. "Isn't nothing to do with me," he said. "I don't do drugs. If it's Lloyd Lewis what brought it in, then you'd best ask him. I seen him, come to think of it, handing over envelopes like this, break time, to some of the older kids. I could give you their names, if you like."

Lloyd's blood was up. He couldn't believe it. "What you on about, Craig Donovan? I wouldn't touch that stuff. My mother died because of that kind of stuff."

"It's okay, kid," the female officer said. "We're pretty certain it isn't you. Besides, when we do fingerprints, it'll show up whose dabs are on the paper, won't it?"

Craig made another grab for the open envelope, but the male officer was on to him.

This time the woman said, "I think you'd best come down the station to answer a few questions, don't you?" She looked at Dave. "Mr Trafford, would you be kind enough to accompany him?"

"Most certainly," Dave simpered. "It's my duty, after all."

It made Lloyd feel sick.

"The WPC will be back later to get a statement from you, Lloyd, if you don't mind, and from you, sir?" The male officer looked at Justin.

"No problem," said Justin, and Lloyd looked unblinkingly into Craig Donovan's face.

"Me too, no sweat," he said.

Craig glared at him, but Lloyd's eyes didn't flinch and he watched intently, as the two officers eased him towards the door.

As he went, he turned to face Lloyd again, and Lloyd saw him mouth the words, "You're dead." But then the police-officers shoved him outside and he didn't see any more.

CHAPTER 15

It didn't bother Lloyd.

If Craig felt better after mouthing off a few threats, that was okay.

He'd sorted him and he'd got him off his back. That was the main thing.

Later the WPC returned and took the statement.

The other kids were quick to pick up that Lloyd had grassed on Craig, and that didn't make him very popular. There was plenty of abuse flying around – and a few pot shots with bread rolls at dinner, but that didn't bother him either.

He didn't know what time Dave got back from the police station.

Justin told him next evening that Craig was being held in some sort of kids' remand home. Dave hadn't arrived back till late the previous night and he'd been at the police station for most of the day. Word was he wasn't too pleased, but that didn't surprise Lloyd.

James and Jenny were setting off from London early the next morning, and they planned to stay the whole weekend.

When they arrived, they greeted Lloyd and Rudi with hugs, and there were kisses from Jenny.

After that they went straight to Dave's office.

He was back now, because the police had charged Craig – he was coming up in front of the magistrates on Monday.

They were with Dave for a long time, and that worried Lloyd.

"Do you think he's trying to put the skids under us?" he said. "To spite me, like, because of Craig Donovan?"

But Rudi shook his head. "He wouldn't dare. The professor wants us to do this, and you know what Dave's like; he can't stand up against big people. He picks on us because we can't fight back, but people like the professor – he won't do anything."

When they did come out, James was on his mobile, and they were both smiling. "Just getting the boy out of bed," he laughed. "He'll be over with his van in about ten minutes. We're to go to the kitchen while we're waiting, for a coffee. Mr Trafford arranged that."

"He don't mind us doing this, then?" Lloyd said.

James grinned. "He didn't have any grounds to object, did he? Besides, he's got other things on his plate – thanks to you uncovering the dastardly deeds of one Craig Donovan."

When Justin arrived they did some manoeuvring of vehicles. James and Justin drove across to Brookley and left Justin's van there.

Then they had a look at the stones from the mound and James confirmed they were sarsen stone – probably, as Justin had said, trimmings from building the hall, but he didn't think there was much chance of finding anything connected with the Beaker folk underneath them.

When they'd finished with the stones they looked at the map and worked out a route so they could trace the broken ley lines back to Brookley Henge. Most of the land between Sarson Hall and the henge was down land, with free access, so there wasn't much danger of trespassing on private property.

Lloyd was excited. He'd come up with a theory, and there was a professor from London University showing him big respect – and now they were on this field trip – just like students doing an archaeological project. And, if his theory worked, it would mean another piece of the jigsaw fitting, and now he felt he was beginning to get his head around this stuff.

It was all good – Rudi and Jenny carrying the picnic basket, the professor and Justin with the maps and compasses and him with the divining rod.

He moved around the approximate line Justin and James had plotted and his mind was focused.

It wasn't long before he'd picked up something too – a small patch of earth force making the divining rod shudder. "There's something here," he called, and the professor watched closely.

"Can you demark the area of the force?" he said. "So we can have an idea of its actual size?"

Lloyd moved around the patch until the divining rod fell limp, while Justin and the professor marked the area with stones.

"It's about four square metres," James said, and they were just about to mark it on their map when Lloyd noticed something.

"It's moving. Look – there isn't nothing there now, not where you put them stones. I'm picking the stuff up over here." He'd moved to the left and the rod was in motion again, not strongly, but the force had definitely shifted. "It's like I figured: these lines, they're like magnetic forces. And they're being pulled in different directions – like – being pulled by Sarson Hall and Brookley Henge and Avebury and, with the different forces pulling them, they don't stay still."

James nodded. "It certainly looks like it," he said.

They set off again, moving steadily towards Brookley Henge and, all along the way, there were patches of force – broken – unstable – never anchored to one spot – and, when they arrived at Brookley late in the afternoon, they found the same instability along the course towards Avebury.

"It's just as you said, Lloyd," James said "Disrupted ley lines. The way you've thought this through with Rudi and Justin – it's quite amazing."

"It wasn't no sweat," Lloyd said. "As soon as I come here, I knew I'd got to get my head around it. Understanding stuff, that's how I get by, isn't that right, Rudi?"

Rudi grinned. "I think the way you get your head around things is brilliant."

Jenny was laughing. She was sitting on one of the up-ended stones pouring coffee. "I think you've all been fantastic," she said. "If you just take a look at that map and see what you've located, and all in one day." She looked at James. "Do you think we should go back to London this evening instead of staying here? The boys' beds are still made up and we can have a picnic on the Heath tomorrow – go somewhere in the afternoon. It might be more fun than just hanging around here – and hopefully, in London, we won't have this weird twilight weather to contend with."

"Would that be okay with Dave?" Lloyd said, and James grinned.

"We did have it in mind as a plan B, so we've already raised the subject with Mr Trafford. He's fine with it."

The idea of going back to London, to the house in Highgate was just perfect, and it was only as they headed back to Sarson Hall to collect their overnight things and the travel bag, that Lloyd thought of Caitlin. If they were going to be away again, it would mean trouble for her. He'd have to warn her before they left.

There wasn't an easy way either.

"Couldn't you not go?" she said, and he felt really bad because, this time, it wasn't a trip connected with the ghost; it was unadulterated pleasure.

They were on the seat outside the main hall and he was getting more confident with her now. He took her hand and looked into her face. "You got to believe me, Caitlin, man," he said. "I'm getting my head around this stuff, and the ghost guy will be gone soon. Then you'll be able to sleep like a baby down the North Wing."

"Yeah?" she said.

"And I'll be back tomorrow night, no sweat."

He didn't know what else to say. Part of him wanted to cry off going, for her sake, but that was a big ask. "You'll be okay. You block up your door like you done last week. Then, even if you do start sleepwalking, you won't be able to get out. You won't go down that cellar."

She didn't look confident, and in her weak smile there was a hint that he'd betrayed her. He felt guilty and, to cover the guilt, he put an arm around her. "You'll be okay," he said again.

En route to London, they dropped Justin's van at Didcot. They'd be returning by train, and they'd need the van to get back to Brookley. The day in London, with the ramble and picnic on the

Heath was magic. They went to Regent's Park in the afternoon, to an amazing open-air theatre; they were doing a matinee there – a comedy, and James had managed to get last-minute tickets.

All day Lloyd felt he was hovering somewhere near the seventh heaven, and Rudi, he could see, was in the stratosphere.

But there was a blow at Regent's Park, and it knocked him sideways.

It happened during the interval.

James was chatting to Justin as they were coming back with drinks and cake.

Lloyd didn't catch everything they were saying but, as they neared the table, he overheard James say, "Get up there by eleven tomorrow morning. I've talked it through with Ted Barnes and he's delighted you're going to be on the trip."

Lloyd looked at them, his eyes questioning and his antennae twitching. "Where you going tomorrow, then?" he asked, and Justin was looking really pleased.

"I'm doing a dig up in Shropshire with one of my old professors and some of the third-year students," he said. "It's like, all this stuff has made me do a bit of a rethink and I'm going to take your advice. I'm going back to university."

Rudi's face beamed. "That's fantastic," he said, but Lloyd was stunned.

"You starting straight away?" he said. "You leaving Sarson Hall now?"

Justin smiled. "Not till the autumn."

"What about this dig, then?"

"It's only for a week," Justin said.

But even that was a thump below the belt. "Don't get me wrong nor nothing, Justin, man," he said. "And I'm pleased and everything, especially about you going back to university, but say something big crops up down at Sarson Hall next week while you're away?"

"I'll give you my mobile number," Justin said. "Anything big we can talk it through on the phone."

Jenny put an arm around his shoulder. "And if it's that big, Lloyd, I'm sure James will be only too pleased to come down at the weekend and help you sort it."

"Is James on this dig too?" asked Lloyd.

James shook his head. "No. I've got commitments back at university."

But Lloyd was blown sideways.

Even if nothing cropped up with the ghost – a whole week without having Justin there – it was like, the rope that kept him at his moorings had been severed, and for the whole week he would be left adrift.

Justin did his best to reassure him, but Lloyd couldn't get on top of it.

He half-hoped everything would grind to a halt for the week, but the other half of him fought against that. He was caught up with the pace of things and any obstacle that threatened to frustrate his progress bugged him.

He had Justin's mobile number along with all the reassurance he could dish out. "I'll keep my phone on," he said. "All the time, so, any problems and you can get through to me straightaway." Then he looked, with what was meant to ease Lloyd's anxiety, and added, "I don't expect there will be anything big, though."

"We haven't gone a week without something big yet," Lloyd said. "I mean, all we found so far has happened in three weeks."

"Yes, but the big stuff – we've found out most of that at weekends, and I'll be back by then. How about I come in on Saturday, first thing, and we go into Brookley – get a drink at Costa or something and we'll talk through anything that's come up."

Lloyd looked doubtful, but he didn't want to put too much pressure on Justin. No matter which way you looked at it, Justin was a great guy and this was a big thing for him. He wanted it to be good, so he just smiled and set his mind on braving out the week.

"That'll be okay, man," he said. "You go off and do this dig and have a great time. That's what we want, isn't that right, Rudi?"

Rudi nodded. "It'll be fantastic," he said. "And it's brilliant that you're going back to university. It's like Lloyd said, you're wasted in this place."

But, as Justin's van disappeared down the drive, there was a gaping hole, and the thick silence of Sarson Hall enveloped Lloyd again.

He didn't see Caitlin until she showed up for the sleepwalking, but she didn't seem over-stressed. There was all the gentle coercion and soft touches and he reassured himself that, no matter what had gone on the previous night, tonight she was going to be okay.

He was nervous in the North Wing though because, with Justin gone, discovery would be an even bigger problem. For the first time, he was hoping the Beaker man wouldn't show and, as he headed into the cellar, he could sense, although the paranormal disruption was there, it was all tired stuff – and the spectre didn't turn up. The spirals just melted back into the floor.

He also made it back to the bedroom without getting caught and, as he sank into bed, he clung to the hope that this would be the pattern for the rest of the week.

Next morning, at school, he was summoned to Mrs Cherry's office. She was perched behind her desk, and her bloated face was ripe for the picking. She had piggy eyes. He hadn't noticed that before.

"Well, Lloyd Lewis," she said. "I must say, you are a dark horse."

"You saying I'm black, or what?" he said.

"Dark horse," she said. "It means you come up with the unexpected, as you well know."

"So long as you aren't referring to me being black – because, if you are, that's racist."

"I'm referring to the matter of you and Craig Donovan. I would have spoken to you on Friday, but I had the police in for most of the day."

It was difficult to gauge her. It sounded as if she was trying to give him credit for something – but it wasn't coming out like that.

"I suppose I should congratulate you for uncovering what has turned out to be a rather nasty drugs operation," she said. But there was still a flavour of spite in her voice and he stared at her.

"That wasn't no sweat, man. I don't have no dealings with drugs. That's what killed my mother."

"I'm sorry to hear that," she said.

"Yeah. Whatever." He shrugged and continued staring, blanking her, because he knew that got up her nose.

"I really think you have a problem, Lloyd," she said at last. "Miss Webb putting you in for extra maths and now the unveiling of the drugs. It's a great pity these obviously good points are obviated by your truculent manner."

"Yeah, well," he said. "It's like this, isn't it, Mrs Cherry, ma'am. People don't show me no respect, and I don't have to show them no respect."

"Don't you think respect has to be earned?" she said. She was turning towards beetroot again. He always had that effect on her and, most of the time, it gave him satisfaction. But he was painfully aware he'd got to tread carefully this week. The last thing he wanted was trouble with Dave – not with Justin away. But he couldn't help himself and he couldn't let her get away with that.

"Yeah, right," he said. "Like you said, it's got to be earned. It's two-way traffic, isn't that right?"

"Well?" She leaned back in her chair, waiting. He decided that, leaning back made her look even more like a barrel and he couldn't figure why she always wore flowery dresses that were shaped like tents.

"Like I said, it's two-way traffic," he persisted. And she let out a withering sigh.

"I suppose it's too much to ask that you identify the boys you passed the drugs to," she said.

It was the way she said it that made him dig his heels in.

"If the police want me to, then that's okay with me," he said. He gave her the famous Gallic shrug.

"It isn't a matter of the police wanting you to, Lloyd; it's a matter of internal school discipline," she said.

"No, it isn't, Mrs Cherry." By this time he'd had enough. "Them kids took drugs. That's against the law, okay? If the police want to talk to them, then I got to identify them, but I aren't going to queer the police's pitch by telling you first." He turned for the door and looked back in a way calculated to do things to her blood pressure. "Is that it, then?"

Mrs Cherry emitted one more explosive sigh and waved a limp hand in the direction of the door. "Just go," she said. He hoped he hadn't gone too far – but he couldn't help it; that woman got so deep under his skin.

He knew she and Dave were thick, and he half-expected to be called to Dave's office when they got back, but Dave was still keeping a low profile.

The antagonism with the other kids about him grassing on Craig hadn't gone, though – and now there was no escape. For the first time since he'd been at Sarson Hall, the route to the garden and Justin had been cut off.

That night, when he went to the North Wing, he was doubly cautious – and, he had to admit, he couldn't wait for the week to end.

Caitlin was already going down the stairs when he arrived.

He steered her back to her room, but this time, as they reached the top of the stairs, she manoeuvred herself so she was walking beside him and he felt her arm slip around his waist – and that surprised him because it was like she wasn't sleepwalking anymore. Her eyelids were still heavy and her eyelashes hooded her eyes in a semblance of sleep, but there was a half smile and he wasn't convinced she was totally unaware of what she was doing. And that idea excited him. All the ritualistic caresses, the touching lips, the soft kisses and the semiconscious looks – they would take on a new significance if she knew what was happening.

He was thinking about this as he made his way down the stairs, but not for long. When he got through the cellar door, things were going on that drove any thoughts of Caitlin out of his head.

Immediately he knew that it was going to be bad news; there was a tension in the place. He could feel it the moment he set foot on the first of the descending steps. The forty-watt bulb was spitting, giving off the effect of ghoulish disco lights and, behind him, the door slammed vehemently. The smell of must and age was stifling, and he knew the Beaker man was going to show again.

As he reached the cellar, the spirals of dust were whipping themselves into a frenzy and their vigour sent chills through him. They were merging too quickly, and then… there was the luminosity, like green slime in the stones, and the form of a crouched creature, long bearded with wisps of hair escaping from its woollen helmet. The apparition was wearing its long robe, and its age-old eyes were darting about the room. It rose from its crouched position almost immediately and began moving towards him.

Great gasping sighs of nothingness filled the place and Lloyd stepped back. But, straightaway, the spectre held out a hand in a gesture of welcome, and it nodded its head, muttering words – and those eyes, mirroring ageless time, probed him.

"How you doing, old man?" Lloyd said. He felt some sort of greeting was necessary and the spectre ejected a long sigh that faded into oblivion.

"You want me to tell you what I've been up to?" he said. He breathed as deeply as the fetid air would allow and then proceeded. "Well, we done the dowsing – all out towards Brookley Henge. We done that last Saturday. We got the professor down from London and he thinks like I do. Them ley lines is all over the place from here to Brookley. We reckon they're being pulled apart because of what the Tudors done, building Sarson Hall with stones from your circle."

The Beaker man raised his head and let out another sigh.

"And you was dead excited when I said about that mound, isn't that right?"

The reaction to that was the same as before. The apparition broke into a barrage of words, gesticulating with its arms, and once again Lloyd was convinced the mound had some huge significance.

"We dug a bit of that up," he said. "Me, Rudi and Justin, and it was like, there's trimmings there, isn't that right? From when they cut the stones to build the hall?"

All the time, the Beaker man was getting more agitated, gabbling away and prancing around. Lloyd almost laughed. "You best calm down, old man, or you'll give yourself a heart attack." He looked at the gesticulating spectre, pale green and translucent, whirling around. It was almost like one of its own spirals. "Trouble is," Lloyd said. "I can't figure what you're getting so excited about. Is there something else in that mound?"

When he said that, the creature stopped suddenly. The eyes pierced through him and, in one swoop, it leant towards the dust and drew something on the ground. This time it was a line and, at the end of the line, two clearly defined circles, one inside the other, then another line shooting off at a tangent from the circles – with an arrow – pointing… The sketch melted almost as soon as it had been drawn, but Lloyd had seen, and he gasped.

"Draw that again," he said, and once more, the creature stooped. It drew the straight line, this time moving a finger up and down it vigorously, and then two circles, and the arrow pointing off.

"I got it," Lloyd whispered. "I got what you're saying, man."

There was a thrill pulsing through him, because the moment the spectre had drawn the first picture, he understood, and the second drawing reinforced his conviction. "That is so clever and it's simple too; I should have thought of that myself."

The ghost stood up then and its look encompassed every centimetre of Lloyd's being. After that it uttered a sigh. It was a sigh beginning with relief and fading into the deepest tranquillity and, with the sigh, the creature faded, leaving the dust to settle while the forty-watt bulb returned to a long, steady glow.

And Lloyd could hardly believe it.

He knew.

He knew exactly what he had to do to bring this manic disruption to an end.

It would be a big job. He'd need Justin and he'd need the professor – most likely with a team of helpers. It couldn't be done till Saturday, when Justin got back and the professor was free. It would need some advanced organising too; he'd have to phone Justin in the morning.

But… this weekend, one way or another, he would see the curse lifted from Sarson Hall – and the Beaker man would be able to rest in peace at last.

He clambered back up the stairs. His head was whirling, and he pushed through the fire door into the main wing.

Then he stopped.

The landing light was on and, standing by the door of his bedroom, with his arms folded and a look of delinquent triumph on his face, was Dave Trafford.

"So," he said. "We've been doing a bit of late-night wandering have we?"

Lloyd didn't move. There was no point in trying the "I've been to the toilet" stunt, because, as Christine had pointed out, the toilets were at the other end of the building. Besides, Dave knew exactly what was going on. James had told him. He knew about his visits to the cellar.

"I had to see the ghost, didn't I?" he said.

But, as he spoke, he could see the malice in Dave's face. His lips were tight and he just knew this was going to be a downward journey.

"I see," Dave said. "Ghosts, is it? What rubbish you do come up with, Lloyd Lewis. I've just about had enough of you. Get down to my office. You've been nothing but trouble from the moment you set foot in this place."

He pushed him through the office door and closed it firmly behind him.

"Sit down," he snapped, and although Lloyd despised the balding blob, the ice-cold tone sent a shiver through him.

Dave sat behind his desk, the harsh low-energy light giving his face an aura of menace. He mitred his fingers and stared.

"You know, Lloyd," he said – and suddenly his voice took on a quiet, lethally controlled tone. "I don't think you've really settled here, have you? It's been one long grouse after another. First the smell, then unbelievable fantasies about supernatural visions, and winding up children. You've shown aggression towards staff and no cooperation at school."

Lloyd opened his mouth, but Dave gave that tiny-teethed, simpering smile. "Oh, yes, Lloyd Lewis. You needn't think your activities at school have passed me by. I've heard about this morning and your calculated insolence with Mrs Cherry. Mrs Cherry and I are in constant touch, you know?

"And then, getting Justin involved in your ridiculous fantasies – and Rudi and Martin. And having the gall to involve outside agencies like Professor Appleyard, to say nothing of the way you take the law into your own hands, flouting rules, going off after lights out and wandering at will about the place. It negates everything we stand for – the smooth running of the home, the discipline, the morale, and, quite frankly, I've had just about all I can take."

He was going to be gated again. He could see it coming, and, more than likely, he'd get put in some room right by the supervisors' common room so he couldn't get out.

But it didn't matter anymore. He knew how to end all this. He'd phone Justin and, at the weekend, the professor would be down and he was certain Dave wouldn't stand up against him. He stared defiantly into the rimless glasses. "Yeah?" he said. "And what you going to do about it?"

A tremor shot down his spine though when he saw Dave lean back in his chair, with his fingers touching his lips and the self-satisfied smirk on his face. There was something coming that he hadn't seen.

"As I said, Lloyd Lewis, I somehow feel this place isn't right for you, so I'm having you moved to another home. I've already contacted Robin. He's making arrangements and he'll be here to collect you on Friday. I think that will be best for all concerned, don't you?"

Lloyd hadn't realised just how near blind panic was to total blackout. This couldn't happen. He'd be out before Justin got back. He'd be out before he could defuse the curse. It was vital for him to be here on Saturday for the other kids' sake, for Caitlin's sake, for Rudi's and Martin's sake, for the sake of the old Beaker man, for the balance of the earth's forces.

His basic instinct was to react, to leap up, stung with the whipping force of it – let Dave Trafford know he'd been dealt a crippling blow. But he wasn't going to do that. No way was he giving that slug the satisfaction.

"Whatever," he said. "You're in control – you get Robin. You move me. See if I care. It won't be the first time."

Dave's face began to redden. "You're right, Lloyd Lewis. I am in control, and it's a great pity you didn't realise that before."

"Like I said, it isn't no sweat," Lloyd said. He got up. "That'll be it then, will it, Mister Trafford?"

"For the moment," said Dave. "Now, for goodness' sake, get back to bed and stay there."

The next morning Dave put in an appearance at breakfast and there was a look of triumph on his face.

Lloyd told Rudi about it. He told him about the ghost and the sketches too – and how he knew what to do.

He told him about what he'd planned for Saturday. "I got to do it, man," he said. "If I don't, this thing will go on forever."

"We'll phone Justin," Rudi said. "Get him back, get him and the professor down to talk to Dave."

As soon as the mob had exploded from the dining room they headed outside where they could get a better signal and Lloyd called the number Justin had given him.

But the message crackling down the phone made his blood congeal. "The person you have called is unavailable," the message said. "Please try again later." And he looked at Rudi.

"He said he'd keep his phone on all the time."

"Can't you leave a message?" Rudi said.

He shook his head. "No way, man. I got to talk to him. He might be in some place where they haven't got no signal. He might not get the message till it's too late."

Rudi stared across the grounds. There was desperation in his eyes. "We've got to do something," he said.

Then Lloyd looked him straight in the face and said, "You know what?" And there was a tremor in his voice. "You ever bunked off school?"

"No," Rudi said. "Why?"

"Well, you're bunking off today, man. We got to get to London, to see the professor."

"But we haven't any money – the train fare?"

Lloyd put an arm around him and still he was looking him full in the face. "We're riding the train," he said. "You got to stick close by me and do what I say and it's going to take a bit of nerve – especially for you, but we can do it. I done it before, with Lee Peddar –loads of times, I told you."

"Say we get caught?" Rudi said.

"We got to take that chance. I mean, there isn't no other way. If we don't get to the professor, they're going to shift me Friday."

"I haven't done anything like this before," Rudi said. He sounded really miserable.

But Lloyd led him slowly back up the steps. "That's okay," he said. "You just follow what I do. We got to go into school just like normal. Then we got to get to Didcot."

He knew this could go disastrously wrong. When he'd done it with Lee Peddar, Lee knew the ropes, but Rudi was a novice and one slip, they'd get caught, and that would land them in the hands of the transport police and they'd never get to the professor.

CHAPTER 16

All the time they were on the school bus, Lloyd was planning. There was no way they could walk from Brookley to Didcot, and they didn't have money for a bus. It would have to be a lift and that wasn't going to be easy.

When they reached school he held Rudi back until the rest had gone in. Then they walked as unobtrusively as they could around by the gate, hoping none of the teachers would notice. Once they were outside they headed for the main road.

"We got to hitch, okay?" Lloyd said. "We got to tell people we go to school in Didcot, and we missed our bus. You better keep an eye open for the police too. And you leave the talking to me. Swing your holdall over your shoulders and don't say nothing."

He stuck a raised thumb out. He'd seen people do this in old films.

A lot of vehicles passed, and most drivers didn't even bother to look. He was careful though; anyone that seemed the least bit shifty and he withdrew his thumb.

All Rudi could do was watch, and there was despair scrawled all over his face.

He looked at the contorted face, dismayed. "Come on, man. This is an adventure," he said. "You got to stop seeming like you're going to be hung."

"We might as well be hung if the wrong person picks us up," said Rudi, but Lloyd just laughed.

"No way. No one's going to lay a finger on us."

He stuck his thumb out again, and this time a car drew up.

There was an elderly couple in it, a man and a woman. They both had grey hair and they looked like some kid's grandparents.

The woman wound down her window and leaned out. "Shouldn't you be at school?" she said.

"We missed the bus," said Lloyd. "We don't go to the school in Brookley no more. We got places in Didcot. It's a better school, see, but we'll be in big trouble if we don't get there."

The man leaned over and opened the back door and they clambered in.

Lloyd squeezed Rudi's arm with a gesture of adrenaline filled triumph. He grinned and winked.

"Have you been waiting long?" the woman asked.

"About ten minutes. It don't matter too much if we're late. We'll tell them we missed the bus. They'll just give us late points."

"How long have you been at school in Didcot?" the man asked.

"Just this term." Lloyd's head was in overdrive. "It's our parents, see? They said you get better results at Didcot. Brookley's a rubbish school, isn't that right, Rudi?"

"And you'd be – how old?" the woman said.

"Thirteen – we're in year eight. We still got plenty of time before we do our GCSEs."

"You shouldn't make a habit of this, you know," the man said. "Hitching lifts – it's a dangerous occupation."

"Yeah, we know," said Lloyd. "But we thought you was safe. You got honest faces."

They both laughed, and Lloyd added, "It isn't going to happen no more – and it was all my fault, isn't that right, Rudi? I couldn't find my homework. I should have packed it last night."

After that, things went quiet, which was a relief because Lloyd was running out of conversation.

The old couple dropped them by the school gate and they went through, waving. Then they hid around the corner until the car was out of sight and, as soon as it was clear, they made their way down to the station.

Their first task was to find somewhere to offload their holdalls.

"We don't want to carry nothing that's going to slow us down," Lloyd explained. Rudi was still looking terrified and that worried him.

"You got to do something about that face, man," he added. "People see you looking like that and they'll know something's up. You got to look like you're enjoying it."

"But if we get caught?"

"If we get caught, we got to bluff our way out, but that's okay; I'll do the talking. If a ticket-inspector comes, then we just slip off into another carriage and come back when he's worked down the carriages. Then we got to push past him while he's checking someone's ticket and, if he says something, we just look all innocent like and say our parents got our tickets and they're down the train. Then we lock ourselves in the toilets for a bit, till he's finished doing his inspection."

They wandered down the path towards the car park until they found a hole in the mesh fence. They pushed their holdalls through, burying them in the undergrowth, and then they headed for the station.

It was no problem getting onto the platform. There was a gate by the path leading directly to the platform ramp.

"We got to take the fast train," Lloyd said. "That's platform two. If we go on the stopping train the ticket-inspector will be up and down all the time. We don't want to be right up the back neither. That's where he hangs out in his little office. We got to be in the middle, say, halfway between the back and the refreshments, and we got to sit at the far end of the carriage, so, if he does show up, we got time to get out the way."

When the train came in, they found a couple of seats, facing the back, just where they needed to be, but as they pulled out, Rudi grabbed Lloyd's arm and he looked really scared.

"You sure this is going to be okay?" he said.

Lloyd grinned. "You just follow what I do," he said. "It won't be no problem."

The journey didn't have the same feeling as the trip with Justin had – or even trips with Lee Peddar. There was a tension all the time, watching for the ticket-inspector, and knowing that, at Paddington, there may be barriers to contend with. Lloyd would need to fill Rudi in about them. And there was the constant feeling that everything was closing in. Dave had got the better of him. He didn't even know where Robin was taking him on Friday, and he just had to be at Sarson Hall. Besides, the thought that he'd be shunted off and not see James or Jenny again, or Justin, really crippled him. And there were other worries. When they got to London, they had to find the university. They'd never been to the university. He knew the office address, but London was a big place. And they'd have to ride the buses. His other worry was that James might not be there. He might have gone to the dig.

When they reached Reading they heard an announcement telling alighting passengers they should have their tickets ready as barriers were in operation, and that made Rudi's face turn even more sickly.

"It's okay," Lloyd said. "There's a gate for people with pushchairs and for disabled people, and when the operator-guy opens that he's usually busy with the luggage and stuff. You can slip through when he isn't looking."

It wasn't so straightforward after Reading either, because the ticket-inspector turned up asking to see tickets from all passengers boarding at Didcot and Reading.

Lloyd pulled Rudi's arm. "Come on," he whispered, and they slipped out of their seats, pushing down the carriages towards the refreshment car. "We got to hang around here for about ten minutes. Then we go back and, if the inspector says something, you leave the talking to me."

Rudi was looking green by now.

"I get the feeling you aren't enjoying this much," Lloyd said, and Rudi shook his head.

The inspector was busy issuing some man with a ticket when they headed back, and they pushed past unchallenged. But by the time they got to Paddington, even Lloyd's nerves were frayed.

They tumbled onto the concourse, and the conglomeration of activity and the cacophony echoing to the arched roof made it impossible to think straight. "Look out for some woman with a pushchair and luggage," he said, but there wasn't anyone and there were hundreds of people milling towards the barriers. No way was this going to be easy. For a while they waited and it looked as if no one was going to need the gate.

At last, though, an elderly man on a mobility scooter came down the platform. He had a huge case, and Lloyd knew that would keep the operator well occupied.

"Stick with him," he whispered; but now, with the crowd thinning, it was difficult to stay inconspicuous.

They attached themselves to the queue adjacent to the gate and, as soon as the operator got involved verifying the old man's ticket and managing his luggage, Lloyd grabbed Rudi by the arm.

"Go, man, and run like hell," he hissed.

They slid behind the man, pushing into the crowd and Lloyd thought he heard someone shout. He didn't hang around to find out who, though. They dodged between the passengers, tore over to the taxi ramp, raced up the hill and out onto the main street, and Rudi was panting and wide eyed.

But, for the first time, he was smiling.

"Good, isn't it?" Lloyd said. "You get a wicked adrenaline rush when you do that."

Rudi nodded, but he was too out of breath to speak.

They could only see one bus stop; it was on the other side of the road. The trouble was, Lloyd had no idea what direction they should go, and so he didn't know if that was their stop.

"We got to get to Russell Square again," he said. "The professor's office is in the Institute of Education. Justin told me that before he went so we got to find a bus going that way."

He watched buses snarling up and down the road but nothing indicated Russell Square as a destination. He did notice that, with Paddington being such an important stop, there were lots of passengers and that would make it easier to get on board without being seen.

"We got to slip in the back door – between them people getting off," he said. "See – the people getting on go in the front so the driver can check them in. We don't want to go near him."

"Wouldn't it be best to walk?" said Rudi. He was looking miserable again.

"London's dead big, man. It could be hundreds of miles to Russell Square."

He saw Rudi give a weak smile. "It isn't that big," he said.

They wandered over to the bus stop and Lloyd stared blankly.

Most of the passengers had cleared, boarding a bus that had just left. There was just one elderly lady there, and he figured she looked quite approachable. He decided to try out a bit of Rudi's diplomacy. He knew he'd got a winning smile, so it was worth a go. "'Scuse me, misses," he said, and it was okay because she was beaming. "Me and my mate here, we got to see this professor guy, in the Institute of Education. We got to get to Russell Square, but we don't know where the bus goes from."

"There's a route-finder," she said. "There's one in every bus shelter." She hobbled down the shelter and she was right. There was a big route-map, and, underneath, all the destinations listed alphabetically, together with the buses they could catch. They even gave you the letter of the bus stop.

"That's got to be neat, hasn't it?" he said. "That makes finding buses in London dead easy." He looked at the old lady with his broadest smile and he could see she was melting.

"So, why are you going to see a professor at the Institute?" she said.

"We got this big archaeological project going – back where we live and he's working on it with us. I made this massive discovery last night, and we got to talk to him."

The old lady's eyes were sparkling and she was really nice. Lloyd was beginning to think, if you got out of the system, out of the reach of carers and social workers and all the others involved with homeless kids, there was a big population of decent people out there.

"You don't know how much you've made my day, dears," she said. "So refreshing to see young people enthused about history and archaeology. I used to work in the Institute library, you know? Have you been there before?"

Lloyd shook his head. "When we met the professor before, it was at the British Museum."

"Well… I'll take you if you like," the old lady said, and suddenly Lloyd's brain went numb. With the old woman in tow, there was no way they could jump the bus.

"I don't want to put you to no trouble," he said, but she just put an arm around each of them and gave her beaming smile again.

"It'll be a pleasure. And I expect you're on a limited budget – would that be right? So… I'll treat you to the bus fare. How would that be?"

It was as if all his winners had come in at once. But old ladies and charm, he had to keep it up. "That isn't right," he said. "I mean, you probably only get a small pension."

"I get my own travel free, with my bus pass," she said. "And don't forget, I worked at the university. The pension isn't exactly a pittance; I'm not on the breadline."

"Well, that's real kind. Me and Rudi, we appreciate that, don't we, Rudi?"

Rudi was grinning as if his face would split. He clearly hadn't fancied jumping a bus.

"The bus goes from over the road," she said. "Just down there. We want a number seven."

They began walking back past the station and there was a bus stop further down the road.

"And your professor – what's his name?" she said.

"Professor Appleyard. He's an archaeologist."

"James Appleyard?" She looked really pleased. "I know him. I remember him when he was a student. He did his doctorate at the university."

"You know James Appleyard, and the guy's a doctor?" Lloyd said.

"Most professors are, but he isn't a medical doctor, so don't try showing him a poorly toe." The old dear was laughing big time, and it was as if she wasn't a proper old woman – Lloyd couldn't believe their luck.

"That's unbelievable," he said. "I mean, London's a big place, and to think, we meet up with you and you know the professor. That's amazing. Isn't that right, Rudi?"

The old lady was shoving coins into a ticket machine. "These things aren't just down to chance, my dears," she said. "I'm a firm believer that there's someone out there watching us, looking after our needs, bringing us together."

"You religious, then?" said Lloyd.

"Not in the conventional sense," she said. "But… these things are governed by some controlling force. I do believe that. There are too many things like this happening for it to be just chance."

A bus pulled in and if they'd seen it before, they wouldn't have needed the old lady at all; it had *Russell Square* scrawled all across the front. But with her they were legitimate, and that was a big relief. It wasn't much fun riding trains and buses with Rudi. He didn't seem to have the build for it.

She insisted on taking them to the Institute when they got to Russell Square, and she was greeted like an old friend.

"Miss Treadwell," the receptionist said. "How lovely to see you."

She beamed. "I've brought two young men on a mission. They're here to see Professor Appleyard."

"Do they have an appointment?" the receptionist asked, and Miss Treadwell laughed.

"I shouldn't think so, not for a minute. Have you got an appointment, boys?"

"No," said Lloyd. "But he'll see us if he's in, no sweat. You just say it's Lloyd and Rudi."

The girl rang through, and after a brief pause she smiled. "He's on his way down."

They had to wait a few minutes, and when he emerged he was looking really puzzled. "Lloyd – Rudi?" he said. "What are you doing here?" Then he stopped because he'd noticed Miss Treadwell and his bewilderment went up several notches. "And Agatha, how lovely to see you; but how did you come by these boys?"

"The guiding hand of fate, James. I met them at a bus stop in Paddington."

"Amazing," he said. He was still looking confused, but almost pleased at the same time. "Come up to my office."

He glanced at the receptionist, raising an eyebrow. "Coffee?" he said. "For Miss Treadwell and me – and possibly orange juice and a couple of cookies for the boys?"

It was all breaking over Lloyd like a surging wave and there was a huge release in him, because now they were with James and that meant everything would be okay.

After he had reconnected with Miss Treadwell, the focus homed in on them.

"Now boys, what on earth are you doing in London? And more to the point, how did you get here and does Mr Trafford know?"

"No way," Lloyd said. "It's because of him we had to come – and because of the ghost, and we hadn't got no way of getting here except riding the train. There's no barrier at Didcot, so it wasn't no sweat and we barged the gate at Paddington."

James looked slightly shocked. "We'll have to phone Mr Trafford," he said. "Let him and the school know you're here. But why? Are you in trouble or something?"

"I seen the ghost again last night and I know what we got to do to reroute the ley lines," Lloyd said. "The ghost showed me. But when I was coming back, Dave was waiting outside my room and he caught me red handed. He said he's going to kick me out. He's got it all sorted with my social worker, and he said they're moving me Friday and that can't happen. I mean, we got to do this rerouting and I couldn't get through to Justin."

All the time he was talking, James was nodding and he was really calm about it. He took a swig of coffee and he didn't say anything about Dave. All he said was: "Tell me about the ghost then and what you found out."

He described the drawings and how excited the ghost had got when he mentioned the pile of stones.

"See – the two things are linked," he said. "The drawings and the stones. What we got to do is this. We got to dig up them stones and we got to make a track with them, from Sarson Hall back to Brookley Henge and then, we got to put stones to replace every stone that's been took from the two circles and we got to lay some pointing the way to Avebury, just to direct the force, and I figure, if we do all that, because all the stones are sarsen stones like the henge, it'll draw the power away from Sarson Hall and back to Brookley and, when it's there, with a bit of luck, the ley line to Avebury will join up again."

He could see the expression of amazement on Miss Treadwell's face, but there was a clear understanding from the professor.

"And that's a big thing," Lloyd said. "Me and Rudi, no way can we do it on our own, and no way can we do it before Saturday when Justin gets back – and I'm not going to be there by Saturday. I didn't know what to do."

"You explained to Mr Trafford why you were down in the North Wing?" James said.

"Yeah, He knew that. It's probably why he put himself outside my bedroom. It was like a trap. He'd already made up his mind he was going to get rid of me. I reckon it was because I showed him up with that drugs stuff with Craig Donovan."

"Well, the first priority is to get your disappearance sorted. Then we can make plans for Saturday."

James had an intercom like Dave's, and he pushed a button. "Debs, would you get my wife?" he said. "And then cancel my tutorials for the rest of the day. I think I'll be doing a bit of damage limitation down at Brookley."

"You going to stop Dave moving me and give us a hand on Saturday, then?" Lloyd said.

"Give you a hand Saturday?" James laughed. "My dear boy, I wouldn't miss it for the world." He leaned back in his chair, waiting for the call to come through from Jenny. "We'll have to mobilise a lot of forces. I'll bring the university pick-up and I'll get some volunteer students. And we'll need to hire a digger to shift that mound of stones."

There was a buzz on the intercom. He picked up the receiver and they listened to his half of the conversation. "Can you down tools and come over?" he said. Then, "Lloyd and Rudi have turned up – some trouble with Trafford down at Sarson Hall." After that

he sort of smiled and said, "They rode the train, the little blighters."
Then: "I'll get Lloyd to explain riding trains later." And: "Yes, I'll
call him, and the school." Up until that point, Lloyd could surmise
the other half of the conversation; but then came an enigmatic bit.
"I think we should both go down, don't you? Talk to him about it.
Put it to him again. I mean, it's what we both want." There was more
talk after that, together with a few arrangements and instructions.
Jenny was coming down with the car; they'd have lunch and then go
back to Sarson Hall.

He phoned Dave and Mrs Cherry, or rather his secretary did, and
she put the calls through. Then they explained to Miss Treadwell all
about the ghost, because she'd been gaping while Lloyd had been
telling James.

When Jenny arrived she gave him and Rudi a massive hug, but
when Lloyd explained riding trains, she looked really doubtful.
"That's a bit naughty, Lloyd," she said, and James laughed.

"They were desperate, Jen. It certainly wasn't legal but, in the face
of extreme adversity, I reckon it shows initiative."

Jenny looked at him with a hint of disapproval. "Don't
encourage them," she said, and it was like having a mum and dad.
Lloyd had to step on that thought before it went somewhere.
That was where the danger always lay. There'd even been half a
thought about Miss Treadwell making a fantastic gran – or at least
a brilliant aunt.

James said they'd take her out to lunch as a "thank you" and
during lunch Lloyd and Rudi told her about Sarson Hall. Some of it
was new to James and Jenny too – about the bullying and the manic
behaviour. They knew about Craig Donovan and his distribution
methods with the drugs, but it was all new to Miss Treadwell and she
was a great person to tell things to.

After lunch she caught the bus back home, and she was fantastic.
"You've really brightened up what would have been a very dull day,"
she said. "And I'm most grateful."

"It's no sweat, man," Lloyd said, and straight away Rudi was in; he
was the real diplomat.

"And we're so grateful to you," he said. "We'd have been lost without your kindness and help."

She looked at James as she dug into her handbag for her bus pass. "Two such charming boys," she said and then, from her seat by the window, she waved as the bus drew away.

After that they headed out of London.

"Do you think we could call in at Didcot on the way?" Rudi said.

"Why?" said James, laughing. "Don't tell me you nicked someone's car to get to Didcot and want to pick it up so you can return it to its rightful owner."

"No," Lloyd laughed. "We dumped our school bags in some grass by the car park. I mean, you got to travel light when you ride the trains."

He felt slightly apprehensive when they got back – but he was certain, with James and Jenny there, Dave would have to tone it down. But it turned out they didn't have to face Dave at all.

The only path they had to cross was Christine's, and her face twisted into all kinds of judgemental contortions.

But when they got to Dave's office, Jenny said, "You boys wait here. We'll go and talk to Mr Trafford. You don't need to worry about that."

They were there for ages, too, but when they came out they were both smiling and Jenny came over and gave them this massive hug and her eyes were glistening like they were full of tears and she said, "It's all right, boys. We've sorted everything."

"They're not going to move me on Friday?" Lloyd said.

James shook his head. "And everything's okay for Saturday. We'll bring a party of students and I'll bring the pick-up. Justin can arrange a digger."

"That'll be really good, man," Lloyd said.

"Now we'll go down and meet your Mrs Cherry, shall we?" said Jenny. "We'll have a chat with her so you won't be carpeted for truancy tomorrow. How does that sound?"

"Brilliant," said Lloyd, and Rudi said: "That would be fantastic. I was really worried about Mrs Cherry."

For the rest of the week Dave didn't say a word to either of them, but Lloyd knew he was seething. Every time they passed in the corridor he would glare, and when he put in an appearance at meals Lloyd could feel his eyes boring into them.

Even when the police came, Dave avoided him. He left it all to his secretary.

The policewoman told him Craig would have to appear before a juvenile court and it may be necessary for him to give evidence.

"But you won't have to be in court," she said. "It'll be video linked and I'll be there to see you're all right."

He didn't mind. As far as Craig was concerned, it was justice. The guy deserved whatever he was going to get.

Through the week he carried on going down to the North Wing, redirecting Caitlin from the cellar, but the ghost didn't show again, even though the force still raged around the rooms and corridors.

On Friday night he hardly slept – not because of the creaks and groans, but because he was excited.

Rudi was awake for most of the night too although they couldn't talk. They'd kept Martin fully informed about what was going on – but, arousing him from indifference and lethargy was a big challenge. All he was concerned about was his sleep and he insisted they didn't do anything to disturb it.

On Saturday Justin turned up first thing, with a friend in tow, delivering a yellow mini-digger.

"It's all been happening, then?" he said "And I'm really sorry I didn't get to answer your call. I knew I hadn't got a signal as soon as I got there. I just hoped nothing would turn up. James told me all about it. He came over on Thursday, to drum up a working party." He looked at Lloyd with his massive smile. "And you're the big guy around college, you know that, don't you? Loads of students wanted to come."

Around eleven o'clock James arrived with Jenny. Their car was stacked with boxes of food and drink, and they were followed by a minibus full of students. The pick-up turned up a few minutes later.

Lloyd noticed they all called James by his first name, although, behind his back, they often said "the prof" – but he could see they rated him. They were really friendly, too. They shook hands with him and Rudi, and it was as if he was some kind of celebrity.

"You're in charge," James said. "You just tell us what to do and we'll do it."

"We got to get all them stones out of the hill first," Lloyd said. "Then we got to lay them. I figured we'd do a count, see we've got enough, because I reckon it's about four miles up to Brookley Henge and if we do, say, a stone every twenty metres it's like – about eighty-eight stones in the mile?"

"Say we go back to the old measurements," James said. "Do a stone every twenty-two yards, that's an old 'chain.' That would be ten stones to the 'furlong,' and eight 'furlongs' to the mile, that would be eighty stones per mile and, if we did that, we'd be in tune with the ancient traditions."

"That's good, man," Lloyd said. "That's what history's all about. Isn't that right, Rudi?"

Dave wanted to make a show of the dig to impress everyone, so he arranged for the hill to be fenced off and he let the kids from the hall come to watch. But that went pear-shaped. Only a few kids turned up and they were sullen and shouted abuse at the students. In the end, Marion had to herd them back inside.

The day had dawned with its usual featureless skies and it was dank and chilly – much like every day since Lloyd had come to the Hall… but today was different.

There was a vibrancy that excited him, and he and Rudi worked with a will.

He issued the occasional instruction and James directed activities with the digger.

They worked on until lunchtime, loading stones onto the pick-up, with Rudi counting them on.

Some of the stones were just chippings, but others were larger, irregular chunks that had broken awkwardly when they'd been cut. Lloyd watched the pile grow.

When they'd been loaded everyone stopped for lunch – and it was great.

The students made him and Rudi part of the group. They included them in their chat and jokes. They all seemed to rib James, but they worshipped him. He and Jenny were like king and queen in their court.

When lunch was over they returned the disturbed soil and replaced the turfs.

The patch was darker than the rest of the ground and, without the stones, it was level again but, apart from that, it was hard to tell where the dig had taken place.

And now it was time.

This was the moment that sent shivers down Lloyd's spine.

Justin, with his map and compass, plotted the route and Lloyd carried his hazel twig. He counted the paces meticulously, directing the placing of the stones and occasionally dowsing to check they were on the right course – and the dowsing blew the students away. They crowded around, firing questions – about the patches of force, about how it felt, about the movement of the twig, about when he first knew he could do it.

For most of the afternoon Lloyd was totally engrossed. His mind was focused… but, as they got near the henge, doubts began to creep in. He tried to put them to one side.

"We got enough stones, Rudi?" he said.

Rudi was wrapped in the spirit of it. "We've got plenty," he said. "I'm putting a smaller stone between each big one, so we've got enough of the bigger stones for the circles."

"That's good thinking, man," he said. He paced on towards Brookley, with the pick-up and a cluster of students following. One of the students had driven the minibus over to the henge, loaded with stuff for tea. "An army can only march on a full stomach," James said. "At least that's the only way to keep this one marching."

It was late when they arrived at the henge and the gloom of lowering clouds gave the place a deeply sinister feel. There was a cold wind whipping around the stones, and it brushed their faces with its damp chill.

One of the students stood beside him and breathed in sharply. "This place is something else, isn't it?" he said.

"It's weird, man," Lloyd said. And it was. In fact, in the encroaching dusk, the atmosphere was thicker than he'd ever felt it, and suddenly the apprehension was back.

He could hardly swallow the sandwich Jenny gave him. There was this force inside him, impatient, impelling him to get the job finished.

The students quizzed him about the next steps.

"We got to locate all the places where the stones used to be," Lloyd said. "But that won't be no sweat – not with so many people. We'll have that covered in no time, isn't that right, James?"

"Yeah, no sweat, Lloyd, man," James said, and the students laughed.

"I'm not guaranteeing nothing, though," he said. It was his insurance. "But, when we done the circles, with the stones what's left, I want us to lay a line across that field towards Avebury. I want the line to be strong, so I reckon it's best to work from the field back. Then, when we join it all up, the line to Avebury will be there in its full strength, to send the force in the right direction. Do you get what I'm saying?"

They nodded and Justin came and sat beside him. "I'll work out a route if you like. So we don't waste time when the circles are finished."

Lloyd nodded. "That's good, Justin, man. I'm not sure how it'll work though, if it happens, and I haven't got a clue how we'll know."

"We'll know, mate. Don't you worry about that," Justin said.

After tea the students set about locating the scars in the ground, fighting their way into the bracken, while Justin marked out the route across the field.

Lloyd went over to Rudi.

"I think I want to watch this," he said. "Like, from a good viewpoint. Could you pace out the stones in the field while I get up on that hedge – so I can see everything right back towards the hall?"

"That's okay," Rudi said. "But what's going to happen when the stones are all in place?"

Lloyd shook his head. "That's the trouble, man. I don't know, do I?"

James directed the students through to the field.

On top of the hedge, he could see everything. He could see small flashes of stones marking out the double henge – and – across the down land there was a faint line dotting the route back towards Sarson Hall.

The students were laying stones across the field towards Avebury – with the pick-up trundling behind them. Rudi was pacing out the yards; James and Justin were directing – and there was a buzz around the place.

Jenny came over to the foot of the wall. "You've done a fantastic job, Lloyd," she said. "The students are really geared up. You can tell when they're having a good time. Are you excited?"

He looked down. She was smiling and it gave him just that bit of reassurance. "I would be if I knew what was going to happen next," he said, and she laughed.

"You don't like surprises, do you?"

"I haven't got no control over surprises – but today's been awesome."

"Can I come up there with you?"

He nodded and leaned over offering his hand. "Grab me and I'll pull you up."

Then they stood, with the damp wind brushing their faces, while the rest completed the path.

One of the students looked up.

"Don't you want to lay the last stone, Lloyd?" he said, but Lloyd shook his head.

"That's okay, man. You do it. I just want to stay up here and watch to see what happens."

The student placed the stone where Rudi indicated and then they all converged on the wall.

The last dregs of light drained from the sky. Down in the valley to their right, the streetlamps of Brookley burned like the afterglow of a fire, and, to their left, out towards Avebury, and ahead, towards Sarson Hall, a thick darkness gripped the land... and there was nothing. No movement, no sound, no hints of any subterranean activity, only stillness and the steady cloying of the air.

Then Lloyd saw it, the faintest pinpoint, over in the direction of Sarson Hall. At first just an electric-blue hint, ephemeral, dancing like the light of a single firefly, but gradually it extended itself, moving towards them, the first trickle of an emerging stream.

"Take a look at that, man," he whispered, and the students strained their heads, peering over the hedge.

Gradually the flame pressed forward, searching out a path between the stones – delicate, like nothing more than the spasmodic flame over marshland – and not a student stirred. No one said a word, and still the flame pushed on, tracking among the grasses, drawing closer until the flitting light was dancing at their feet, pushing across towards the stone circles. With wisps like marsh gas, it searched out the two circles, shooting anticlockwise, finding first the inner ring, then the outer, until both circles flashed in an evanescence of pale-blue light. Flames were leaping across a path from Sarson Hall all the way to Brookley Henge now, and then, a gasp of awe and incredulity as a line, like lightning, split the land, and shot out across the fields towards Avebury, streaking away from the Henge.

Flash followed flash until the piercing arrows merged into one consistent line.

And still no one spoke.

They just watched and stared.

Whatever it was – this fragile blue light – something big was happening and Lloyd's heart was pounding.

Then, from the distant horizon, he saw the line slowly extinguish itself, from Sarson Hall outward.

The ensuing darkness followed the same pattern as the light, on towards Brookley Henge until the flashing flames danced only around the two stone circles.

For a few minutes they all watched as the fire leapt from stone to stone. Then, with a crack, like a splitting thunderbolt, the flames went out and a line of livid-blue shot across the land from Brookley Henge towards Avebury and then... it was gone.

Nothing – no sound, no light, no movement, and no one breathed... until one of the students began to clap; a slow, steady clap – and others joined in, clapping and cheering. And crazed across the sky, edges of the cloud broke and, lighting up the clouds' tips, they saw, for the first time, hints of moonlight.

They watched and clapped and cheered and stamped, while the clouds continued to break, ripping open the sky, and stars glinted through.

And Lloyd stared, his heart thumping. He was watching, as the landscape across the downs reflected, at first patches, then a flood of silver... the skies cleared – and the plains between Brookley and Sarson Hall were bathed at last in unbroken moonlight.

CHAPTER 17

There were congratulations and back slapping all the way back to the entrance.

The students crowded into the minibus while Rudi and Lloyd went with Justin, Jenny and the professor in the pick-up. All the way back Justin had his broad smile on and Jenny and James couldn't stop talking. They were like kids, especially Jenny, going over what had happened blow-by-blow.

Rudi was just as bad, reliving the moments from the first sighting of the blue flame to its final extinction, but Lloyd wasn't so drawn in to the excitement. He was drained and suddenly it was more like a dream. Everything was happening so fast.

"There'll be changes down Sarson Hall, don't you reckon?" he said.

And there were changes.

There was a calm – a feeling of tranquillity that had never been there before. Most of the kids were watching TV, and they probably hadn't even noticed. It was just that they weren't bickering. They were sprawled out on the chairs and couches. A few were sleeping – exhausted by the nightly ravages. There was a bit of good-natured banter, but no malice... and that dreadful, sickly sweet smell had gone.

Christine was on duty. She greeted them at the door, and there was still an air of disdain with her. "You two boys had better get cleaned up for supper," she said. "I'll take the professor and his wife down to see Dave."

Their bedroom had a different feel to it as well – the same peaceful ambience that permeated the whole building. "Can you sense it?" Lloyd said. "It's like there isn't no grief nowhere anymore."

Rudi sniffed, as though he could smell the changes. "It doesn't feel the same," he said. "I can't put my finger on it, but it isn't like it was."

James and Jenny had booked into a hotel in Brookley for the night. They hadn't planned for Lloyd's project to end so quickly, but Jenny said it would be good to stay anyway – it would give them all another day together.

It was when she said that, that Lloyd felt the first pang. This was what he'd been afraid of. There was a finality about the coming day – one last chance to prolong the dream... and then... it would be over. Once James and Jenny had gone, there'd be no reason for them to come back.

Rudi went to the television lounge, but Lloyd stood on the doorstep, watching the retreating lights of James's car.

He needed to be alone, to get a grip on his thoughts – to lick the suppressed dreams back into reality – because he didn't want to be hurt again. He wanted to face the "goodbyes" tomorrow as the inevitable step in the process. It was the passing ships syndrome; it was what seemed to make up so much of everyone's life.

Eventually he wandered back indoors, just as Caitlin came out of the television lounge. She looked at him with the half-disclosed smile – and that always made his adrenaline surge. "You notice anything?" he said, but she just looked blank. "I mean, there isn't no bitching. Didn't you notice?"

She smiled. "No – but, now you've said."

He walked with her up the stairs. "That's because we broke the curse."

"I saw you mucking around with them stones you dug up," she said. "But that didn't do nothing – I mean, it was just a load of overgrown kids playing games. I seen babies do that – making lines with bricks."

"We wasn't mucking around," Lloyd said. "We laid the line of stones to draw the curse out of Sarson Hall. We took the power back to Brookley."

"Yeah, right," she said, and there was an expression of mocking disbelief.

"You come down the North Wing with me, and you'll see. I'll guarantee there isn't no bad stuff going on down there."

They passed through the fire doors and it had to be obvious, even to her.

For a start there was no chill – in fact, there was a warmth permeating the air, generated by the central-heating system… and the smell – that was always the first thing that hit him; but the smell wasn't there anymore.

They went into Caitlin's room and that was different too – warm, almost cosy, and there was no tremulous flicker when he flicked the light switch, no sense of anything out of the ordinary.

"If you still don't believe me," he said, "come down the cellar."

He felt her tense up. But he grabbed her hand. "It's okay. Trust me."

When he turned the light on in the cellar, even that had a different feel to it. There wasn't any eerie intimation – just dim rays of an inadequate but functional bulb.

"It isn't scary, but that's because I'm with you," Caitlin said.

He looked at her and shook his head. "You're not going to get scared no more, man," he said. He was still holding her hand and his throat was caught by an inexplicable hitch.

"What about tonight, when I do the sleepwalking?"

"You aren't going to do that. That's all done with. You aren't going to do any of that ever again."

"But what if I do?"

He sighed. "Okay, like always, I'll come down tonight – just in case. But you got to believe me. It's finished. It isn't going to happen."

She gave a suppressed giggle. "I'm going to miss it if you don't come down," she said, and that made him look harder into her face.

"What you saying, man?"

She was gazing at the floor, her long eyelashes hiding the look in her eyes, and he watched as her foot moved gently over the ground. "You, tucking me in every night. It was all right, that was."

He gave a self-conscious laugh and he was looking at the floor too. Suddenly he moved forward, brushing her lips and then he pulled her into some kind of a hug. She was holding him as tightly as he held her. He knew his face was filling with colour... and he didn't know what to do next.

Caitlin was blushing too and, after a minute, she pulled away, still looking down. But, even in the dim cellar light, he could see her face was on fire.

At last he said, "Yeah, but if I got caught doing that every night we'd be in big trouble with Dave. And we don't have to do it. I mean... we got each other – like, there's this sort of closeness, isn't there – between you and me? That isn't going to go away. Least ways, I don't reckon it is."

Her hair was brushing her cheeks and she shook her head. "No. I don't reckon so neither," she said. Then she looked up and her eyes were beautifully soft, so much so he let out a gasp. "You're well nice, Lloyd Lewis," she said. "You're the nicest guy I ever met."

"Yeah. That's good that is," he muttered. "I appreciate that, man. That shows respect, that does."

They stood there then, both awkward, both staring at the floor. "Anyway," he said. "Tonight, I'll be there, okay? Just in case you do the sleepwalking, so you don't need to worry." And, slowly, they made their way back up the steps to the North Wing.

For the rest of the evening the feeling around the place was completely tranquil. Many of the children were in a state of exhaustion, and most of them were dozing in the television lounge.

Dinner was quieter than in the most disciplined of homes.

No one commented. It was a bit like when the tide turns and the change passes unnoticed, but change was there. Marion and Christine were sitting, poised to launch their usual offensive – and they were left with guns primed and nothing to shoot at. He could see the bewilderment in their faces.

Dave's face didn't give anything away. He just sat at his place, waiting for the first miscreant and his snide warning at the end of dinner showed just how little he was aware of what was happening. "Now, you lot, you'd better stay quiet," he said. "Because we'll be keeping a close watch. I can tell when there's something brewing, and believe me, this dinnertime has been infused with hatching plots. We're not stupid, you know? If you've got any schemes in mind, don't even go there, because if I have to come out to you once tonight, there'll be real trouble."

Lloyd looked at Rudi. "I'd still love to smack him one," he said. "What we done didn't change nothing in that guy's head."

But Martin noticed the change. "You done something out there today, haven't you?" he said. "I can sense it." They were settling into bed and, for the first time, there was no pandemonium outside. Even Christine had been silenced. "What went on with you and them students up there?"

They told him, and, for the first time, he looked really interested. He didn't show any sign of lethargy and Lloyd laughed. "It's changed you too, man. Yesterday, if we told you that stuff, you'd be sleeping by the end of it."

"No way," Martin said. "That is so brilliant, what you done. I wish I'd gone up there. It would have been awesome to see that light coming across the downs and everything. It's dead impressive, that is."

He hadn't changed that much though, because, five minutes later he was buried in pillows and duvet, his curls splayed out around him and he was fathoms into sleep… only this time the sleep was deep, dreamless and cleansing.

When the lights went out and he was certain Marion and Christine had gone back to the common room, Lloyd crept down to the North Wing, just to put Caitlin's mind at rest. And it was calm. There wasn't even a groan from the floorboards, and Caitlin's door never opened.

He'd known that would happen, but there was something about it that confused his feelings. It was like everything else connected with the ghost. There had been good bits, and this ritual with Caitlin, there was something special about that – guiding her back to her room, the hooded glances and that enigmatic half-smile. And it was finished, just like all the other good things.

He knew none of it would ever happen again and it left part of him with an empty feeling.

James and Jenny were there soon after breakfast the next morning and, before they picked up Lloyd and Rudi, they went off to see Dave.

Dave came out of his office with them when they'd finished, and he was his usual simpering self with James and Jenny. His pale eyes peered at Lloyd and Rudi and there was that self-righteous malevolence in his voice. "You boys have certainly landed yourselves in clover, haven't you?" he said. "And you'd better make sure you appreciate it." He looked at James and Jenny with that smug smile and added, "I suppose I should say – how is it the Americans put it? 'Have a nice day' – is that right?"

Even the good wishes had an edge, and it made Lloyd's hand itch. "One day," he whispered to Rudi. "One day I'm going to rearrange that guy's face."

Rudi hushed him up, but he saw James glance at Jenny and grin.

They went up to the henge and it was almost as good as being on Hampstead Heath. The sun was out and it was warm. Insects droned among the grasses and, for the first time, the henge, like Sarson Hall, was at peace with itself.

Justin joined them and they kicked a ball about. They rambled the moorland and chatted, joking and teasing.

Lloyd dowsed the trail towards Avebury, and the forces of the ley line infiltrated every nerve in his body. "It's okay," he said. "And that is so weird. I mean, it's like, it hasn't been doing this since Tudor times – not since Queen Elizabeth the first and Shakespeare."

"And it's all down to you," James said. "Your tenacity and powers of deduction, and the skill and logic, that's what made it happen."

"I'm really proud of you," Jenny said, and she gave him a kiss on the cheek.

"That's respect, man," said Lloyd. "That's appreciated, that is, isn't that right Rudi? Because you done your part. I mean, without you and Justin, I wouldn't have done nothing."

It was great and, for the whole morning and early into the afternoon, there was this feeling that he didn't want any of it to end. But then reality punched him in the very depths of his gut.

James and Jenny began packing the picnic stuff into the car.

"We'd best be making a move," Jenny said. "James has got a lot of preparation to do before college tomorrow." And immediately the thought flashed through his head.

It was over.

The project, the archaeology, the exercise to stamp out the curse, they were all done. James might write up something for a journal – but, after that, it was finished. He would go back to his students and his seminars and tutorials, and that was the last they'd see of him.

Lloyd had been sitting on the car rug, but when Jenny said about moving, he stood up and looked around. It was as if he wanted to take a mental picture, so the memory would stay with him forever.

"That's it, then," he said. He wanted to say more but the words wouldn't come. He did manage to make a few noises. "I don't reckon we'll be seeing you no more. Not till I come up to university – and, I'm going to do that, man – as soon as I got the qualifications – and Rudi too, isn't that right, Rudi? Until then, well… like I said."

He was watching their faces and he saw Jenny look at James.

"Perhaps…" she said. "We'll see."

It was a bitter blow. All the pain and resentment was surging in him and he knew he'd done it again. He'd let his guard down. He'd let two people into his life and into his affections. He'd let them into his hopes and they were about to drop him, like everyone else did. Only this time it was worse – worse even than Jean and Bill, because… with Jenny and the professor it was like… not an adult–child relationship. It was more like man-to-man, and still they were going to let him down.

He could have wrung his own neck for allowing it to happen, but it had happened and he'd got no defence against it.

"Perhaps… We'll see." That's what she'd said. It was like they didn't even believe him and Rudi would make it to university.

He wasn't going to let them see the hurt though, even though he knew his face had coloured up. That was a big advantage of being black; it was harder to see that kind of thing. With a bit of luck they wouldn't even have noticed.

"Yeah, right," he said. "And it's been great. I want you to know that. Like I said, I couldn't have done none of it without all of you."

Suddenly Jenny had her arms around him, giving him the biggest hug ever and she was kissing him on the cheek. Then she did the same with Rudi, and James hugged him too. They hugged Justin – but Justin was all right. He was going back to university in the autumn. It wasn't over for him.

Then they said goodbye all over again and got into the car… and, for Lloyd, there was such a bitterness hearing the engine roar and seeing the cloud of dust hover over the road when the car had gone. It was all so empty, and there was desolation bleaker than anything the curse had thrown onto Brookley Henge.

"I told you," he said to Rudi when Justin had dropped them back at Sarson Hall. "Up there, when we was staying in London, I told you. You can't trust none of them. It's always the same. It's like, they play with you – being your friend because it suits them, being close, giving you treats, but it don't last. It's like, with them, friendship is something you turn on like a light when it's dark, and when you don't need it no more you just turn it off. You see it all the time, man. People going off on holiday, they go to functions and stuff – they meet up with other people and do things together like they've known them all their lives and then they walk off and forget they've ever seen these people. That's the way they work. It don't do to trust none of them."

Rudi nodded and it was as if he was beginning to understand. But Lloyd knew the guy was hurting and he wished he could have saved him from that.

"I did warn you, man," he said.

"I know."

They were sitting on the seat outside the hall, and it had a cruel irony because the grounds were bathed in the afterglow of a perfect day; its beauty seemed to mock the emptiness.

"But didn't you hope, too, just a bit?"

Lloyd didn't answer for a very long time, and it wasn't because he didn't know what to say. It was because he was too choked. At last he nodded and said, "Yeah, deep down, and all the time I was trying not to because… well… the disappointment, it's like… it's like a knockout punch, isn't that right?"

They stared ahead of them, almost afraid to catch each other's eyes. "We still got each other, though," Rudi said. "And Justin. Like you said, he'll stick by us."

"Sometimes I'm afraid, even with Justin," Lloyd said. "Because – well, it's like he's still a kind of kid himself now, but he'll grow up and then he isn't going to be bothered with two kids he met in no home – no more than the rest of them."

"What about you and me?" Rudi said. "We'll grow up, too, one day."

But Lloyd looked him full in the face then and said: "I tell you what, Rudi, man. You're the best guy as I ever met. I know I only been here for what – a month? But I haven't never had no friend I trusted like I trust you, and that isn't going to change, not even when I'm a hundred, and that's the truth."

Rudi sat back on the bench and he was smiling. "That's all right, then," he said.

During the next few days, things began to settle into a routine. The suppressed peace of exhaustion gave way to more boisterous banter as everyone woke from deep, uninterrupted sleep each morning, and the weariness of the past wore off.

The carers were still edgy. It was as if they hadn't yet worked out what had happened. They couldn't gauge the difference in behaviour and there was still the haunted look on their faces. They even kept up the surveillance and confrontation, but now the kids weren't answering back so much, and, after a couple of days the eruptions became less frequent and less prolonged.

Dave still brooded in his office and he still had all the malice and malevolence that made him what he was. There was the edgy sarcasm and the retention of grievances. Lloyd could see it in his eyes.

At mealtimes he presided with the pale-eyed stare and the aggressive looks. His grudge against Lloyd, for still being there, for getting his way with the dig and the stone-laying, for managing to lay his own ineptitude bare with Craig Donovan; all these were telegraphed whenever Dave caught his eye.

But Lloyd didn't care.

After the initial disappointment when Jenny and James disappeared back to London, he made a superhuman effort to readjust.

Four more years... that was all, and then freedom – university, being up there with James, doing the things he loved, being free to travel the world. Jenny and James didn't believe he'd do it, but he would, and so would Rudi.

On Monday he began his extra tuition at school with Miss Webb, and other teachers noticed him too. In fact, the changes with all the Sarson Hall kids were noticed. And the whole school seemed different, as mornings dawned with skies that floated fair-weather clouds, with sunshine, the odd shower and a warmth that put spirit into the staff as well as the kids.

Even Mrs Cherry showed signs of humanity.

But in spite of his newfound ambition, there was still a huge hole for Lloyd. The quest was over. There was nothing to strive for and no immediate purpose, and there was still, deep down in the gut, an indefinable flatness and disappointment about Jenny and James.

He and Rudi went in search of Justin every evening.

They agreed not to tell him about the Appleyards. In the day's full light, it did seem stupid to expect a passing acquaintance, no matter how amazing, to develop into anything bigger and, after a couple of days, the nagging hurt and the lack of mission melted into a kind of normality. The new mission for Lloyd was to get through the next four years... and he was just about coming to terms with it. But when they got back from school on Thursday night, it was as if someone had twisted the clock back, because, as the minibus drove onto the gravel drive, there was Christine, grim faced with her arms folded, standing on the steps.

As soon as they got out, she yelled, "Lloyd Lewis, Rudi Singh, you'd better come with me. Dave wants you in his office."

He couldn't think why they should be summoned to Dave's office, but when they got to the door, all the feelings that, for the last few days had been repressed and repelled, suddenly exploded in his head and, for a moment, his eyes lost their focus.

Dave was sitting with his usual smug expression and his mitred fingers, but sitting opposite him were James and Jenny.

"Well... you two... As I said before, it seems, wherever you fall, you come up smelling of roses," Dave said.

"Why? What we done now?" said Lloyd. He was knocked too far sideways to remember the common courtesies; he'd barely acknowledged James and Jenny. His eyes did go towards them and he did nod, but he didn't know why they were there, and it was as if they'd got into some kind of league with Dave because, when he said about smelling of roses, it was like they had this private-joke going.

"Just sit down, Lloyd, and you too, Rudi, and we'll explain," Jenny said. "And you don't have to do this, not if you don't want to."

"No," said James. "And there's no pressure. You can have as much time to think about it as you want."

It wasn't usually Rudi that led the charge but, this time, with Lloyd's head still plunging around the intangibles, it had to be Rudi's level-thinking diplomacy. "Think about what, Professor Appleyard? You haven't said what we don't have to do if we don't want to."

James laughed and Lloyd could see he was on edge, and so was Jenny. Her cheeks were all flushed. "Sorry," James said. "Nor have we." He glanced at Dave and nodded. "Mr Trafford?"

Dave leaned back in his chair and his expression was the same supercilious mask of smugness, and Lloyd's hands began to tingle.

"Okay, then," he said. "Let me explain: Professor and Mrs Appleyard here seem to have taken it into their heads that you two are rather nice boys. And, for reasons, Lloyd Lewis, that entirely elude me, they would like you to leave Sarson Hall and go and live with them."

Lloyd's eyes grew so wide they were stretching out of his head. "What? Sort of foster carers you mean?" he said.

Jenny was still uneasy and her face was burning red. "Yes, to begin with," she said. "Till you've got to know us better, but, eventually, we were hoping, James and I, that you might like to become our adopted sons – become part of our family. We haven't any children of our own you see, and we'd love you to... I don't know, become our boys."

Lloyd's heart was thumping and his eyes were filling up. "You want to adopt me and Rudi? Proper like? Forever?" he said.

"If you decide you'd like that," said James. "Both of us have taken to you in a big way. We think you're wonderful boys and we want to give you a home... No – that sounds like charity. What I'm trying to say is, we want you to be our kids, to love us and be our family. But we understand that's a big step and you must have space to think about it. We'd only adopt you if you decided you wanted us as parents."

All Lloyd's instincts were to rush across and throw his arms around them both, and hug every gram of life out of them, but... here, in Dave's office – that didn't seem right, and nothing in his life's experience had prepared him for this. He looked at Rudi and the sight of his face said it all. He didn't think he'd seen a grin that big in his whole life. It was bigger than Justin's, and his eyes were dancing.

"I reckon – me and Rudi like... we think... well, that would be great," he gasped out. "Isn't that right, Rudi?"

James and Jenny were laughing, and suddenly Jenny opened her arms and he didn't need a second invitation. He was over there, hugging her like a bear – and so was Rudi.

Dave Trafford was lost. He just sat, staring out of his pale-blue eyes, shielded by the rimless glasses, and he was playing mitred finger against mitred finger. At last he did his throat-clearing act, to restore order, and Lloyd and Rudi returned to their chairs.

"We've talked it through," Dave said. "And, subject to your agreement, which, from my observation, you seem to have given... I mean, you do quite like the idea, don't you? So, if Professor Appleyard and his wife collect you, say, on Saturday – that will give you time to pack and say your farewells here and at school. It'll also give us time to get the paperwork and the formalities finalised. How do you feel about that?"

Lloyd just leaned back in his chair, his head swimming and he said, "That sounds good to me, man, don't you think, Rudi?"

Rudi was still beaming and it looked as if he was too full to speak. He just nodded and then there were hugs all around again – well, James and Jenny hugged Lloyd and Rudi. No one hugged Dave.

At the first opportunity they found Justin and told him.

"I knew something was up," he said. "Jenny and the professor were asking all kinds of questions about you – your background and everything, and I knew they were taken with you."

"We thought, when they went off Sunday like, that was the end," Lloyd said.

"And you'd like to be their kids?" said Justin.

"Yeah, right we would. I mean, how's this for a plan? We'll get them to adopt you too and then you'll be our proper brother, because we'd be dead pleased with that, wouldn't we, Rudi? I mean, it's like you've been our brother ever since we first saw you."

Justin was laughing. "I reckon my parents would have something to say about that," he said, and Lloyd looked abashed.

"I'm stupid. I'd forgotten you had parents. That's really tough though, because… well… James and Jenny… they'd be great parents, wouldn't they? And you haven't got no brothers and sisters – apart from us."

"No," Justin said. "And I promise, even without James and Jenny as parents, I'll still be your brother, for as long as you want, okay?"

"That'll be forever," said Rudi. "And it will be great in the autumn, when you're up at university again."

Caitlin wasn't quite so pleased.

It was his one regret, because he'd really got close to Caitlin. "Like I said, you're the nicest guy I ever met," she said. They were out on the bench. And it was late Friday evening. Time was getting short.

"It isn't going to be the end for us, though, is it?" Lloyd said. "I mean, we'll email each other and do texts and stuff, and I can get you on Skype. We'll even see each other on that."

"Yeah," said Caitlin, and this time there was no hooded restraint or concealment. "But, being together, that's what makes it nice, and, it's like, you can't get close on Skype, and not with emails."

He caught hold of her hand and he knew, at the end of this, he was going to hold her tight, no holds barred and he was going to kiss her. "James and Jenny, man – they're really nice people. They'll let you come and stay weekends. I know they will. I mean, it's like… you're my girlfriend in a way."

"Am I?" she said.

"Yeah, dead right you are," he said, and that was it. It was the time for the hug and the kiss… and it was okay, him and Caitlin. She was a great kid.

The rest was one massive whirlpool, totally out of Lloyd's control – but for once it didn't matter.

Rudi and Lloyd opted to share a bedroom when they got to London. James and Jenny gave them the choice and James said, as they grew older, they might need more privacy, so the second bedroom would always be available.

They had a huge Chinese meal delivered for Saturday night and it was great, even better than before, because now Lloyd didn't have to fight his hopes. He could dream about a family life, because he'd got one. James and Jenny were going to be his family, and Rudi, and Justin – and Jenny said it was okay for Caitlin to come whenever she liked.

That night he wrote two letters. One, a long letter, to Bill and Jean, telling them about the quest at Sarson Hall and about James and Jenny – and the other, a shorter one, to Miss Treadwell, because he knew she'd be really pleased.

When he'd finished, he sat up and stared through the window onto a moon-swathed heath. It wasn't the eerie moonlight of a disrupted earth that he'd seen from the windows of Sarson Hall either. This time it was the genuine flood of silver, hinting at a long and amazing summer.

Suddenly, with a surge that welled from the depths of his belly he brought his left fist against his right palm and whispered: "Yessss!" Then he looked across at the irregular contours of Rudi's duvet and saw a hand emerge, fingers clenched and a triumphant thumb aiming to the sky.

And he rolled over, switched off his lamp... and fell into the deepest, most contented sleep ever.

Lightning Source UK Ltd.
Milton Keynes UK
UKOW04f0236091217
314159UK00001B/29/P